TOURISM

Nirpal Singh Dhaliwal is thirty-two years old. A freelance journalist, he writes for *The Times*, the *Guardian* and the *Evening Standard*. He is married to the journalist Liz Jones and currently lives in Hackney. *Tourism* is his first novel.

NIRPAL SINGH DHALIWAL

Tourism

VINTAGE BOOKS
London

Published by Vintage 2006

2 4 6 8 10 9 7 5 3

Copyright © Nirpal Singh Dhaliwal 2006

Nirpal Singh Dhaliwal has asserted his right under the Copyright,
Designs and Patents Act 1988 to be identified as the author
of this work

First published in Great Britain in 2006 by Vintage

Vintage
Random House, 20 Vauxhall Bridge Road,
London SW1V 2SA

Random House Australia (Pty) Limited
20 Alfred Street, Milsons Point, Sydney,
New South Wales 2061, Australia

Random House New Zealand Limited
18 Poland Road, Glenfield,
Auckland 10, New Zealand

Random House (Pty) Limited
Isle of Houghton, Corner of Boundary Road & Carse O'Gowrie,
Houghton 2198, South Africa

The Random House Group Limited Reg. No. 954009
www.randomhouse.co.uk/vintage

A CIP catalogue record for this book
is available from the British Library

ISBN 9780099493044 (from Jan 2007)
ISBN 0099493047

Papers used by Random House are natural,
recyclable products made from wood grown in
sustainable forests. The manufacturing processes
conform to the environmental regulations of
the country of origin

Typeset in Sabon by
Palimpsest Book Production Limited, Polmont, Stirlingshire
Printed and bound in Germany by
GGP Media GmbH, Pœssneck

FOR MUM, LIZ AND BUNMI

xxx

TOURISM

September 2003

EYES HALF CLOSED, pretending I'm asleep, I watch her. She moves lazily; every few steps she stops, kicks up a spray of Italian sand, then glances around to see if anyone's looking. She gets closer. I sit up and look at her body, which is petite, slim, with fine legs and a lovely chest. She pays me no attention and lies on her sunbed, several feet away from mine. Rolling onto her stomach, she unfastens her bikini and spreads the straps out either side. I've been waiting to see her topless, without luck. But her swimsuit shows her nipples, jutting beautifully whenever she steps out of the water. I think of them in my mouth, between my teeth.

When I first saw her, some days ago, I thought she was eighteen. My estimation has since fluctuated between fourteen and twenty; like a hologram, she switches shape according to the light. Sometimes she's the perfect ingénue, unsure of her wonderful new body; other times she's so assured, flirting with the lifeguard, playing with her hair, amused as he hangs on her every word.

We tried talking this morning. We smiled, we nodded, we said '*Buongiorno*' and then we floundered, unable to bridge the gap between her English and my Italian, gawping in silence like imbeciles instead. Saving the moment, she offered me her bottle of water. I took a swig and gave it back. Looking at me, she held it to her lips then, not quite accidentally, let it spill onto her chin and into her cleavage. I said nothing as she sat there open-mouthed, her gaze darting between my face and her breasts – shining like polished apples – as if it were the most amazing event. She got up, said '*Ciao*', then walked away, waving and disappearing into the phalanx of beach tents. She returned an hour or so later with her companion, and subsequently ignored me.

He's as curious as she is. He's old, well over fifty, and he's with her almost whenever she's here. I don't think he's her father – there's no great affection between them. Their conversations sound perfunctory, to the point. She sunbathes and occasionally swims; he keeps himself chalk-white under their tent, quietly watching the world through huge Versace sunglasses, sipping daiquiris and smoking Gauloises with merciless contempt for his body. His hair is immaculately cut, dyed black, oiled and combed back over his skull. He sits like an old duchess taking tea; a hand rests on his knee, one leg slung over the other, his cigarette held between thumb and forefinger, a signet ring glinting on his upward-pointing little finger. The flesh is draped loose and rumpled over his bones; his shoulders poke obscenely from either side, his breasts hang like soggy dishrags. There's a hideous dignity to him, like an expensive, now haggard and disused leather bag.

When he's here she doesn't look at me, but she still toys with the lifeguard who goes out of his way to walk past her. What does the old man disapprove of? My colour? The girl, caramelised in the sun, is as brown as me – there's the occasional Italian who's darker. Maybe he's seen some trait I share with the Afghans who shuffle about the beach, hawking trinkets and shawls. Maybe the duchess might like me for himself. His manner – weirdly content as he sits inert and blank-faced in the shade – is either the boredom of the very rich, or the hauteur of the very gay. Quite possibly both.

I look at him for a few seconds, with no idea if he's looking back. I nod, and his features unfold into the emptiest, most ingratiating smile I've seen in months. His teeth are unreal, perfect and brilliantly white. He tilts his head and says, '*Ciao*.'

4

'Ciao.'

Rasping slightly, he sighs a few musical sentences of Italian, then laughs with the grace of a courtesan.

'No speak Italian,' I tell him. *'Parli inglese?'*

'Oh! You are Ingleesh? So sorry!' He is effusive, and speaks open-armed, like Christ.

'Don't apologise. I ought to speak more of your language.'

There's a stiff silence; he continues smiling.

'I've only been here a few weeks,' I say.

'I seee. You are on 'oliday?'

'Yes, I am.'

'Very good.' His joyous, obsequious grin holds fast and he asks, rather intrusively, 'Where you are staying?'

'Ostuni.'

'Oh good. Very good. That is very very good place.'

'It's lovely.' I look at the girl who watches us empty-eyed, not understanding a word. She has feline cheeks, pale brown eyes with thick lashes, and tight black curls. She is an original, very natural beauty.

'Thees ees my . . . my . . .' – he looks up and searches the air for a description – '. . . my seester's doe-tah.'

'Your niece.'

'Si . . . My niss.' He speaks to her in Italian, and she smiles at me as if we've just met. Her name is Chiara, he tells me, as though introducing a contestant on a game show, a seventeen-year-old student from Bari. Being a little stupid, she doesn't speak English, but she's a lovely girl and a wonderful dancer who ought to be in an academy instead of all the time watching television, or fretting on the telephone with her friends about make-up and boys. Her mother, Maria, had an operation on her kidney, so Chiara stays with her uncle at the family cottage while his sister recovers quietly at home. His voice is louche and seductive, reverent enough to address the Pope, and his name is Marcello Massimo Marchiagiani.

He's a television producer who splits his time between

his home in Milan and his office in Rome, where he makes a plethora of celebrity shows. He has spent the summer in Puglia since he was a boy. Unsolicited, he tells me all this and more, making tart, shameless remarks while dropping names into his monologue – Berlusconi, Deneuve, Prodi, Zoff . . .

He asks me what I do.

'I'm a writer.'

'Oh! Very good!' His face loses none of its ersatz euphoria. 'What you are writing? A novel?'

I look down at my journal on the table beside me. 'Yes,' I lie.

'What about?'

I extemporise a quick plot that involves desperate young men, a bank robbery and a dismal bloody end.

'Brilliant!' he cries with unabashed mendacity, sitting up and clapping his hands. A silence follows. I sense a movement behind his dark lenses and know he's appraising my crotch. I recline a little, giving him a better view. 'That is *good*,' he murmurs. '*Very good* . . . If you don't mind . . . I can read it?'

'Well, I've only written notes for it so far.'

'It can be a brilliant film, I think.' He shifts forward in his seat. 'I know many people making films. Producers are always needing the scripts.' He pauses, lowers his voice: 'I want to make a film myself, but I need a script. Maybe we can help each other?'

'That's an idea.'

'We must talk about it.'

'Sure.' Unsurprised by his insistence, I'm still somewhat unnerved.

'But not now,' he says, his smile as sheer as a cliff face. 'Let's eat now . . . Please, you will join us?' He turns and speaks to Chiara who, curious and uncomprehending, still watches us. She nods and encourages me with a smile.

'Thank you,' I reply. 'I'd love to.'

He calls for the attendant.

*   *   *

The beach is near-empty. The last of the swimmers make their way out of the water, the tide foaming at their ankles. Behind them several yachts are moored short of the horizon, their black outlines visible against the sky. Marcello's on one of them, dining with business friends. He invited me to his cottage tomorrow night, and I accepted. Still weighted with the lunch he bought me, I'm anchored to my deckchair. How gluttonous did I look, eating enough to save myself dinner tonight, maybe breakfast too?

The sun sinks slowly into the hills behind me. The light wanes and the view tinges orange; each moment is palpably quieter, darker than the last. Here I can see evening fall, like watching a scrap of paper held up by the air drift slowly down to earth. I spoil my mood, thinking I've only been here a fortnight, when I should've been here all summer. And now I'm broke. I wish I'd had foresight, not flitted and squandered from one city to the next. What was the point of Amsterdam? Months of narcotic indolence, some lechery; nothing of interest nor value. Munich was worse; I was mad to go there in winter, alone and freezing. I thought that in isolation I'd focus myself and write. But every city has its easy pastimes, easier women. Barcelona was better, for its weather and for having suspended my plans: I'd write, so I told myself, when I'd finished scratching my itch.

Nonetheless, this past year: bullshit! It's brought few rewards, little joy, no peace. I was born into city life; when I hit my filthy little jackpot and had to get away, I didn't think of coming here. I had nothing to guide me, just urban habits and a knowledge of Europe based upon its football teams – Ajax, Bayern, Barca. That logic took me to Turin, then Milan, where, on a whim, I chose to come here. And now I can write. The view from my room helps; it overlooks a wooded hillside, dotted with hamlets, beyond that the Adriatic and the horizon. Ostuni is a lovely town, quiet, rustic, peopled with a few unobtrusive rural types. Its mood liberates me, its emphasis on the simple, the beautiful. I'm calmer here, less afraid. As the last of my blood money trickles away – on food, shelter, a little wine – more of me returns. I know what to write. The clamour in my skull, urging me to wait, questioning the point, is silenced by the fact that *if I don't write this, I'll write nothing.* It looms too large in my imagination for me to think of much else.

I'd always thought there was a novel in me. I thought my change in fortune, my windfall, would let me write it. Except I can't. I've scribbled thousands of banal sentences during these months, and can't find it. It's not there. If it is, it's behind this *thing,* this colossus that's blocked my sight for twelve months. I look into the sky and I see *it*; I stare at the wall, the floor, the mirror, my fingernails, and I see *it.* So I've jotted down my memories, preparing for my project, my opus – my confession.

I pick up my journal and hold it with both hands, fearing I won't finish it. I've enough money for a day or so, not even the fare to reach the British embassy, let alone get home. Mum would die seeing me now, the opposite of all her hopes and immigrant zeal – penniless and indifferent, cadging my lunch off an old poof, scheming to cadge more. From what Marcello says, his cottage is huge; he and Chiara go whole days not seeing each other. Maybe I can slip myself in there. If there isn't space for three, I'll find a way to share. I hate to think how, and with whom.

In the darkness bright instances flash across the water's surface. I look around and realise I'm the only one here; the only sound, the gasps of waves expiring against the shore. A breeze cuts through the warmth, ripples my skin. I want to return to the hotel, but decide not to. All my things are in the satchel hanging from the arm of my chair; I'll skip my bill and sleep here until the weather changes, or until I find somewhere else. Meanwhile I can wash in the public showers, and write at café tables. I'll eat, tomorrow at least, at Marcello's.

The breeze unsettles me. I grope in the darkness for my

sweater, discarded somewhere about my feet. I find it and pull it over my chest; the coarse fibres scratch my skin. I contract into my chair, draw my knees up and hug them close. My toes start to chill; I rub them, contemplating the task I've set myself. It's quite a story, one I don't know how to tell, other than from the beginning . . .

I

LUCA TOLD ME to go to a prostitute; he visits them regularly. Buying sex helps him fuck other women; it empties him of sentiment, so he handles them with ease. He's good-looking, has a sweet nature and a quick mind; plenty of women linger for his phone calls, his intermittent affections. In some ways we're similar; we're the same age, and the useless first sons of expectant families. I hadn't been laid in a while and I was pissed off, so decided to do as he does, treat sex as sex and, as I would a pint of milk, buy it as necessary.

It was the first Saturday in May and the first truly hot day of the year. I prowled around Victoria looking for 'Amy'. I'd nearly met her a week before, with Luca, after we rang the number on a card stuck inside a phone booth.

'The lovely Amy is eighteen years old,' answered a woman. 'She has a 36-26-36 figure. She is five feet, six inches tall, with blonde hair and brown eyes.' She invited us to a flat in Churton Street. We made it to the front door; Luca then waited as I took a while to decide not to knock. We'd visited Luca's mother in hospital that morning; I said it was 'bullshit' to then take her son whoring. Luca, to his credit, didn't argue.

I retraced my way to Amy's flat. Sunlight hit the surrounding masonry in a painful glare; the heat was dry and stifling. Cars filled the road in a slow conga; the drivers wore tired, bitter faces. My skin itched under a film of sweat and pollution. Wanting a drink, I stopped at a pub en route. It had a mock-Tudor facade, laced with ivy; inside it was dark and sparsely furnished. I walked to the bar and waited to be served. A pack of beer-bellied white men stood in a loose circle nearby; they stopped mid-conversation to throw me a collective, unwelcome stare. Someone mumbled something, probably about me. I avoided their gaze and ordered a beer. They resumed talking with absurd cockney gravitas.

'You heard wo' Mickey done? When 'e come dan?'

'Na.'

'Dincha?'

'Na.'

'Fackin ittim inni'!'

'Wanka!'

I could see bits of them from the corner of my eye – bristled chins, stout bellies and thick forearms, faces red raw, excoriated by the sun. Two cockney crones sat beside me, regaled in ridiculous, inexpensive jewellery – lime-green beads, gaudy supermarket bracelets, enormous plastic earrings – and wearing pink-rinsed bouffants. They gave me approving smiles; my manners obviously pleased them. Asking for a drink 'please', saying 'no thank you' to the offer of ice, were elegances outside their usual experience. Their hair was thinned to a pink haze above their scalps; thick blue veins and purple spots contested the space beneath the decrepit, translucent surface of their hands. Their smiles beamed 'what a nice boy'. I smiled back at their cracked, powder-dry white faces.

I paid for my drink and asked the barmaid for directions to the bathroom. Visiting the toilet took me through the room which curved kidney-shaped around the bar; twenty people might sit in it at once and in comfort. The seats were upholstered with green velvet, on which sat the locals, ageing quietly and staring at a television screen, at Thierry Henry mopping sweat from his temple. These people were, I guessed, from the council estate at the end of the street. A listless man with oily hair and a limp moustache sat beside the television. He wore an ancient pin-striped suit and sipped a glass of Scotch, a forgotten cigarette cindered between his fingers. There were a dozen others like him, with pasty sunless faces, dressed like thrift-shop mannequins, silently watching the football.

I returned to my drink. The men were still talking.

'Whachu fackin on abah?' said one. 'If 'e comes dan, I'll sor' it ou'. Na warries.'

'Crafty fackin cunt, incha?' admired his friend.

They all laughed; one smiled at me in boozy goodwill. I smiled back, and finished my drink. Stepping outside I squinted. The street was empty but for myself and a cluster of screaming children – the grimy white and mulatto children of the poor. A brown-skinned girl, with loose curls and mucus-gilded nostrils, wandered free from her friends and fixed me with spectacular green eyes. She wore plastic sandals and a T-shirt for a dress. She stared at me, then lost interest and took to exploring the soiled hem of her shirt, her fingertips black with filth. I turned towards Amy, now only a block away.

Her flat was next to a restaurant, the Star of Bombay; a bowing, turbaned sahib was painted on the window. I knocked on her door. There was no reply. I knocked once more. Again, there was no reply. I waited a few minutes then left; I didn't want to be caught loitering by someone from next door. Petty disapproval meant nothing, but the prospect of a knowing gaze, a wry Gujarati smile, was too awful to bear. There was a phone booth across the street; I went to it, scanned the cards stuck inside the windows and began dialling. 'Athletic Brunette' hadn't time to see me that day; 'Sexy Nineteen-Year-Old' didn't answer her phone. In the event, 'Busty Swedish Blonde' was the one. The voice on the end of the phone was soft and polite and directed me to an address in Warwick Way. I said my name was 'Paul'.

Her flat was below a B&B; I walked down the steps to a sturdy, well-secured front door and rang the bell. A woman – a withered dissolute, at least fifty years old – opened the door and welcomed me with a tobacco-charred smile. 'Hello,' she sighed. She was a dried husk, with open pores and lank black hair; wearing couch-potato jogging bottoms and a moth-eaten sweater, she reeked of cigarettes. Her face was crumpled, exhausted, but there was a coquette's charm in how she tucked her hair behind her ear, lowered her eyes and ushered me inside. She led me into a living room which had a couch, a plain rug and a coffee table. A television in the corner showed Columbo ambling boss-eyed around an empty car. 'The lady,' she said, 'is waiting for you.' She walked me to a door at the far side of the room and pushed it open.

The bedroom was small and dim, the curtains drawn. The lady stood beside a neatly made bed with a clean, lemon coloured duvet. She was middle-aged, with a bottle-blonde coiffure, sharp features, slim legs and pert, if unnatural, breasts. She wore stilettos and a taut black bikini; her thick labia bulged through the flimsy crotch. She nodded me inside.

We stood either side of the bed while she studied me, taking stock of my face, my height and breadth. Her eyes settled on my chest, on the bright yellow polo shirt snug against my torso.

'Vot voot you like?' she asked in a Slavic, very un-Swedish accent.

I didn't know. I asked about her prices. Hand relief was thirty pounds, fucking was sixty. I paid for a professional handjob, hoping it would be an improvement on my own. My money in her hand, she began making small talk.

'It is hot outsite?'

'Very.'

'You voot like to use the bussroom?' She gestured to an en-suite toilet.

I washed my cock in the sink – it was only polite – while she left the room, probably to give the money to her receptionist. I stood waiting by the bed, my trousers unfastened, my prick tingling with the sensation of cold water. She was ending a conversation as she walked back in: 'Quiet assa church mous, isn't he?' she said, walking through the door. Seeing me she stopped, then smiled. She sat on the bed, removed her shoes, and asked me why I was in Victoria.

'I had dinner at a friend's last night, and stayed at his place . . . He lives sort of nearby.'

'That's nise.' Her voice drifted and tangled itself around the room. She stood up and untied her bikini; it fell about her ankles. She stepped out of it, flicking it off her toes as though shaking water from her feet. Arms outstretched, she walked over to me and held my waist; she toyed with the hem of my shirt, then slid her hands under it and upwards along my sides. I raised my arms; she lifted my shirt from me and dropped it on the floor. She kissed my jaw; her nipples brushed my chest. Our breath mixed enticingly in the space between us. I slipped my hands into my pockets.

'You are okay?'

'Yes,' I said. 'Can I touch you?'

'Mmm-hmm,' she nodded. 'You can tahch my tits, tahch my pussy, everisink.' Holding my shoulders, she stepped back to look at my body. She ran a finger across my chest; her eyes bright above a wide smile, she bit the tip of her tongue between hard white teeth. 'Vee vill haff fun, yes?'

'Yes.'

'Vot is zat?' She looked at the gold *khandha* hanging from my neck.

'It's from India.'

'You are Intian?'

'Yeah . . .' I kicked off my Nikes. 'I guess I am.'

'It is beautiful.' She gazed at it, pulling open my combat trousers. 'You're not vearink any pants!' she said, staring at my limp penis.

'I never wear them,' I said. 'It's too hot anyway.'

'Oh . . .' She raised an eyebrow and picked up a towel from her dressing table; she stooped to lay it over the duvet, smoothing away the creases with an open palm. I looked at her slim white body, her sleek calves flexing under her weight, her flat buttocks, slack with age. She was almost beautiful. She lay down, patting the bed, and invited me to join her.

It felt easy lying next to her. Before entering the flat I was troubled by a seedy guilt, but the lady's uncomplicated manner relaxed me. She poured oil onto her palm, rubbed her hands together, and began stroking my cock. I kissed her shoulder; her warm skin felt good. I slid my hand down her spine and squeezed her buttocks.

'Your hants are colt!' she gasped.

'I'm sorry.' They were still chilled by the cold water. 'I'll warm them up.' I slid my hand under my thigh.

She squeezed my prick and smiled. 'You are attractif.'

'You think so?'

'Don't girls tell you you are attractif?'

'Sometimes.' I watched her working my cock, thickening it between her fingers. 'You don't have to say that just because I've given you money.'

'I've got your mahney!' she laughed. 'I've got it, so I don't haf to say annisink!' She was sweet; her laughter was girlish and lovely. She sat upright; my cock was now hard and she worked it with one hand, stroking my thighs and testicles with the other. I kissed the side of her belly.

'I want to touch you.'

'No . . . Your hants too colt!'

I pulled out my hand from under me. 'I think it's warm now.'

She laughed again, in a glitter of clean white teeth. 'You can look at my pussy.' She pushed forward her trimmed pubis, manicured into a neat rectangle: 'You like it?'

'It's lovely. You take very good care of it.' I slipped my hand between her buttocks, then down between her legs; I parted her labia with my finger, and pushed it inside her. She was warm and greasy; I slid in another alongside it.

'Mmmmmmmm,' she mewled. She closed her eyes and slid a firm grip up and down my erection, winding her hips while I fingered her. This continued for some time.

15

'You vont me to kiss it?'

I nodded, thinking she just wanted to get her job done.

'I get a contom.'

She reached across me and fetched a sachet from the bedside table, unwrapped it and rolled the latex over me. Kneeling beside me, she sucked my cock; the heat of her mouth felt good. She sucked hard; her cheeks flexed in and out. I lay back and listened to the sound, like water lapping against stone.

After a while, she sat up. 'You vont to fahk me?'

I said nothing.

'Fahk me,' she insisted.

'Okay.'

'From behindt,' she instructed, shifting onto her hands and knees. 'Only from behindt.'

I knelt behind her; she reached between her legs, held my prick and guided it inside. I grasped her shoulders and fucked her; leaning forward, I grabbed her breasts, groping for the silicone bags inside. Her cunt wasn't very tight, and I was wearing a condom: this fuck would be just another dull and laboured chore. I sighed in resignation. She moaned, and my attitude softened; her indulgence was a compliment. I stirred her cunt with a firm, winding rhythm. I teased the edge of her vulva then sank back in, stroking the soles of her feet, taking my cues from her sighs, the rustle of her breath. Churning twists of the hip brought roars of approval; I fucked her with some force, before my attention drifted elsewhere, to the blank walls, the shabby furnishings.

'I want to look at you.'

'Okay,' she groaned. 'I get up ant I do it vit my hant.'

I lay down. 'You can sit on it if you like.'

'No . . .' She sighed and peeled off the rubber. 'I do zis.' She took me in hand again. She only wanted sex from behind: a nameless, faceless fuck administered by a stranger. There must be something nasty in the faces of the men she fucked for money – leers, stupidity, slobber and hatred – that she didn't want to witness. She was

16

working hard, wanting the job done; she grimaced with effort. 'Come on! Time to shoot!'

'I want to look at you,' I said, 'because you're so pretty.' She was; her beak-nose, thin chin and brown eyes were more attractive than her bare back, her blonde plume and the hairless, pink squint of her arsehole. The words calmed her; she tossed me off less cynically. I tried helping her, pumping my groin against her hand. I sat up and kissed her breast, drew the teat into my mouth, grating it against my teeth.

'You like zat?' she smiled. 'You like ze titties?' She began working with both hands, to no effect.

'I'll do it.'

'Yes, you do it!' She let go and ran her palm over my chest. I masturbated in my customary manner.

'Kiss me.'

She kissed my face, my neck – not my lips – then licked my nipples; hardening the points with her tongue, she took them each in turn into her mouth. I felt my sap rise.

'Hold it!'

She resumed control and I came, spouting warm seed that splashed over both of us. I wanted to spoon it into her mouth with my fingertip, but didn't ask. She continued masturbating me a while, the meat waning in her hand. Smiling incessantly, she fetched a handkerchief and mopped the semen from our skins.

'You vork in restaurant?' she beamed.

'No.'

'Ver you vork?'

'Mostly from home,' I said. 'I work mostly from home.'

'Oh?' she nodded. 'Vot you do?'

'I'm a writer.'

She paused, not knowing what to make of me. 'You write books?'

'Yes,' I lied.

'Oh.' She was impressed. 'You lif in Lonton?'

'Yes.'

'Ver?'

'Hackney.'

17

'Vy are you in Victoria today?' she asked again, absent-minded.

'I had dinner at my friend's place last night, and slept over.'

'Oh! You hat a barbecue party!'

'No, he cooked it in the kitchen.'

'Vot foot?'

'Chinese.'

She nodded. 'I like Chiniss foot . . . You lif in house or flat?'

'A flat.'

'Zat's goot. You not haf to vorry about ze garten.'

'No, but a garden would be nice.'

Her face brightened with a happy thought: 'Zen you can haf barbecue party!'

'Yes.' I got up. 'Can I use your bathroom?'

'Off course.'

I washed the oil from my cock, then returned and got dressed.

'If you are in Victoria again,' she said, fastening my belt for me, 'I vork Montays, Zursdays, ant Suntays. Com see me. Vee can haf nise time.'

'Yes.' I moved to the door.

'Vait!' she cried. 'Your pen. You forgot.' She handed me a biro that had fallen from my trousers. Taking the pen, I reached into my pocket for my wallet, thinking she might've stolen it while I was in the bathroom; I stood in the doorway in case she tried to lock me out. Relieved to find it, I felt ashamed and stared at the floor. She stepped forward and kissed me on the cheek. 'Be a goot boy.'

'I will.'

'I see you soon?'

'Yes,' I lied. I stepped away, glanced at her and asked her to take care.

'See you!'

The dried husk showed me to the door with perfect manners, greasing my exit with a shopkeeper's thanks and a flurry of queries: 'You will come again, won't you? It's

18

not too hot outside, is it? Would you like a drink, to cool down before you go?'

I said a polite goodbye and left immediately. I walked slowly to the station; the streets were vast and still, the grey concrete doused in the amber glow of the evening. I breathed easily, enjoying the breeze on my face. I stopped at a phone booth and made a call.

'Hello?' he answered.

'Luca—'

'Puppy! You arsehole, where the fuck are you? Why have you left your phone at Rory's?'

'I'd better go and get it off him.'

'There's me trying to call you, and I have to talk to that cock instead. Where are you now?'

'In Victoria.'

'What for?'

'Because.'

'Because what?'

'Just because.'

'I haven't time for your fucking games,' he groaned. 'Why are you in Victoria?'

'I was at the Tate.'

'Very nice . . . What are you doing now? I'm going for a booze-up, you coming?'

'Where?'

'The Peacock.'

'Who with?'

'Sarupa.'

My heart leapt. 'Yeah?'

'Among others, yes. So it's in your interests to make an appearance, don't you think?'

'Definitely.'

'I think her fella's coming too.'

'Fuck him.'

'That's the spirit. I'll see you in about an hour then?'

'I'll get my phone first.'

'For fuck's sake . . . Just call Rory and ask him to come too.'

19

'Okay. I'll see you in a bit.'

'Bye-bye.'

I hung up then dialled Rory's number, leaving a message on his answering machine with details of the evening's entertainment. I walked hurriedly to the station, enlivened by the sound of Luca's voice and the perilous, exquisite prospect of Sarupa. I nearly skipped with anticipation; my nerves pulsed, ready for adventure.

2

THE TIP OF the redhead's cigarette flared as she took a long drag, her lips tight against the filter; her head cocked, her eyes raked over me. I turned towards her and she looked away, affecting an interest in something or someone else, just as I had a moment before. She sat on the huge leather sofa opposite mine, tucked against the arm with her thin legs crossed. She clutched her stomach with one arm; the elbow of the other was folded against her side, wrist straight, her cigarette poised between two vertical fingers. A straight white line slashed against the black leather, she occupied minimal space, her pose borrowed from the pages of *Vogue* – a copy of which rested on her knee.

I held my gaze until she met it. When she did, her blue eyes narrowed. I smiled. Flushed with satisfaction, she looked away; she'd cast her bait and I'd bitten. Her lips swollen, she rolled some self-important thought around her tongue. I laughed. She glanced back.

'You got a cigarette?' I said.

She hesitated, then flustered, 'Yes!' She reached for the packet of Marlboro on the table between us, and her pose unfolded into a mass of angles. I peered down the front of her dress, at her flat chest, her soft apathetic pink nipples. She stood up, leant across and offered me a cigarette. I slouched against the sofa as she stooped ridiculously in mid-air, her thin arm extended towards me. I took one and she collapsed back into her seat, her magazine pose a shambles, a muddle of long limbs and bony joints. Her gaze flitting everywhere but at me, she blushed and ran her fingers through her short hair; picking up her phone, she searched through text messages she'd read only minutes before.

'A light?' I asked.

'Oh, sorry!' She rifled through her Louis Vuitton holdall and produced a Zippo. She held out the flame and looked away. I leant forward, enjoying her discomfort, and lit my cigarette.

'You waiting for someone?'

'Yes.' She kept her face from me. 'Yes, I am.' Her words were beautifully enunciated, glossed with a fine English polish.

'A friend?'

'Yes.'

'Me too.'

She finished her cigarette and immediately lit another; she was rapt with her phone, desperate for it to ring and deliver her.

'Is that your magazine?' I asked.

She looked up. 'Yes?'

'Can I read it?'

She looked at me, puzzled, and slid it across the table. I picked it up and flicked through shining pictures of thin white girls with big feet and pantomime make-overs, dressed in gaudy outfits by Gucci and Versace. I looked up and caught her staring at me; she looked away.

'I hate waiting for people,' I said. 'Don't you?'

'Yes.'

'Thanks for letting me read your magazine.'

'That's okay.' She looked towards the door.

'You get it every month?'

'Yes. I like the fashion.'

'You work in fashion?' I glanced at the hem of her pale yellow minidress, draped over her thigh. 'That's a lovely outfit.'

'Oh, thank you!' She sat up and smiled.

'Where did you get it?'

'Valeron Da Silva lent it to me,' she gushed. 'He's a

22

close friend.' She brushed the hem with her hand. 'It's one of his favourites.'

'I bet he looks great in it.'

She laughed and cocked her eyebrow in mock admonishment. 'He's brilliant! He's my favourite designer.'

'Yeah.' I nodded, knowing nothing about him. 'Mine too. You work in fashion, then?'

'I work at Val's studio, in Hoxton.'

'Hoxton? I live near there.'

'Really?' she said, butting in. 'I help him out with lots of things, like PR and stuff.'

'Sounds great,' I lied.

'It's fantastic. And I model as well. For his shows and stuff . . . I *really* love working with him.'

'Yeah?'

'Definitely! He's got so much . . . *energy*! You know? I don't think established designers have the same fire. That *edge*.' She spoke with passion, her stare was intense; she made me want to laugh. 'You have to take risks when you're starting out, to get seen,' she said. 'But when money rolls in, they get stale, conservative. No *energy*! No *edge*!'

'None.'

'I write about that kind of thing. I'm a writer too.'

'Oh?' I sat up, interested.

'I've just finished a piece for *Cosmopolitan*.'

'Oh.' I glanced around to see if Luca had arrived. I was annoyed at being punctual, knowing he never would be. I wanted to call him, but remembered I'd left my phone at Rory's. I sighed; if Rory got my message, I'd suffer him for a second night in succession. I thought of the night before, of how Rory had prattled on for hours about his new man ('He's *so* handsome. But then I think Asian men generally are . . . He's a Muslim, and I'm C of E . . . Do you think that's a problem?').

'It's a good magazine.'

'Huh?'

'*Cosmopolitan*,' she said. 'A lot of people read it, you know.'

'Yeah,' I sighed. 'Anorexics, and women who can't fuck.' She looked at me open-mouthed. 'What kind of idiot needs to read a piece on how to suck off her man? Its features are either on how to get a man, how to fuck a man, or how to keep a man . . . It's bullshit.'

She laughed, mistaking my tone for cockiness.

I smiled and rose to my feet. 'Fancy a drink?'

'I'd love one.' She stood up, holding her bag. She was an inch or two taller than me. 'Vodka and slimline, please. I'll just visit the bathroom.' She looked me in the eye then strolled away, one arm dropped by her side, eyes lowered to the floor with studied nonchalance. I watched the hard outline of her hips, her tight waist and the long stride of her lean white legs.

I stood at the bar, waiting for my drinks. I used to drink at the Peacock quite often, but now it felt oppressive. In less than a year it had changed from my rendezvous of choice into a hub for backpackers. The place was full of Australians and South Africans, the air jammed with their noise and the smell of cheap beer. London was full of these people. I didn't like them; they were shrill and full of berserk enthusiasm. Like a strange Galapagos finch, these honkies had evolved in isolation from the rest of their kind; they were now deeply unsure of themselves, deeply paranoid. Beside me, a man stood wearing a Springbok jersey speaking loudly to his friends in Afrikaans; his body upright and stiff from trekking the plains, tilling the soil, tormenting the *kaffir*.

The drinks arrived and I took them back to the redhead, who was sat against the arm, toying with her hair and pretending not to notice me. I sat down beside her.

'Oh, hi!' she smiled. She'd prettied herself with rust-coloured lipstick and black eyeshadow; her eyes were pale and glacial.

'Your friend still hasn't shown up?'

'No,' she said. 'She told me she'd be here at half-seven. I don't know what she's doing.'

24

'You're not meeting your boyfriend?'

'No.'

'You got a boyfriend?'

'No,' she smiled.

'Oh-kay.' The word dropped lazily from my lips.

She gave me a wide stare. 'What does that mean?'

'What does what mean?'

'Okay.'

'It's an American word for *yes*. You've not heard it before?'

'I know what it *means* . . .' she laughed. 'It's the way you said it. I want to know why you said it like that.'

'Like what?'

She gave me a coy look. I smiled.

'You're very naughty.' She giggled, shaking her head.

'Am I?' I relaxed into the sofa, arms outstretched.

Watching me, she asked, 'Who are you, anyway?'

'I'm the boy your mum warned you about.'

'Oh, really?' She turned away, trying to seem bored.

I leant towards her and rested my palm against her back; I could feel the hard nodes of her spine. 'My name's Bhupinder.'

'Boo-Pin-Darr.' She tried to pronounce it right, but anglicised it completely, as if it originated in Pimlico not Punjab. 'I'm Sophie. Nice to meet you.' She smiled and offered me her hand.

I held it and brushed her knuckles with my thumb. I looked at her clean, long fingers, and neat unvarnished nails. Her feet were equally honed, her soft toes naked in a simple pair of sandals, a Chinese character tattooed on one ankle. I raised my drink: 'To absent friends.'

'Indeed!' she laughed.

We touched glasses. She caught sight of something behind me and glared over my head: 'Sarupa!' she cried.

I shuddered.

Sophie clambered over the back of the sofa. 'Baby, you look fantastic! How have you been? How was the holiday?'

'It was great, thanks. Sorry I'm late . . . I'm *really* sorry.'
The voice was smooth, tantalising as ever.

'Where's Duncan?' asked Sophie. 'Have you left him at home?'

I waited anxiously for the reply.

'He's on his way. He's looking for somewhere to park.'

I took a deep breath and turned around. She was much darker than before, had the burnished copper glint of brown skin that's captured the sun. She wore a pair of tight denim hipsters, her wonderful flesh almost exploding from them. Her belly was exposed beneath a short electric-pink top; her big tits bounced beneath the chiffon. She glowed with health and money. She saw me and narrowed her eyes – almond-shaped, lined with kohl – wondering why I was there. Sophie's gaze followed hers.

'Oh sorry,' said Sophie, 'I forgot all about you. Sarupa, this is Boo . . . Boo . . .'

'Bhupinder,' I said. 'My name's Bhupinder.'

'Yes, of course. This is my friend Sarupa.'

Sarupa stepped forward. 'You know Luca, don't you?'

At how many parties had I stood talking to thin air while she ignored me? How often had I made a fool of myself trying to get a word from her? Now, after years of tweaking my ego, she chose to recognise me. I sat there prick-teased and dumbstruck like a stupid teenager. I became aware of my silence and daft expression. I opened my mouth, sifted my mind for a reply and found none. Sophie watched me.

'Yeah!' I gasped. 'I'm sorry for staring . . . You look *just* like my mum.' I was lying off the cuff.

Sophie laughed; Sarupa raised an eyebrow.

'When my mum was young,' I added. 'It's uncanny.'

'I hope that's a compliment,' said Sarupa.

'My mum's a peach.' I stood up and walked around the couch. 'I think I have seen you around. You're another of Luca's many friends, aren't you?'

'We know a lot of the same people.' She looked at her watch; it was an Hermès classic with a beige strap. 'I bumped into him last night,' she said. 'He's meant to be here. He said he'd swing by for a drink.'

'He's never on time.'

'No?'

'No.' I couldn't look into her eyes, so stared at her chin, at her thick glossed lips.

She looked at Sophie and I. 'How do you know each other?'

'We were just chatting!' chirruped Sophie. 'We've just met. I had no idea you two were friends!'

'We're not,' she said. 'Not really. We just go to the same clubs sometimes.' She stared at me; her gaze was impossible to hold. My eyes flitted to her sleek eyebrows, then downwards to her necklace; a diamanté teardrop rested on the brink of her dark fat cleavage.

'God, it's a small world,' laughed Sophie. 'I'm here meeting Sarupa, you're here to meet her friend, and here we are meeting each other. Hilarious!'

'And your mate even looks likes my mum,' I said. 'What a small world.'

Sophie laughed. Sarupa looked irritated.

'I was just getting to know Sophie here,' I said. 'We had a great chat about her work. Very glamorous, isn't she?'

Sophie wrinkled her nose and looked at the floor. 'I was telling him about the piece I've written for *Cosmo*,' she said.

'You're writing for *Cosmo*?' Sarupa looked surprised.

'And I've just pitched something to *Vogue*. I might be going to St Lucia, to write about a new spa. Isn't that great?'

'That's brilliant,' said Sarupa. She touched Sophie's dress: 'That's lovely. Where did you get it?'

'Val lent it to me. Have I told you I'm working for him now?'

'No. Doing what?'

'Well . . .' Sophie paused bashfully. 'Val wants me to model for him. I'm doing a shoot for him in a few weeks!'

'That's fantastic.' Sarupa's tone was warm and generous, though not actually impressed. 'We should have a drink then, to celebrate. Champagne.' She turned to me: 'You'll have a glass, won't you?'

'I'd love one. Thank you.'

I watched Sarupa walk to the bar in her denim hipsters; her big arse swung like a bell. Sophie and I sat back down on the couch.

'Congratulations,' I said. 'You must be thrilled.'

'I am,' she grinned. 'I couldn't wait to tell Sarupa, she's one of my best friends. Isn't she gorgeous?'

'How do you know her?'

'Through my cousin, Duncan. They're engaged. Do you know Duncan?'

I shook my head. 'Not really. I've seen him around.' Hearing his name grated on me. I sipped my drink. 'How long have they been together?'

'He's thirty-three now . . . So I guess it's about seven years. They're getting married next summer.'

I stared into my whisky. 'And how old are you?'

'I'm twenty-four . . .' She paused. 'He's amazing, Duncan. *So* successful!'

'Yeah?'

'He's got this loft-house on Cheyne Walk. It's *beautiful* . . . We had a *lovely* dinner there at New Year's.'

'What does he do?'

'He works in the City with his dad. It's their family business . . . It's like a hundred years old or something.' She lit herself a cigarette and stared at me. 'You know what?'

'What?'

'You haven't told me a thing about yourself, Poohpanda.'

'Bhupinder. My name's Bhupinder.'

'Oh, I am sorry.' She blushed. 'Boo-Pin-Darr. I'll remember that. Boo-Pin-Darr.'

'My nickname's Puppy,' I smiled. 'You can call me Puppy.'

'What an odd nickname. Who gave you that?'

'My mum.'

'Whatever for?'

I thought of explaining how *Papi* is a common Punjabi pet name – which my friends mispronounced as 'Puppy' – but I couldn't be bothered. 'I don't know,' I said.

Sophie narrowed her gaze: 'You're a curious man, Puppy.'

'How so?'

'You just *are*.'

'Not as curious as you.'

'What do you mean?' She leant forward to use the ashtray, enough for me to see her boy-tits, the bony contours of her sternum prodding through her skin.

'It's not every day I hang out with a supermodel.'

'Hardly!' she laughed.

'You're very beautiful . . .'

Her face glazed; I'd touched a nerve that numbed her.

'. . . *Very* beautiful.'

She shrank with embarrassment, peeking at me through streaks of red hair she ruffled over her face. I watched her silly behaviour; she was dim and easily flattered, but very sweet. We sat quietly and sipped our drinks, exchanging smiles and glances.

Sarupa returned holding Duncan's hand. He stood beside her, dressed in the Gap mufti of the English middle class: khaki trousers, a white T-shirt and desert boots. He had a blond short back and sides with a long foppish fringe. I could barely look at him.

'Dunky!' squealed Sophie. She jumped from the sofa and wrapped herself around him. 'How are you, darling?' She kissed both his cheeks. He was almost a foot shorter than her, squat and barrel-chested; he looked like an enormous toddler. He untangled himself from Sophie's embrace, raised a flat palm and gave me a stiff wave.

'Hi,' he said. 'I'm Duncan.'

We shook hands. He looked atrocious: dusty flakes of

skin peeled from his nose; his face was pink with a rough brownish texture, like braised salmon.

'Sophie,' he said, turning to her, 'I had to stop Sarupa getting the drinks in. We haven't time. The table's booked for half-eight.'

'You guys going?' I addressed Sophie, but thought of Sarupa; this was the closest I'd ever been to her. 'Won't you finish your drink?'

'Of course we will!' said Sophie. She dropped back into her seat. 'Sit down guys. We'll be fine.'

Duncan shrugged and sat beside his cousin. I felt Sarupa's belly skim my forearm as she sat next to me. Our knees touched; I didn't move away, nor did she.

'Sarupa says you've got exciting news,' said Duncan. 'What is it?'

'Let's wait until dinner,' replied Sophie. 'I don't want to bore Puppy by saying it all again.'

'It's worth waiting for,' I said.

'Well, they do say that no news is good news.' Duncan chuckled at his own inane humour; Sophie indulged him with a smile.

'You two been on holiday?' I asked. 'You look like you've been in the sun.'

'You have such an amazing tan, Sarupa,' said Sophie. 'I'm *so* jealous. I can't go in the sun at all.'

'You burn easily?' I asked, noting the state of Duncan's face.

'Not really. It's my agency, they like me to keep my complexion fair.' She nodded at Sarupa: 'I mean tans are great. You look stunning. But if you're a model, there's more work for you if you've got . . .' She paused apologetically. '. . . The *classic* look.'

'The English rose,' I remarked. I felt Sarupa harden with irritation, and turned to her: 'Your friend's very beautiful, don't you think?'

'Incredibly,' she mumbled. She reached for the cigarette packet on the table.

'How was your holiday?' asked Sophie.

30

'Lovely,' said Sarupa. She took Sophie's cigarette to light her own. 'It was just perfect.'

'I bet it was,' said Sophie. 'I'd *love* to go to Kenya.'

'You went to Kenya?' I asked, unsurprised.

'Got back the other day, didn't we sweetie?' Sarupa swapped glances with Duncan. 'We borrowed my dad's place in Mombasa for a fortnight. It's right by the beach, which is amazing. It's just beautiful. I love it there.' She reached across me to use the ashtray, her big tits brushing my arm. I could smell her hair; it was black and sun-streaked, washed with some fruity, girly lotion. She sat back, stretched out her legs and put her shoes on the table; she wore a scuffed pair of Adidas Superstars. I looked at her bare ankles.

'You like my trainers?'

'Pardon?'

'You're staring at my feet.'

'They're great.' I looked up, and her gaze snagged on mine for an instant. Her brown eyes unnerved me, and I broke away to smile at Sophie who was smoking her cigarette. Duncan was staring stupidly into space.

Sarupa stood up and looked at her watch. 'We really ought to go,' she said. 'We'll lose our table.'

'Okay,' sighed Sophie. She looked at me: 'It was nice meeting you, Puppy.'

'Lovely to meet you too.' I spread my gaze to catch all three of them, especially Sarupa.

'Tell Luca we waited for him, won't you?' she said.

'Sure.'

She didn't reply and walked to the door, her boyfriend in tow. Sophie sat fussing with her magazine and cigarettes, taking a deliberate while to put away her things and leave. She glanced sideways at me.

'Looking for something?' I said.

'Just making sure I've got all my stuff,' she murmured. 'Don't want to leave anything behind, do I?'

'No, you don't.'

She blushed, zipped up her bag, then hastened away. 'Byeee!' she cried.

I stared over her shoulder at Sarupa standing in the doorway with Duncan. He was a bland, perplexing enigma. How could he, an obvious mediocrity, have a woman like that? How was it allowed? I was appalled and desperately envious. Sarupa saw me looking at her. She linked arms with Duncan and whispered something in his ear; he grinned and held her waist. She kissed his lips; as she did so, she latched her eyes on mine. The taunt was irresistible. Sophie joined them in the doorway where the three of them had a quiet word before leaving. I dithered, trying to kid myself that another, better chance would come to meet Sarupa and make my play. I ran out after them.

The street was empty. I heard Sophie's laugh and chased it. I spotted them walking down a side road.

'Sophie!'

She turned around and froze; I jogged up to her.

'Sophie . . .' Her gaze flitted from my face to the floor and back again. 'Sorry to run after you like this,' I said. 'I couldn't just let you just go like that . . . I'd love to see you again. Maybe I can call you sometime? We can go out and have coffee?' I looked into her eyes. 'What do you think? Can I call you?'

She paused, looking shocked and bemused, and said, 'No.' The word landed on me like a rock. 'I don't give guys my number just like that.' Sarupa stood beside her, trying not to smirk.

'Oh . . .' I felt myself heat with embarrassment.

'But I'll take yours.' Sophie reached out and touched my hand.

'Huh?'

'*I'll* call *you*.'

I laughed with relief and told her my number, which she keyed into her phone. Duncan smiled encouragingly. Sarupa watched me carefully.

'You will call me?' I said. 'Won't you?'

'Don't worry.' Sophie held my hand. 'I will.'

'Soon?'

'Soon.' She held my wrist with both hands. 'I've got to

go.' She kissed my cheek and smiled, then turned to walk away. Duncan grinned and said goodbye. Sarupa said nothing and walked on.

I stood watching her big arse swing its way down the street. I wondered if she'd spoil things, tell Sophie how often I'd tried hitting on her in the past. But that would look like sour grapes. She wouldn't say a thing. I knew I'd see Sarupa again, and on better terms. I strolled back to the Peacock to wait for Luca.

3

BEHOLD!, THE ASIAN family: unit of tradition, moral strength and business acumen. Behold!, my mother: matriarch and fulcrum, proud bearer of sons, stately in her new sari, her one eyebrow draped across her forehead like a trophy pelt, her moustache downy like an adolescent boy's.

It was a lousy type of revenge. For her disappointments, we suffered a mother who looked like an animal. Walking with her through streets, down supermarket aisles, we felt ashamed, revolted, and guilty for feeling so. And there was the weight: a stone gained when each of us came of age not meeting her expectations. She was five feet tall, weighed as much as a man and sported a beard; her bulky plait trailed down to her arse. It started when Dad left, continued when I dropped out of university, and accelerated when my sister married outside the caste. Now it was my brother's fault. His obesity robbed her of a dowry, of a beautiful daughter-in-law who would fulfil her duties, make up for our failures.

Religion played its part. When Dad left she visited the temple most days and listened to the day-long service. Some idiot told her the truly devout did not pluck or trim a hair on their body: it was her calling. She took *amrit*, then observed every tenet. The beard, the thick adjoining eyebrows, became bullish assertions of faith, admired, even coveted, by her peers.

Putting a hand on each armrest, '*Wa-he Guru Jhi Ka Khalsa*,' she muttered, girding herself. '*Wa-he Guru Jhi Ka Fateh*!' she groaned, pushing herself out of the chair.

She had rheumatism and angina; she was fifty years old and called on God just to get out of bed, or climb the stairs. Stooped, hands on hips, she hobbled finding her balance, then shuffled out of the living room to the kitchen. The waist of her sari was drawn needlessly tight; a tyre of crinkled fat bulged from it.

Breathing noisily, my brother sat next to me in his smartest sweater and smartest trousers; his tasselled loafers were unpolished, worn and misshapen. Our silence had lasted a few minutes. It was now impossible.

'She seems like a nice girl,' I said.

'Yeah . . . She's alright.'

'Have you two talked about a date yet? For the wedding?'

'No.' Hari looked at me. His fat face gleamed with almond oil, applied after every bath since he was born. 'Mum'll do that,' he said. 'She'll chat to her folks and they can sort out all that. Leave them to it . . . I can't be fucked.' He paused nervously. 'Pups, you like her? Honest?'

I tried recalling the girl who'd sat opposite me. She was quiet, shy, not at all attractive nor repulsive, but so plain her face was a blank. I remembered she was dark; she had a Dravidian trace, a possible wiriness in the hair.

'You could do a lot worse,' I said.

'Yeah,' he grinned. 'She's fit.'

'Yeah.'

'I'm really glad you like her, Pups.' Deeply touched, he put a hand on my shoulder, his eyes shining on the edge of tears. Smooth-faced, with a greasy side parting and a heavy bosom, he looked like a lesbian. His need for my approval unsettled me. I shifted in my seat.

'You'll be great together.' I gave his hand an assuring pat.

'See how it goes . . .'

'You'll be fine.'

'Pups . . .' The boy's voice wavered. '. . . I'm really glad you came. I ain't seen you in *time*.' He put his arm around me. I looked at the floor. 'I never see you these days, he said. 'Don't be a stranger.'

'I won't.'

'Don't.' He hugged me. 'You're my big brother, isn't it?'

I looked up and saw he was crying. I looked at my sister, stood by the wall, regarding me with disgust. She was the anomaly among us; thin, with an ever-pinched expression, animated, like my mother, by a fitful peasant energy. Wearing a sari, she looked ridiculous; she did so as a child, prancing barefoot around the stage with some other kids at Diwali, in a dance full of twirls and hand-claps – the school's yearly nod to multiculture. She and my mother rarely wore saris; I wondered why they did today.

'They ain't givin' us nuffin'!' spat Rani. 'No gold, nuffin' . . .'

'Eh?' I cocked my ear to her.

'They ain't given no money, no jewellery, fuckin' nuffin' . . . And Hari's got a fuckin' shop!'

She annoyed me, playing marriage politics. Five years ago she eloped with someone we'd known since child-hood; for years I defended her, helped rehabilitate her with my mother. Yet still she was an old-world recidivist, who raised my nephews too sternly, harangued her husband to earn more money, buy more houses. She was baleful that Hari hadn't won a dowry.

'. . . And she's fuckin' ugly!'

Hari's face reddened; he looked away, tight-lipped. I was incensed. Jaw clenched, I told her to shut up.

'Fuck off!' She stepped away from the wall, arms still folded, her sharp face pointed at me. 'Who are you, tellin' me to shut up? My dad? My fuckin' husband? . . . Fuck off!' She stood over me, glowering. 'You know what, Pups? You're a cunt! You ain't never 'ere . . . You don't give a fuck about nuffin'! . . . You just do whatever you do – fuck knows what! – then come round 'ere tellin' us

36

what to do!' Purple with hate, she screamed, 'You don't give a fuck about Hari! Stickin' up for that fuckin' black fuckin' bitch!'

My brother squirmed uncomfortably. My anger subsided into my usual exhaustion when confronting my family. 'If Hari likes her,' I said, 'that's what matters.'

'Fuck off!'

'*Papi*!' roared my mother in the kitchen. I sighed, thinking she might join the fray. '*Papi*!' she cried again.

'What!'

'*Ti-li-foon*!'

I got up and walked to the kitchen. Mum stood over the stove, watching a pan of tea come to the boil. The room was thick with the smell of cardamom. My mobile phone was ringing on the table. I picked it up. The call was from Sophie; I diverted it to voicemail and put the phone in my pocket. I pulled a chair away from the kitchen table, sat down and watched my mum.

Tied in a bun, her hair was a thick whorl of ash-grey and white. Her feet were bare; her heels were calloused, nails blunted, by a lifetime of cheap, painful, ill-fitting shoes. She looked out of the window onto the small concrete backyard, littered with empty boxes from the shop. Hari left them there, piles of rotting cardboard and cellophane, for months at a time.

'*Cha pinha?*' She poured a cup and offered it to me.

'*Nhai.*'

She sipped it herself. She pulled another chair from the table and sat beside me. She asked me what the row had been about. I told her Rani was a bitch. She nodded and sipped her tea. I asked after her health. She said it was okay. She asked me about my work. I said it was okay. I asked if she'd heard from Dad. He'd phoned a few weeks ago, she said. He was okay.

I chewed my thumbnail, wanting a cigarette.

'*Naw nhi khaneh!*' she cried, slapping my hand from my mouth. The irritation swelled; I restrained it, exhaled slowly, and put my hands on my lap. We sat there, saying

37

nothing. I looked around the kitchen. Dishes filled the sink; the draining board was laden with cutlery. Old jars of chilli powder, cumin and dried coriander lined the windowsill beside a listless house plant, its leaves yellowing, decayed. An artless print of Guru Gobind Singh, riding a white horse above the temple at Amritsar, hung over the stove, on which sat the remains of lunch – a pan of spinach, a pan of cauliflower and a pot of rice. The lino – a gaudy mosaic of green and yellow – hadn't changed since I was a boy. The white plastic tablecloth was indelibly stained with turmeric.

She got up and put her cup in the sink. I watched her treading the old lino, and thought of the money I'd frittered, while she bore the brunt. She sighed and walked over to the kitchen cabinet. She rummaged inside it and found an old cocoa tin. She opened it, pulled out a roll of twenty-pound notes and held them out for me. I thanked her and told her I'd pay her back next month; I told her that my work, though slow of late, was picking up. As usual, I was lying. She frowned, saying nothing. She knew the cash was the only reason I was there. I couldn't look her in the face, so gazed at the floor. I took the money. She walked past me, back into the living room. I followed soon after.

Rani was stood by the wall, hot with anger and biting her nails. She tore a piece of cuticle from a finger and chewed it shrew-like. I sat on the sofa, next to my mother. On the wall before me were two pictures garlanded with synthetic flowers. One was Guru Nanak, haloed and beatific; the other was a black-and-white photo of my maternal grandfather taken after he'd died. Eyes closed, sullen-mouthed, he looked like a sleeping drunk. Wearing a white turban, he was draped in the hammer and sickle of the Communist Party. Another photo on the sideboard showed his body held aloft amid the hundreds who were at his cremation. He was the village *sarpanch*, a cadre who gave his all to the cause, though he was a complete illiterate. Soon after independence, an itinerant politico came to his village espousing Marxism, or rather a boiled-down version: everyone should be equal, and the rich are to be hated. So began a fifty-year collaboration between the Sidhu family and the Communist Party of India.

Also on the sideboard was a framed picture of Raja, our dog; part Alsatian, he died when I was seventeen. There was also a school photo of Rani and I, staring empty-eyed at the camera: Rani's hair was in two plaits that fell either side and out of shot; mine was in a knot on top of my head, tied in a Donald Duck handkerchief. Soon after, in time for high school, I wore a turban, blighting my adolescence. When I got rid of it and had a haircut, Mum spent three days in fast and prayer, interrupted only by sleep and fits of tears. My father never wore one, and my mother wasn't then baptised, but England brought out the zealot in her. I didn't eat a hamburger until I was eighteen, didn't have a proper shave until I was twenty.

I tried making conversation with my sister. 'When's Nav coming?'

She didn't reply.

'Will he bring the boys?'

Ignoring me, she sighed and walked to the armchair, sat down and resumed chewing her nails. My mum sat quietly beside me, dwelling on her own thoughts. Hari wasn't there. I guessed he was in the shop.

I went downstairs. It was the same messy hybrid of confectioner's, newsagent, grocery and liquor store as it was when I worked there. Behind the counter was the same chair I'd sat on after school and at weekends. Hari was standing outside the front door, smoking a cigarette. I walked up to him.

'Alright?'

'Fuckin' hell!' he gasped, turning around. 'I thought you were Mum!'

'She doesn't know you smoke?'

'Don't be stupid. You think I want a smack in the mouth?'

'Give me one.'

My brother gave me a cigarette and lit it for me. My phone buzzed in my pocket. I took it out. It was a text message from Sophie: 'wot r u doing? xx'.

I replied: 'why?'

Hari watched me as I sent the message. 'Who was that?' he asked.

'Some bird.'

'Your bitch?'

'No.'

'You got a bitch?'

'Not right now.'

'Man, you ain't had a woman for *time* . . . What's up?'

'I haven't got your magic touch,' I smiled. 'Look at you, getting hitched.'

'Yeah.' He nodded solemnly. 'Time to settle down, isn't it? I've had my fun.' He was nineteen years old. I wanted to ask what fun he'd had, with whom, and why he was set on this marriage. Looking at him – podgy fingered, smoking with overstated machismo, his guileless face, chequered jumper and soft belly – the questions answered themselves. My heart sank with regret.

I patted him on the arm. 'Playing days are over, yeah?'

'Yeah.'

'Well, good luck to you.'

'Pups?'

'Yeah.'

'You're coming to the wedding, isn't it?'

I paused, not wanting to lie: 'Course I am.'

'Yeah. Definitely,' laughed Hari. 'You're gonna be my best man and that.'

I said nothing; I looked at the street.

We smoked our cigarettes looking at Allenby Road, the front line separating Southall from Great Britain. This street is where the Punjabi tribe starts in force, leading downhill into the brown-skinned, petit bourgeois suburbia of Lady Margaret Road, which itself leads to the bustle, often mayhem, of the Uxbridge Road, Southall's high street. Cross over the road, go down the other side of the hill, and you come to Ruislip Road, Greenford's main street. The faces are whiter there, the pavements aren't full of people hawking Bollywood soundtracks while their asylum claims are processed.

My phone buzzed; again it was Sophie: 'i'm all alone! xx'.

'&?' I replied.

'You're busy with that phone,' said Hari. 'You got some dealings?'

'It's just a mate. Wants to hook up for a drink.'

We looked at the semi-detached houses opposite. One pair was painted the same harsh white and shared the same front garden and driveway; a gold Mercedes saloon was parked in it.

'Does Guv still live there?' I asked.

'Yeah. That's his motor.'

'The house looks different.'

'They bought the house next door, too,' explained Hari. 'He lives there with his mum, dad, missus, everyone.'

'Govinder got married?'

'Yeah. Time ago.'

'*No*. Really?'

'Serious. Some girl from India. And he's got a kid, a little boy.'

The newly fitted double glazing glinted in the evening light; a brick wall enclosed the buildings, finished with an iron gate and mock-Mogul decorations. A window in the roof opened onto an attic conversion.

'He's doing alright for himself,' I said.

'Yeah man!' said Hari. 'He's making 'nuff bucks. He's an accountant. They've done it wicked inside, knocked doors through the wall. They've got like a shared lounge and kitchen and that.' Hari nodded admiringly. 'Guv's a safe bloke. He's always coming in the shop with his kid. Kid speaks wicked Punjabi. *Ha-jhi, nhai-jhi, uncle-jhi*, all that . . . Wanna go say hello?'

'Another time.'

'His wedding was massive.'

41

'You went?'

'Yeah, me and Mum. They had Sunrise DJs and some comedian from Punjab. It was *bad*! Best wedding . . . Proper *desi* wedding.'

I looked at the house and thought of Mum seeing it every day, reminding her of the life she'd hoped for, the life she'd come here for. I sighed; I wanted to get away.

My phone buzzed; Sophie had sent me another text: 'want 2 cum round? bring sum wine? xx'.

'giv me 1 hr . . .' I replied. I squeezed my brother's arm: 'Hari, I've got to go.'

'Yeah?' He was visibly disappointed.

'Sorry mate. You know how shit it is getting across London without a car. If I don't go now, I'll be stuck on the Tube for ever.'

Hari opened the door and began walking inside. 'Go say goodbye to Mum,' he said.

'No.' I stopped him. 'It's a bit awkward up there. Just tell Mum I had a phone call. Say it was work.'

Hari stared at me, nonplussed.

'I don't need any more heat off Rani,' I said. 'I'll catch up with you soon. Promise.'

Hari walked back onto the street and held out his hand. I shook it. He stepped closer and put his arms around me; I hugged him close.

'It was good seeing you, Pups.'

'Good seeing you, too.' I kissed the side of his face. 'Give my love to Mum.'

'I will.'

We let go and looked at each other.

'Be cool,' I said.

'I will.'

'I'll call soon.'

'Yeah.'

'See you later then.'

'Laters.' Hari stepped back inside and closed the door, watching through the glass as I turned away.

I walked to the corner of the street. The old man at the

video store was standing outside; on the window behind him was a poster for a Bollywood film, bearing the face of an actress I didn't know and a title I didn't understand. I looked at the floor, pretending not to see him, and headed to the bus stop.

4

I'VE ALWAYS LOVED women. Not in the way they want to be loved – exclusively, with unwavering attention – but in my own selfish, utterly sincere way. Even as a child. I hadn't begun school when I stole my sister's dolls. I'd kiss their mouths, buttocks and chests; I smelt their nylon hair, their plastic skins. Breathtaken by this petting, I'd hide them naked behind the sofa, exhilarated. It wasn't just the slim, long-haired Sindys I loved, but also the big squat baby dolls who were brunette, red-haired, sometimes bald. Some were brown-skinned; one was black with Dionne Warwick curls. I loved them all. I loved women, girls; I longed to be loved by them.

My parents, progressive in a way, sent me to school in Greenford; they thought white kids were smarter, and that this would help me. There were three other Asians in my class: a Sikh boy, a Sikh girl, and Asaf, an impoverished Pakistani dressed in oversized hand-me-downs. I was the most conspicuous, my hair coiled behind my head like some prissy *Frau*. I was nine years old when Mum tied it in a *joodha*, a bun wrapped in a handkerchief, like a little suet pudding.

At first Asaf and I went to a special-needs group (my English wasn't very good; we never spoke it at home). Twice a week Asaf and I were collected, along with children from other schools, in a small bus fitted out like a classroom. The teacher had auburn hair, dark eyes and elegant hands; she'd kneel behind me, put her hand on mine and guide my finger over letters of the alphabet. I'd hear my breathing slow down in an envelope of calm. I craved her; I was in love. I also made my first friend there, Russell, who was fat and gypsy-coloured; we'd take turns throwing each other onto the school-yard concrete. My English improved and I left; I never saw those two again.

Asaf, however, was a bane who tailed me for years. We were pariahs for being explicit wogs – I for my tribal plaits, while Asaf had a tart dank stink, like a latrine. The two Sikh kids – both with haircuts and fluent English – made friends with white children and kept their distance. Asaf was later joined by my sister, who was a year younger. They followed me at break times; we'd wander in silent single file around the playground, watching the others having fun and hearing their laughter. We never spoke. In fact, I hated them; their presence underscored my loneliness. And they never spoke to each other: Rani was raised to hate Muslims; Asaf was raised to hate girls.

PE lessons were hell; I was invariably paired with Asaf. He never had a gym kit, so exercised barefoot in his musky vest and Y-fronts. We'd make intimate shapes with our bodies interlocked; his skin was tangy with sweat and *garam masala*. I'd retch holding his clammy feet.

Summer held the worst, most dispiriting occasion. The class performed a country dance routine, rehearsed for weeks and staged in the playing fields. The ritual began with the girls choosing their dance partner for that year. The boys would line up in the practice hall; the golden boys were picked first, blond-haired tykes with ear studs and scabbed elbows. I watched the girls, flushed and bronzed, pink-cheeked and lovely: with each decision I was destroyed. The boys were whittled down to the runts, but even the mad hyperactive black kid who stabbed us all with his pencil was chosen. Finally there were Asaf and I and two girls, who picked each other. Our bastard form tutor, a dumpy grey-haired sow, oversaw all this. Each year she alternated the male role between Asaf and I, while the other fawned and curtsied, mortified before the whole school, who sat cross-legged on the green – my sister among them.

* * *

I rolled onto my side and pulled the sheet over me; I nestled myself in silk, savoured it against my skin. The blinds were half drawn; sunshine poured through the window. I closed my eyes and still saw it, an orange haze behind my eyelids. I shifted again, to get comfortable and drift into sleep.

'You're such a wriggler,' yawned Sophie. 'I've never known anyone wriggle so much.'

'Sorry.'

'I love sleeping . . .' She put her hand on my shoulder, ran her finger along my biceps and stroked faint circles on my elbow. '. . . And you keep waking me up.'

I pulled the sheet off me and sat up.

'What are you doing?'

'I'm waking you up. I'll let you get some sleep.'

'Don't go.' She put her hand on my hip. I lay down again, facing her. She pulled the sheet over me and drew herself close, draping her leg over mine, resting her face in my chest. Her body was warm. I put my hand on her thigh; with my fingertip I drew the same circles she'd caressed me with. I kissed her hair.

'Mmmmmmm.' She tucked herself closer. 'I *want* you.'

'What do you mean? I'm right here.'

'*I want you*,' she whispered.

'You want sex? *Again?*'

She slid her hand onto the small of my back, pulled herself closer and nuzzled me. '*I want you.*'

'You want me . . .' I thought about it, resting my chin on her head. '. . . In your life?'

She nodded, her eyes still closed. I lay there, taking it in, holding her quietly. She glided her foot along my shin. I kissed her cheek; I stroked her earlobe, kissed that, too. She sighed, rolled onto her back and inclined her head, offering her throat. I kissed it, pinching her nipple, then ran my hand over her stomach. I licked the skin just below her ear, put my hand between her legs, rubbed the opening of her cunt and felt it dampen. She reached for my prick and held it.

'You're always so *hard*,' she grinned. 'Let me suck you.'

'No.' I rose onto my knees and placed myself between her legs; lifting her hips, I pushed a pillow beneath her back. Arms splayed, she watched me. I held her calf, raised her leg and looked at her pussy; I licked my thumb and rubbed her clit. I pressed the tip of my erection against it, then slid it along the seam. She giggled.

'You want me to stop?'

She shook her head. I pushed it inside her, and she sighed. I laid myself on top of her, fucking her deep and slow, my cheek pressed against hers, my breath whispering in her ear. My body weighed her down; she hugged me close and grasped my hair, wrapping her legs around my waist. Her cunt grew loose and wet; I raised myself up and rammed her hard. I forced the pace, grabbing the bedstead one-handed for purchase, hearing it rattle. She clawed my hips, her eyes screwed shut; teeth gritted, her breath was short and hoarse. The skin was taut across her ribs; she had a thick brown mole beneath her right breast. She didn't really have breasts, just nipples, pink and stubby like eraser tips. I closed my eyes and concentrated.

'Ow!' she cried.

I slowed down. 'Am I hurting you?'

'You're pulling my hair!' My other hand, resting by her head, had trapped a few strands. 'Don't stop!'

I held the bedstead two-handed and fucked her as hard as I could. My thigh muscles started to burn. Eyes fraught, Sophie gripped the sheet in each hand; neck strained backwards, her nostrils flared, showing empty hairless sockets. I shut my eyes and focused, forcing the same tempo. I came and collapsed beside her, fighting for breath, prickly with heat. She rolled onto her stomach, grabbed my hand and clasped it to her vulva, squirming to give herself a climax. She finished with a groan and lay there panting. I got out of bed and rifled through the clothes strewn on the floor. I found my jeans and a packet of cigarettes; I picked them up and went to the kitchen.

Like the rest of the apartment, it was ultra-modernist, ultra-minimal, with a tiled limestone floor and matching chalk-white walls. The refrigerator and appliances were bright chrome; halogen lamps were recessed in the ceiling. At the centre of the room, circled with tall blond-wood Jacobsen stools, was a wooden console incorporating the hob and the sink, filled with accumulated pans. Rice, slices of mushroom and other debris floated in the grey water. The work surface was littered with pottery bowls – some daubed with Sophie's tasteless ragout, others caked with breakfast cereal – amid a puddle of red wine that crept into the wood.

'What a fucking tramp,' I muttered.

Half a loaf of desiccating bread sat by an ashtray piled high with lipstick-smeared butts. I cut two slices and put them in the Dualit toaster. I looked for a coffee jar and found none. I came across some beans, then searched out a grinder, then a mocha pot full of mouldering grinds. I emptied it, figured out how to use it all, then lit the stove. Finally I made some coffee, but the mugs were either in the sink or had cigarette ash in them. The milk in the fridge was sour. Drinking my coffee black from a clay bowl, barefoot and bare-chested, sat on a breakfast stool in the dishevelled luxury of Sophie's kitchen, I looked the epitome of beatnik chic. Thinking this, I laughed and lit a cigarette from the hob.

'What are you laughing at?'

I turned around. Sophie walked into the kitchen, wearing my T-shirt and rubbing her hair, a short spiky mess. Still warm with sleep and sex, she hugged me. She kissed my shoulder, bit the skin.

'Don't get too close,' I said. 'I need a shower.'

'You smell lovely.' She hugged me tighter.

'Like what? I stink.'

'Like a *boy*,' she smiled. 'Like a naughty little boy. All smelly.'

She looked at me, her eyes blind and vacant without her contacts. We French kissed, our mouths dry with the

48

night's drinking and smoking, the taste of one another's come. My prick stiffened. I held her buttocks; I gripped one and she moaned, moving her head back and forth, sucking my tongue. I fingered her arsehole; she liked it and pushed her hips back, easing it in further. I dug my finger in deep, pulled her close and sucked her mouth hard. I thought about fucking her again, but saw no reason to spoil her. I drew my face away and nodded to the bowls of coffee, the two slices of toast lying on the work top. 'I've made breakfast.'

'*Ooh*,' she cooed. 'You're so sweet.' She kissed my cheek and climbed onto my lap, her pelvis jabbing through her flesh into my thigh. She nibbled at the corner of her toast, sipped some coffee, then reached for the ashtray. Sifting through the butts, dropping some on the floor and dusting her fingers with ash, she found a half-smoked joint. 'Got a light?' she asked.

I gave her my cigarette; she lit the joint and inhaled a mouthful. She held her breath, then blew out a cloud of sweet-smelling smoke. She took a few more drags then gave it to me. I finished it, and was stoned immediately. I wrapped my arms around her. She was as slight as a boy, like Hari when he was ten. The thought stung me. I sighed, remembering Hari on my lap, laughing demonically when I tickled him. I thought of him sitting quietly on my bed, reading my comic books while I did my homework, or just happy to be there and have my company. I thought of him rapt and delighted as we watched *Wildlife on One*. I thought of how he worshipped me, and how I left him with my mother and her failure, with no one to make him laugh and nothing to do but go to school, work in the shop, and eat himself into a stupor.

'What's the matter?' asked Sophie.

'Huh?'

'You look sad.' She stroked my cheek. 'You alright?'

'I'm just stoned,' I said. 'My head's going all over the place.'

'Aaw.' She gave me a frown. 'Come on, lazy. Why don't you go out and get some more fags?'

'No,' I said, irritated. 'I'll take a shower.'

We sat in silence. Eventually I mustered the wherewithal to get up and stretch my limbs. I washed my bowl under the tap, filled it with water and drank. Sophie sat on the stool with her eyes closed, smiling to herself, her slim-fingered hands cupped in her lap. My T-shirt hung shapelessly on her frame, just over her thigh; her long white legs tapered to the floor. She rubbed a buffed, pedicured foot against her tattooed ankle. Her toes were svelte, the nails varnished raspberry, her soles black and filthy.

She opened her eyes and looked at me with blue unseeing eyes. 'What are you doing?'

'Nothing.'

'You're doing *something*.' She narrowed her gaze.

'How can you tell?'

'I just *can*,' she said. 'I can tell when you're being naughty.'

'I'm just looking at you.'

'Oh don't!' She hid her face in her hands. 'I'm a mess!' She bent into her lap, showing only the back of her head, her dark-red hair cropped and tousled.

'You look lovely.'

'I don't.'

'You do,' I said. 'You look lovely in my top. Very day-sha-billy.'

She sat up and laughed. '*Déshabillé*,' she corrected, her accent perfect.

'Is it French?'

She nodded.

'I didn't know that.' I was embarrassed. 'I wish I spoke French. All I speak is English and Punjabi.'

'That's got to be some use.'

'Is it fuck. You don't know many Punjabis.'

She smiled uncertainly.

'They're good at drinking,' I said, 'and fighting. Sometimes spin bowling. That's about it.'

Sophie paused thoughtfully, then asked, 'Is that what you're like?'

'I'm not that talented.'

She sat thinking to herself. I squeezed her shoulder and told her I was taking a shower.

The shower had a room all to itself; it was my favourite room in the flat. Limestone tiled, with chrome fittings and lamps in the ceiling, it had the same clinical austerity as the kitchen. I imagined some howling cretin locked inside, being hosed down against his will. I stood under hard jets of hot water, trying to wake up. I looked at myself in the mirror, and liked what I saw. I'm a typical Singh: broad-chested and thick-limbed, I have heavy eyebrows, my father's good skin and my mother's long eyelashes. I showered leisurely, helping myself to Sophie's avocado and oatmeal scrub, her vanilla conditioner. I finished with a sharp burst of cold water, gasping from the shock. There was no towel. I wrung my hair and brushed the excess water from my skin with my hands, then walked through the hallway, leaving damp prints on the bare, expensively restored hardwood floor. I was tempted to go back and mop up, but Sophie, languid on the bed in a cannabis daze, didn't seem to care. The T-shirt was hiked around her navel; her sleek belly rose with her breath. I looked at her beautiful pussy – a waxed-thin strip, brown and mousy, unlike her head.

I put on my jeans and cast an eye over her bookshelf. She had *The Celestine Prophecy* and its sequel, both Bridget Jones novels, all things Harry Potter, Martin Amis and Zadie Smith, a lot of books on horses, and a couple by Deepak Chopra. On the shelf below were her CDs – Blur, Moby, Madonna . . .

She sat up. 'Do you fancy going out for lunch?'

'Where?'

'Nearby. Sarupa called. She wants to go out.'

Faking disinterest, I asked, 'Does she want me to come too?'

51

'I forgot to say you were here. But she won't mind. Why should she?'

'I don't know. Maybe she just wants to meet up with you.'

'She won't care. Come on, it's a lovely day.'

'Okay,' I said. 'I will.'

Sophie stood up and took off my T-shirt, dropped it on the floor and shuffled naked to the shower. I picked it up and put it on, then lay back on the bed and stared at the high ceiling, thinking of Sarupa.

It was Saturday afternoon. I looked from the café balcony onto Portobello Road. It was a miscegenist heaven: white women clung to well-wrought ethnic studs who pushed tricycle pushchairs laden with fat brown babies; demure young white men guided Asian girlfriends through stalls selling hookahs, avant-garde sneakers and sun-dried tomatoes.

The café was crowded, full of people drinking Spanish beer and eating parmesan and rocket salads, enjoying the pluralist esprit de corps of Notting Hill. I hated the area: a vapid would-be bohemia, it was too fey for imagination and radicalism, but had odd pockets of deprivation, the remnants of the old West Indian quarter. It was home to the corporate rump of the creative media – scriptwriters, agents, marketing impresarios – and a hub for the under-belly of the English bourgeoisie: antique-dealing heroin addicts, thespians-turned-coke-dealers, New Age charla-tans selling Ayurveda to the upper classes. I preferred where Sophie lived, in Holland Park, in a Georgian town house converted into three flats, all owned by her stepfather. There, everything was pristine; almost everyone was white. It felt beautiful, stepping out of the house and into her car, exchanging nods with the couple who lived opposite, obvi-ous millionaires who assumed I was one too. Money alchemises people, the mere suspicion of it changes *every-thing*. The gentilesse of Sophie's street – people sharing glances and smiles, stepping aside for one another on the pavement – came from the mutual assumption of wealth. They were a beloved elect: Europeans, Arabs, Americans and Jews; each saw the other through a prism of money, and loved what they saw. I lived in Hackney where people had nothing, or just enough to inspire resentment. Hackney's rich owned Land Rover Discoveries and Smeg fridge-freezers; Holland Park's owned *the world*.

Sophie sat beside me, her red eyes hidden behind sunglasses. She pored over the latest copy of *Tatler* and sipped a Diet Coke. We kept a seat free for Sarupa, but had to share our table with a delicate young couple who were reading the *Guardian* and drinking fruit smoothies. One read a piece on GM crops; the other glanced through a feature on Iranian art-house films. Both wore short hair, Levi's, sandals and black rectangular spectacles; their faces bore the idealism, the vague suicidal melancholy of white English liberalism.

Smoking my cigarette felt uncomfortable in the heat. I shifted my chair, moving my face from the glare of direct sunlight. My stomach quavered; I didn't want to be there, but daren't lose the chance to see Sarupa. She arrived on the balcony; Sophie waved excitedly and called her over. I sat still in my seat, staring at my coffee. The girls greeted each other, kissed each other's cheeks.

'Hello,' said Sarupa, standing over me. 'I didn't know you were coming.' She wore a grey sports bra beneath a short denim jacket, blue jogging bottoms and running shoes. Her hair was tied back; her skin was bright, freshly showered.

'I was at Sophie's when you called,' I said. 'She asked me to tag along.'

'Well, it's a nice surprise.' She looked at us. 'Look at you two. You're quite an item now, aren't you?'

'Yeah,' smiled Sophie. She took my hand and interlaced our fingers.

'You look lovely together,' smiled Sarupa. 'How long is it you've been seeing each other? A month?'

'Just about,' I replied.

She walked around the table, sat on the spare seat and took off her jacket. I couldn't bear to look; her breasts, her succulence, killed me. Every bit of her – belly, lips, ankles – was plump and enticing. I wanted to bite her, make her bruise. The white guy beside me sat up and gave himself an eyeful. His girlfriend noticed and he went back to his paper.

We chatted briefly about the weather. Sarupa asked a few innocuous questions about life and work, and asked after Luca. Then the conversation switched to gossip about people she had in common with Sophie. They spoke between themselves. I felt stupid having come along to sit at the margin with nothing to say, nothing to do but flick through Sophie's *Tatler*. They talked for over an hour about their friends, their friends' relationships, and their friends' homes, cars, holidays and clothes. I looked at the words in the magazine but read nothing. I stole glances at Sarupa and boiled quietly, riled by her indifference to me.

Sarupa looked at her watch and said she had to leave. She leant around Sophie and looked at me: 'Nice to see you again, Puppy.'

I smiled and nodded.

'We should all go out again sometime,' she added. 'I'll bring Duncan.'

'That'll be great.'

She turned to Sophie: 'What are you doing on Wednesday? I've got tickets for Eminem, but I can't go. Do you want them?'

'Where is it?' she asked.

'Brixton.'

Sophie looked at me: 'Shall we go?'

'I hate hip hop.'

'Oh?' said Sarupa, looking surprised.

'That fucking crap,' I said, 'is for bums and retards.'

They both gave me blank stares.

'And children,' I added. 'Do you know what I heard on the radio the other day?'

They shook their heads.

'Some idiot rapper. Listen to this shit.' I mimicked the hoarse voice, the rhythm, the ghetto gravitas. ' "*I ain't complacent in yo' facent, baby, I got what you need. Mercedes. DVDs.*" '

Sarupa laughed.

I laughed too. 'DVDs? . . . Mercedes? That's fucking bullshit . . . ! Rap is *so* dumb. It's for the dumbo sub-proletariat. It has to be dumb; they won't go out and buy it otherwise.'

'A lot of Asians listen to it,' said Sophie.

'What's that? A ringing endorsement?'

Sarupa laughed again.

The white couple looked up from their papers, staring at me with revulsion. Her sunglasses resting on her head, Sophie stared intently at the table; she was annoyed.

'What does "proletariat" mean?' she asked.

'Working class.'

She sat up and gave me a scathing look. 'Hip hop's not working class,' she hissed. 'It's *black*!'

I was about to argue back; we were on the point of our first argument. I checked myself, remembering Sophie's world view (she once said her dad must be paying her Filipino cleaner a fortune: 'Why else would she do such a shitty job?' Sophie was naive, out of sync with reality. But she was sweet; she had a moral logic). I said nothing and nodded. She looked back down at the table. She was hurt because I'd refused a night out with her.

Sarupa looked at us. Unsettled by the static, she stood up and said she had to leave.

'Me too,' I said. I held Sophie's hand. 'Come on, let's go.'

'No.' She drew her hand away and kept her face from me. 'I'll stay and finish my drink.'

I snuck a glance at Sarupa; she was frowning at me. I kissed Sophie's cheek and told her I'd call her later. She said nothing and glared impassively ahead. I stood up, took a twenty-pound note from my wallet and laid it on the table. Sarupa said an embarrassed goodbye. Sophie smiled at her, but didn't look at me. She put on her sunglasses, breathing heavily; she was going to cry. I didn't care.

Sarupa looked at me with irritation. 'I'm going,' she said, and walked away.

I looked back at Sophie – scowling behind her shades – then followed Sarupa into the café, down the stairs and into the street, still crowded with people. She was looking around, getting her bearings.

'Which way are you headed?' I asked.

'I'm parked that way.' She pointed towards Notting Hill Gate.

'I'm going to the station. Mind if I walk with you?'

She didn't reply and set off ahead of me. We picked our way through the throng, past stalls of tie-dyed skirts and incense burners. A tanned, bare-chested white man with blond dreadlocks sat on a milk crate, begging outside an off-licence. An old yellow Creole stood beside him in a dirty linen suit and a fedora, hobbling drunkenly to calypso playing from inside.

'I love this town,' I said, stepping around them, over the puddle leaking from the old man's trousers. Sarupa saw him and shook her head.

'Oh Lahd,' he sang, gawping at her. He doffed his hat and smacked his lips. 'Lahd ha' mercy . . . Sweet Lahd ha' mercy!'

I laughed. Sarupa blushed, then laughed too.

'Lucky girl,' I said. 'Centre of attention today, aren't you?'

She tried not to smile and glanced back at the imbecile. He waved his hat at her. We turned into a quiet side street lined with tall, grey town houses, and walked in the middle of the road, side by side.

'I shouldn't have mouthed off back there,' I said.

'If you don't like the music, you don't like it.'

'I acted like a prick, didn't I?'

'Yes, you did.'

'I shouldn't have walked off.'

'You were being a turd.' She stopped by her car, a silver BMW coupé. 'If you did that to me,' she said, 'I'd have nothing more to do with you.'

'She's really pissed off, isn't she?'

'She's very sensitive.' Sarupa opened the door. 'You have to be gentle with her. A'ight?' We stood a moment and looked at each other. 'Don't mess wid ma homey,' she smiled. She got into the leather seat, shut the door and started the engine. She opened the window and looked at me. 'Make sure you call her.'

'I will, when I get home.'

'Where do you live?'

'Hackney.'

She moved the car forward a little, then stopped. 'I'm meeting Duncan near Liverpool Street,' she said. 'I can drop you there if you like.'

I looked at her squinting at me in the sunlight. I said thanks and walked around to the passenger door.

5

I WOKE WITH a start. I'd slept only a few hours and was shaking with exhaustion. My head throbbed, my heartbeat pulsed in my ears; my mouth was dry, cloyed with viscous saliva. I closed my eyes, but the pain in my skull was awful. My soul, tired of me, was kicking its way out through my forehead. I was fully dressed, with my shoes on, lying face up on my duvet. The window and the door were shut; the air smelt like shit. An empty bottle of rum lay beside me.

I got up and stumbled to the toilet. My urine was dark yellow, almost brown. I retched into the bowl for a few minutes but nothing came. My nausea eased a little and I flushed the toilet. Holding the banister with both hands, I walked slowly downstairs to the kitchen.

Michael was at the table, reading the *Telegraph* and drinking coffee. He saw me and laughed. 'Fancy a drink?' He threw me one of several beer cans sitting on the table. I made no attempt to catch it; it hit my thigh, bounced onto the floor and rolled behind the fridge. He laughed louder, and asked if I wanted a coffee. I nodded. He stood up and switched on the kettle. I sat down and he brought me a mug of very strong, very sweet coffee.

'Thanks.' I picked up a cigarette packet from the table and lit myself one. 'Is Luca here?'

'Yeah,' said Michael. 'He's on the floor in the lounge.'

'I can't drink with him again. He'll kill me. He's a fucking alcoholic.'

'He's a fucking monster,' agreed Michael. 'I'm glad I left when I did, or I'd be looking like you.'

Drinking my coffee, I woke up a little and remembered last night. 'What happened?' I asked. 'Get any pussy?'

'A little bit.'

'How much?'

'Fingered one of them a bit.'

'Get her tits out?'

'Yeah.'

'Didn't close the deal?'

'No.' Michael shook his head. 'Couldn't be bothered.'

We sat quietly reflecting on the night before, on how we'd squandered another portion of our time, our money, our precious little self-respect. At least once a week, Michael and I went out and got drunk; last night Luca came with us and drank us to a pulp. We went to a Moroccan bar in Stoke Newington; we sat on cushions in the corner, annihilating ourselves with beer and whisky chasers. Around midnight, three women – all in their thirties, none of them pretty – came and sat with us. Two were French; the third was a ruddy-faced Mancunian with a wide snout and a filthy grin. She pawed at Luca all night while the other two fawned over Michael. I tried making conversation but no one spoke to me.

The French women got up and made Michael dance. They were brunettes, with lacquered perms, and wore cheap tight jeans high over fat stomachs, fastened with glossy black belts. One wore a blue waistcoat over a white T-shirt, the other wore a glitter bra-top over enormous, shapeless breasts. They sandwiched Michael between them, writhing without rhythm; they stroked his body and pressed their groins against him. The French are the world's great negrophiles; no one loathes or adores negroes quite like they do. Michael could see what the deal was; his happy, cocoa-buttered black face shone. He was having a great time.

After a while they picked up their things, cajoled Michael into going with them, and left. Luca lay blind drunk and prone in the corner, straddled by the Mancunian. She sucked on his face until closing time, then she left, taking Luca with her. The women said they were teachers; all three had rings on their fingers. The Mancunian was engaged; the other two were married and, judging by the flab hidden unsuccessfully in their trousers, probably mothers too. I went home alone, drank what I could find, then fell asleep.

Michael made us each another coffee. I lit another cigarette.

'Did you try chatting up one of those French birds?' he asked.

'No. I wasn't on their agenda.'

'What was their agenda?'

'Black cock.'

'I hate that,' he groaned unconvincingly. 'I've got more respect for women who just want some cock, than for chicks who want it black.' He looked at the coffee mug cupped in his hands. 'They thought you were Arab.'

'Yeah?'

'They hate Arabs.' He eyed me sceptically. 'I reckon you've got some Mogul blood in you. They could smell it. *L'odeur d'Islam*, that's what they called it.' He laughed. 'I love France,' he said. 'It's the only country I've been to where the lowest section of society isn't black. They hate niggers more than the English do, they just don't hate them most of all.' He raised his coffee. 'The French! That bunch of cunts!'

I raised my cup in solidarity. 'What happened after you left?' I asked.

'I went back to their place. Actually it was their mate's place, the one with the pig nose who was on Luca's case.'

'Where was that?'

'Just round the corner from there.'

'And?'

'I got there, had a bit more to drink, then had a little smooch with them.'

'Both of them?'

'Yeah. But then the ugly one . . .'

'Which ugly one?'

60

'The *really* ugly one, in the black. She got a bit moody and went to bed.' He frowned. 'Thank God she left. I was so pissed, I might've fucked her.'

'So you were with the fat one, with the boob tube?'

'Oh God . . .' Michael held his face in his hands.

'What?'

'You don't want to know.'

'What?'

'I kissed her feet,' he groaned. 'We were making out and I started kissing her feet and sucking her toes.'

'You smooth bastard!' I laughed out loud. 'You're so fucking smooth!'

He shook his head ruefully. 'I was fucking pissed. I didn't know what the fuck I was doing.'

'Then what happened?'

'Nothing special . . . Fingered her a bit, got a blowjob, then Luca showed up with her mate. He was totally wasted, couldn't even stand up. So I got a cab back with him. You were asleep when we got in.'

'At least you did something to talk about.'

'You know what?' said Michael, suddenly inspired. 'I'm gonna write a book about this shit, about black men and white women. There's a story there.'

'Write about your experiences,' I said. 'You've had enough.'

'Yeah!' he laughed. 'I'll call it *The Black Cock Diaries*.'

'That's a great title.'

'*The Black Cock Diaries: My Struggle With Miscegenation*, by Michael Andrews.' His eyes gleamed with the idea; in his excitement it seemed an actual possibility. He looked at me: 'What about you? You could do something from the Asian perspective. Aren't there women out there desperate for some Asian cock?'

'Some . . . A lot of fags are like that.' I thought about it for a moment. 'Crackers don't hate us that much anymore,' I said. 'They don't have too much of a complex about us.'

Michael nodded and finished his coffee. I watched him

61

get up, put his mug in the sink, and leave the room. He was well over six feet tall, and was an interesting Caribbean mix – tar-black skin, hazel, European eyes and sleek, almost Asiatic features, combined with a powerful West African frame, perfected by slavery, its harsh conditions of natural selection. It's great to know that in his grab for wealth, Whitey created the body his women want to fuck the most. We'd been flatmates for nearly six years; our friendship worked largely because he was Trinidadian. In Trinidad a lot of people are Indian, and they rub off on the blacks. Michael was a clever guy, shrewd but calm; he didn't have that dumb-fuck attitude a lot of brothers have – Jamaicans especially.

I stood up and opened the fridge. A cube of butter sat on a saucer on the top shelf, an ancient carton of soya milk stood on the shelf below; otherwise, there was nothing. I sat back down, feeling hungry and desolate. I looked at the kitchen: old wallpaper peeled off the cracked walls; the ceiling was unpainted, the bare plaster sagged around the damp patch directly beneath the bathroom. We never bought a curtain rail for the bath; whenever someone showered, water ricocheted all over the floor, then leaked through it and dripped into the bucket in the centre of the kitchen. There were no utensils to be seen – they were in boxes in the hallway – and there was nothing on the shelves. Cleared of everything but its original fixtures, the room, for once, looked clean, eerily spacious. I shut the fridge door and went to the lounge.

Luca was lying face down on the carpet, limbs akimbo, as if he'd landed there from a high fall. I crouched down to inspect him; he was still breathing. He stank of liquor and stale sweat. Michael sat on the couch, a shabby velvet-covered relic; it was the only furniture in the room – everything else had left days ago. Michael was getting ready to move out; he was moving in with his girlfriend, who was expecting their first baby. I couldn't afford to rent the place on my own, so I was moving too. I hadn't decided where to.

There were no curtains anymore; sunshine flooded through the windows and splintered against the bottles and beer cans discarded on the floor. The room – barren, enormous, bathed in calm white light – felt reassuring, like a home at last. I walked over to the window; a wasp raged against the glass, leaving dabs of venom on the pane as it fought to get out. I pushed the frame upwards, waved the wasp outside and sat on the ledge, looking at the street.

Our flat was above a parade of shops; beneath us was a bookmaker's. A group of young black men loitered on the pavement, wearing florid tracksuits and pristine running shoes, their bikes propped against the wall. They were couriers for crack dealers who operated inside, taking orders on mobile phones then despatching them via a flunky. One of these flunkies was bare-chested; he stood leaning on the railing at the edge of the road, caressing his six-pack. A young, very pretty black girl walked by; he said something in lewd, inaudible patois, and the men laughed. Her face turned to the pavement, she walked a gauntlet of gold-capped sneers. The flunky with the six-pack walked behind her in a lopsided prance copied from MTV; he made catcalls as she disappeared around the corner. I wondered how those arseholes kept it up – the incessant posture, the swagger – even when they wobbled around Hackney on bicycles built for children.

Michael came and sat with me.

'I've got to get out of Hackney,' I said. 'It's making me a racist.'

'Me too,' said Michael. He sighed, looking at the men below. 'Fucking mutts . . .'

A flunky looked up, spotted him and gave him a nod. Michael nodded back; he nodded to anyone black, whether he knew them or not. 'I'm so fucking glad I'm going,' he sighed.

A woman walked out of the betting shop and stood talking and laughing with the men. She was always around: thin and white, she wore an Arsenal shirt, faded flower-print leggings and white stilettos; crusted scars flared on the backs of her ankles. The men gathered around her; pasty-faced and ever-pregnant, she seemed to be their communal wife. She sucked a lungful from a cigarette, scratched her swollen belly, and made banter in the Caribbean slang that is the lingua franca of London's multi-ethnic underclass.

I wondered if the young men were genuine Yardies, or a stupid sham. In adolescence many blacks, encouraged by the anomic rantings of rap music, adopt a sordid boorish persona that bears no relation to their actual lives. It's often their defining choice.

In childhood I had a friend, Marlon; at primary school he was one of the few children I had any interaction with. We were the only two from our year who chose Hadley Grove, a boy's-only institution, as our secondary school (my turban, my humiliation in the presence of girls, and my early development of acne had me terrified of mixed-sex comprehensives). Marlon's mother was lovely; a kind and decent Anglican woman, she came from Barbados and raised Marlon alone after divorcing his father. She dressed him impeccably in trousers and smart shoes, while the other children wore sportswear; she kept his hair trimmed in a neat cubic hedge, and sent him to a maths tutor on Saturdays. She hoped he'd be a doctor one day, or run a business. He wasn't at all precocious, but an earnest, well-turned-out mediocrity stands every chance in this life, and she knew that.

For a time he was my best friend. On our first day at Hadley Grove, he arrived at my house at seven in the morning so we could go to school together – though I lived a thirty-minute bus ride from there, while from his house he could walk there in ten. It was the most touching display of comradeship I've ever known. My mother kissed him on the cheek and made him breakfast while I dressed.

For the next two years we were close; we both supported Liverpool, idolised John Barnes, and were the first at school to own home computers. Then, around the age of thirteen, he began to speak a coarse West Indian vernacular, as did the other black kids: none had spoken it before, not with such brusque assertion. They would flagrantly disregard the teachers, goad them during lessons, and never do their homework. Their project was to *keep it real*, an idea imported from the States, discernible in American popular music and shows like *The Fresh Prince Of Bel Air*.

In this programme the lead character, played by Will Smith and also called Will, is a bright handsome son of the Philadelphia ghetto, sent to live with fabulously wealthy relatives in Beverly Hills. He is a rapper, a great dancer, an excellent basketball player, and a consummate seducer of women; he is also (given that he now attends an expensive school with excellent resources) an academic prodigy. This ludicrous conceit is rooted in the resentment and guilt, the schizophrenia, of African America. Middle-class blacks are alienated from the malaise and suffering of the poor; Will represents the impossible fusion of louche gutter panache and upward social mobility. By believing in Will, America's black bourgeoisie and sub-proletariat can still believe in racial unity. Will is juxtaposed with his cousin Carlton who, born into wealth, missed the rituals for actualising his blackness – dancing, fucking and basketball – that abound in the slums. Will is *real*, while Carlton is a *sell-out* who longs to be white. *The Fresh Prince Of Bel Air* was the blandest example of *keeping it real*, and Will Smith went on to become the most successful children's entertainer in the world.

But for Marlon and his friends the allure of such shows brought disaster; they thought themselves sell-outs unless they assimilated the inanities of a foreign dispossessed. My once studious friend now eschewed schoolwork and non-black company; he cried out 'Batty-man!' when I answered a teacher's question correctly in class. The last I heard of Marlon was maybe two years ago: he was a postman and still living with his mother.

It was one o'clock. Luca was still asleep face down on the floor, his limbs sprawled into a swastika. He broke wind: a prolonged discharge followed by a series of quick bursts. Sitting on the window ledge, I smelt a hint of it drift by: it was revolting. His farts had the thick, beery stench of a true alcoholic's.

Michael looked at him and frowned. 'Fucking animal.' Michael was irritated; he disliked human weakness, and Luca had plenty of it. 'Look at the fucking state of him.'

'Luca! You okay?' I half shouted so he might hear.

Luca slowly rolled onto his side, collapsed on his back and stared, mouth open, at the ceiling. 'Aaaaaaaaaaaaaaah,' he exhaled. He lay still, blank-faced and unblinking; several times his mouth silently opened and shut as though he didn't know how to use it. Michael laughed.

I got up, walked over to Luca and crouched down. 'You alright?' I ruffled his blond hair with my hand.

'Aaaaaaaaaaaaaaah,' he sighed. He tried to sit up; I helped him onto his knees but he fell forward on all fours, his head lolling uselessly. I left him alone. He stayed like that for some time, then crawled to the couch and slumped against it. 'Waaah,' he gasped. We looked quizzically at him. 'Waaah,' he said again.

'What the fuck is he saying?' said Michael.

'What is it Luca?' I said. 'What do you want to say?'

Luca brushed his hair from his blanched, oily face. He inhaled, to summon energy, to force out two pained syllables: 'Waaah . . . Tah.'

'Water?' I asked. 'You want some water?'

He nodded. I went to the kitchen, filled a plastic pint glass from the tap and brought it to him. I helped him to hold the beaker steady as he took a few gulps, then hauled him onto the sofa and sat him upright. His body was slack; it slumped into its seat as if he were filled

66

with straw. I looked into Luca's face; he stared back with huge, uncomprehending eyes. I felt sorry for him. His drunkenness was once amusing; now it was boring and desperately sad.

Michael and I looked at one another; we wondered how long it would be before he sobered; then we could go out and have lunch. I was starving.

I was pissed off. The waitress, a Slavic blonde with a pockmarked face, had brought me the wrong food. She smiled weakly as I explained my order again – a mozzarella salad and some bread. She narrowed her brow; she didn't understand. I waved her away.

A man, authoritative looking and dressed in black, waited a nearby table. I caught his attention. 'Why don't you hire people who speak English? You're in a service industry.' I waited for his reply. He bit his lip nervously; he didn't speak it either.

'Eastern Europeans,' said Michael. 'They make niggers look smart.' He took two cigarettes from the packet on the table, gave one to me and lit them both. 'The best thing that's happened to black people in this country was letting these idiots in.'

'Yeah?'

'There's nothing better for the people at the bottom than having a bunch of other saps brought in and dumped beneath them. Niggers won't catch so much flak now these dummies are here. You already see it in the media. The papers don't make a big deal about Yardies anymore, they're obsessed with these Albanian gangs now.'

I looked at Luca, who sat listless in his chair opposite me.

'That guy's got to straighten out,' said Michael, looking at him too. He leant closer to me, eager to return to his thesis. 'Eastern Europeans are way more fucked than black people. Look at those gypsy-looking types you get hanging around charity shops at night, going through the rubbish bags and stealing the clothes. You don't get niggers doing that.' He sucked his cigarette, let a cloud of smoke hover before his open mouth, then inhaled it. 'And these people, they've got some big fuck-off attitude. When you drive around town they give you the most grief, honking their fucking horns and giving you shitty looks. You know why?'

'Why?'

'Because they're *white*. They come to this country and they think, "Hey, why am I being treated like shit? *I'm white*! I'm as white as the English!" But they get lumped in with the Somalians and every other tramp that comes here. They're just another bunch of tramps, fighting the rest of us in this pigpen for the same fucking crap. It fucks them off. It *really* fucks them off.'

I laughed.

'I'm telling you . . .' Michael began laughing too. '. . . These dummies are making life easy for black people. Same as Muslims are good for black people. 9/11 was a break for niggers. White people are cutting us some slack, now we're not top of their shit-list. Right now, they need all the friends they can get.' Michael sipped his coffee and smiled. 'Niggers might rob you and rape your girlfriend, but they won't land a fucking plane on you. Another stunt like that, and we'll be in the clear.'

I laughed. I almost said the black underclass was a rich source of potential Islamists, but that would've sparked a proper conversation. I was tired, so nodded instead. The waitress returned and laid a cheese sandwich with French fries in front of me. I gave her a smile; she'd almost got it right. Michael had ordered the mixed grill – glistening shapes of processed offal steamed on the plate before him. He opened the accompanying sachets of mustard and smeared them on his sausages. Luca wasn't eating; his cappuccino sat untouched. Michael took his fork and tore the meat into large chunks and stuffed them into his mouth, bolting them almost unchewed. I found the sight distasteful; raised a vegetarian, I've never liked eating meat. I ate half of my sandwich and a handful of fries, then lost my appetite and smoked another cigarette. I switched on my phone. It buzzed into life, informing me I had seven messages: three texts and a voicemail from Sophie asking how and where I was, a text from Hari saying hello, and one text and a voicemail from Rory inviting me to his health club later in the day. I sent Rory a text saying I'd meet him there in a few hours.

'You got any ideas about where you might move to?' asked Michael.

I shook my head. 'I haven't thought about it. How much longer are you hanging around?'

'A few days. Evie's back from her show on Tuesday, so I'll be moving into hers anytime between then and next weekend.' He paused and wiped his mouth with a napkin. 'You know, I'd love it if you crashed with us. But she's really into the idea of us doing the couple thing. I couldn't chuck a gooseberry into the mix. I'd get my ear chewed off just for asking.' He looked at me guiltily. 'There's no room there anyway. The place is full of her stupid equipment.'

'Don't worry about it,' I said. 'I might crash at Luca's for a bit.'

'What about this girl you're seeing? Couldn't she sort you out for a while? You never know, you might like it there.'

'I've only been seeing her a few weeks.'

'That's long enough. People start families quicker than that.' He smiled to himself. 'I have to hand it to you, Pup, you're doing alright. You've got some rich white girl you can mooch off. You can have a great time, don't knock it. Just don't get her pregnant and fuck yourself up.'

'She can't get pregnant.'

Michael raised his eyebrows.

'She doesn't have periods,' I explained. 'She doesn't eat

enough. She models and stuff, so she doesn't eat a lot. She's had like two periods in her life.'

'Fuck . . .' He paused, nonplussed. '. . . That's handy.'

'I suppose it is.'

I reached for the packet of cigarettes, Michael went back to his meal. We were sat at a window table; in the sunshine outside was Upper Street and a traffic of afternoon shoppers. Luca sat beside the window, resting his head on the glass; he was still drunk, insensate. After Michael had gone to bed, Luca had drunk through the night on his own. We managed to get him to drink some coffee and wash his face before we left home and he'd perked up, some of his colour had returned, but now he was catatonic and on display. I watched women slow down to have a good look at him, even the ones accompanied by their men. Luca was beautiful: blond-haired and blue-eyed, he had dark skin and an open, gentle, almost stupid-looking face. Women loved him. His face had a cleanliness; it hadn't been twisted with rage or bitterness in its life. That's what women loved about him most, his obvious lack of malice and cunning.

I looked out the window and watched people walk in and out of a shop across the street. It was a great store, selling beautifully restored antique furniture. Often I'd go in there and sit on a box-shaped couch from the 1930s, covered in dark tan leather, enjoying it for a moment before it was taken by an advertising executive, or a psychiatrist, or anyone else with a taste for classic design and the money to buy it. Luca's house – or rather his mother's house – had furniture like that. He lived there largely on his own; his mother was often abroad. The house, located in Belgravia, was Regency period and stucco-fronted. On the top floor was what he and I called 'the war room', a sumptuous, sombre space with a mahogany table at its centre, surrounded by Eames chairs. At one end of the room was a burgundy leather recliner and matching ottoman stool. Glass doors opened onto a decked balcony; we'd stand out there, the morning after a drinking session, breathing clear air and looking over one of the finest areas in London. It was through knowing Luca that I saw how charmed and beautiful other people's lives can be.

Luca had no idea how lucky he was, so pissed away his time as a twenty-first-century roué. He even had the twenty-first-century roué's career of choice: he was a DJ. He composed electronic dance music, synthesising a hybrid sound with samples taken from hip hop, film scores, indeed from anything, including *qawali* and the theme tunes of soap operas. It was quirky, technically ingenious, and condemned to obscurity. He had potential: good-looking and musically proficient, with the right guidance he could produce something marketable and become a phenomenon. But he didn't have the essential force for success; he wasn't *obsessed*, neither with himself nor his music. An obsession with venting either his talent or his ego would've sufficed, given him the energy to take flight. Luca muddled along, cutting the odd record and playing at the occasional club. He didn't need fame, everything was already on his plate: money, friendship, sex. He was, however, about to launch an album, the culmination of nearly ten years' work. A compilation of his six best recordings, he was releasing it under the name of 'White Man'; the album was called *Share My Joy*. The pseudonym was the nickname Michael and I occasionally had for him.

The three of us – Michael, Luca and I – had met six years before, on a journalism course at the East London Community College, in Whitechapel. The course was created to help the unemployed and members of ethnic minorities enter the news industry. Funded by the European Union, it was then running for its second year. Peter, the teacher who initially interviewed me, was a grey-haired, bearded, obese and nervous white guy; he boasted that several ex-students now had careers with papers such as the *Barking and Dagenham Gazette*,

Eastern Eye and the *Caribbean Times*. He assured me his course was 'comparable' to the one offered at the London College of Printing, which cost £2,500. His course was a proven success; it empowered the disenfranchised and injected diversity into the news industry – and it only cost a fiver. I signed up immediately. I hadn't finished my degree, so had to sit a test to decide if I could join the 'fast track' stream of graduates whose course lasted only four months; those who failed it would spend an entire academic year plodding through the syllabus at a snail's pace.

The next day, a midweek afternoon in late September, I stood outside Peter's office. A note on his locked door stated he was late, that those sitting the media exam should wait until he arrived to invigilate. Nearly twenty people were standing in the corridor, waiting. The group was a mixture of chattering Bangladeshis – teenagers, nearly all boys – and an assortment of Afro-Caribbeans, some middle-aged. I noticed Luca straight away; he was the only one who was white and approximately my age. He was wearing combat trousers, a hooded sports top and a woollen Kangol hat; he carried his stationery in a plastic bag from a record store. We exchanged bored uncertain nods. The Bangladeshis all seemed to know each other; their cockney patter had a quick Bengali rhythm. The black people were uniformly annoyed at having to wait; after an hour, most of them had left. I was on the verge of leaving myself, when Peter arrived holding the exam papers. Without an apology, he led us to the exam room; we waited at the door for another half an hour while the class inside finished its lesson. We were in our seats, the test papers face down on the desks before us, Peter chalking the finish time on the blackboard, when Michael strode in. Tall, handsome and dreadlocked, wearing Levi's, a sky blue Pringle jumper and pair of Police sunglasses, he flashed Peter a disarming grin and strolled nonchalantly to the back of the room. The test was a cinch; the questions included, 'Who is the Chancellor of the Exchequer?' and 'Give two examples of what the term PC stands for'. Nonetheless, of those who sat it only we three – Michael, Luca and I – made it onto the 'fast track'.

On our first day in class, we recognised one another from the test, so congregated at the same table. Other than Michael and I, the 'fast track' was entirely white: darkies with brains don't waste themselves in journalism. The other students were tedious, middle-class left-wingers with arts and humanities degrees; they'd all been claiming unemployment benefit at the time of joining the course, so qualified for enrolment (even Luca, who'd filled out the DSS forms days earlier; he'd missed the deadline to enrol at any other college). They were enthused and managed to turn every lesson into a political rally. It was 1996 and the Tory government was on its last legs; New Labour was about to bring a new era, they thought, full of ideas and compassion. These kids wanted to be at its heart, the media nexus, managing the debates. Luckily, they had neither the talent nor connections to get anywhere near it. Michael and I didn't care for the coming election – we both admired Thatcher's 'pull-yourself-up-by-the-bootstraps' brand of politics, which resonated with our upbringings – and Luca was a political ignoramus. The three of us were natural bedfellows.

We were each at a loose end. Having plied his music for a couple of years without success, Luca was disillusioned. Michael was an occasional writer for a listings magazine, but wasn't progressing. In 1995 I dropped out of university; for eighteen months I moped aimlessly at my mum's. The journalism course at the East London Community College solved all our problems: it was something to do. It entitled us to a free travel pass – valid throughout London for the duration of the course – and a grant of £300. It also gave us our first real experience of East London: Luca lived in SW1, I lived in Southall,

Michael lived in 'Hell's Den', his apposite soubriquet for Harlesden.

The general college population was mostly Bangladeshi and Afro-Caribbean, with some Turks and whites (among the last of East London's white working class, i.e. those that hadn't fled to Essex when the immigrants arrived). Racially similar to the Burmese, Bangladeshis are a slender, elegant people with clear skin, large eyes and delicate movements. Some of the young men wore beards and a sort of *kurta-pajama*; the rest had a common haircut, a shaved short back and sides with gelled, jet-black coiffures. Like the blacks, many wore outsized jeans and sportswear which, on their small frames, looked more clownish than usual. They wrote graffiti on the walls; their favourite statement, BANGLA CREW RUN TINGS, was written in a hip-hop scrawl. I have a typical Jat-Punjabi chauvinism, so made no effort to befriend them.

I tested their sensibilities by flirting with their women. I sat next to Bangladeshi girls in the cafeteria, their beautiful faces often framed in a hijab, and made gentle conversation. Like all women, they enjoyed polite male attention and exchanged smiles, eye contact and pleasantries; embarrassed, they tried to ignore the mass of boys who gathered nearby, proprietorial and suspicious. The boys loitered and threw me caustic stares; stymied by religion, their love lives consisted of bitter, solitary masturbation. I made no advances towards the girls; it would've caused a riot.

Much of East London was, is, a shithole. Michael and I moved there a few weeks after our course began. It took me over two hours to commute to college from Southall, so I often didn't bother going. Within a month I received an official warning for poor attendance. Michael had his own problem: he'd got drunk and slept with his overweight, ferociously ugly landlady, with whom he shared a house in Harlesden. She was a middle-aged Cypriot who worked for Brent council and hadn't had a man in years. It was a vigorous, mean-spirited grudge-fuck; it was the fuck of the century. Michael exacted his revulsion for her and her dirty habits (fouled underwear strewn on the bathroom floor; stinking cartons of uneaten take-away food left in the lounge; the often unflushed and putrid toilet). She misread the event and fell in love. Desperate for her lithe young stud to repeat his performance, his refusal gave her convulsions of hatred and despair.

He needed a new home and I needed to live nearer the college, so we rented a shabby two-room flat in a pre-fabricated building near Hackney Town Hall. It had no central heating and the mite-infested carpet made me asthmatic. There was never enough hot water for both of us to wash in the morning, and every word in the adjoining flats could be heard – especially those of the Portuguese family below, who communicated in shrieks. We lived there for a year, on housing benefit like everyone else in the building. Michael, being an early riser, let me have the bedroom for myself. He slept in the lounge which led to the kitchen; he reasoned he'd be awake by any time I wanted breakfast, so I wouldn't disturb him. He was generous, laid-back and easy to live with: he was a good friend. We later moved into a bigger flat, when we both had jobs. We'd be stuck in Hackney for years.

I heard my breathing slow down; the mentholated steam had cleared my sinuses. Droplets formed in my scalp, rolled down my forehead and into my eyes. I tried lying on the plastic bench to relax, but it was too hard. I felt leaden and uncomfortable, utterly sullen. I hate steam baths. I see no benefit in subjecting myself to unnatural heat, basting in my own fluids. Fat and lazy people often use steam baths and saunas as a substitute for exercise, equating sweating to weight loss. Rory made this mistake, so was still fat. He'd been a member of this health club for months, and came here several times a week. Wearing a gold, Juicy Couture velour tracksuit – he'd seen Geri

Halliwell wearing one in a copy of *Elle* – he always spent half an hour in the gym: a short waddle on the tread-mill, then some pathetic repetitions on each machine, the weight set as low as possible. Afterwards he'd idle in the steam room, or in the jacuzzi, watching the men, hoping to catch the eye of a chubby-chasing hunk. It never happened.

I sat in the steam room alone; Rory had gone to the changing room to wait for his boyfriend, Shamir. Shamir was running late and Rory didn't want him to get lost looking for us in the club. The health club was a labyrinth of utilities: massage rooms and hydrotherapy units; halls for yoga and Pilates; a swimming pool and gymnasium; a martial arts dojo and a 'higher-consciousness space' devoted to meditation, t'ai chi and alternative medicines.

I didn't want to wait in the changing rooms with Rory. When I arrived, at six o'clock, the changing rooms thronged with businessmen undressing for their midweek workouts: a tundra of cold white bodies. They had taut pinched expressions, thin physiques and hairy nipples. The sight of their flaccid pink cocks upset me. Most of them headed for the treadmills and the cycling machines, while others rowed: the emphasis of their workouts was on endurance. These men were executives, administrators of modern capitalism; they needed to stay lean, hungry and alert. The air stank of sweat and bourgeois angst. They moved to the hard rhythm of techno music that blared from speakers mounted on the walls – a metallic clamour, like a thousand trash cans rolling down concrete steps.

I watched them while I lifted weights. There were plenty of women among them, hard-bodied corporate divas. Their buttocks rippled under their Lycra legwear; their torsos honed into V-shapes, they had square shoulders and flat stomachs. One or two made eye contact with me, giving me harsh, greedy stares. They would've fucked me dry, thrown my husk to the wind. The thought of it unnerved me.

The heat made me queasy. I hadn't fully recovered from last night's drinking binge with Michael and Luca. The steam opened my pores, washing out the booze and cigarette smoke; I smelt it on my skin. I decided to stay put for a while and sweat out more toxins. The name of this health club, the Next Level, was embroidered on the corner of the towel wrapped around my waist; the club also provided free bottles of mineral water bearing its name. Membership cost Rory £200 a month, in addition to a joining fee of over £500. The club was in Knightsbridge and had a vital role in the lives of the haute bourgeoisie. It was at once a purgative for their bodies, and an idyll where they could indulge in feng shui and crystal therapy, a world away from the intense rationality of their working lives. Clubs like this revitalise capitalists, so they can manage capitalism more effectively; billions are made worldwide from such ventures. I thought of Sarupa. She was a member of an Ayurvedic health club, called Bhakti Zone, in Notting Hill. She'd had a yoga class there on Saturday, before she met Sophie and I for lunch.

Hatha yoga was her preferred form; it's less strenuous, placing great emphasis on one's breathing. She spoke about yoga for over ten minutes as we sat in her car. She told me about the meditative aspects of yoga, the lucidity that her 'practice' brought her; she enthused about her 'Guru Ji', his methodical expertise as a teacher. She described, in anatomical detail, the benefits of yoga, such as suppleness and longevity.

'Hatha is the classical form of yoga,' she said, 'unlike, say ashtanga, which was developed later.'

Her monologue began when we stopped in a traffic jam, caused by road works in Kensington High Street. Being polite, I feigned a mild interest and asked a few questions. The conversation, like the traffic, hadn't moved since. There was a spare pair of dark sunglasses lying on the dashboard; I put them on, turned to her and covertly ogled her tits. I smiled and nodded. She didn't notice my ploy.

'Ashtanga's the yoga that Madonna and Sting practise. It's very popular in the West.'

I nodded again. Her tits looked great in a sports bra; her nipples bulged like thick welts.

'You can see why Westerners like it, can't you?'

I hadn't a clue. 'So they can lick their own arseholes when they're eighty?'

She almost smiled; she looked through the windscreen at the cars in front of us.

'Tell me,' I said. 'Why do Westerners like ashtanga?'

'No. You'll only make fun of me.'

'I won't. Go ahead, tell me.'

She stared ahead. 'I'm not talking to you.'

I leaned towards her and patted her thigh; her skin smelt fresh and soapy. 'I was just being facetious . . . I'm sorry.'

'No you're not.' She looked at me: 'I bet you wind Sophie up all the time.'

'Not *all* the time.'

'Women don't appreciate men who can't be serious.'

'Don't they?'

'I don't.' She looked ahead; the cars in front were moving. Her car was an automatic; she shifted into drive mode. She weaved into the spaces between cars, picking her way through the traffic; soon we were driving along Kensington Road, towards Hyde Park Corner. She handled the vehicle with ease, steering nonchalantly with one hand. The superb suspension of her BMW meant her breasts didn't bounce; this was a disappointment.

'Bit of a princess, aren't you?' I said. 'You don't like jokes at your expense.'

'I like a good joke. In fact, I think you're quite funny.' We slowed down at a red traffic light; she turned and looked at me. 'You've got a quick wit, Bhupinder, and you're forthright . . . I actually like that about you.' She smiled, her eyes hidden behind her sunglasses. 'But

78

you're a little too flippant. That's what annoys me, your flippancy.'

We sat quietly for a minute. The light changed to green and she took her foot off the brake.

'Tell me more about yoga,' I said. 'I promise I won't be flippant.'

'I was going to say, before you made your comment, that Westerners like ashtanga because it creates a very chiselled, very muscular body shape. It's a very Western concern with the surface.' She looked into the rear-view mirror, checking on a taxi that was tailgating us. 'Yoga's primarily an inner process,' she said. 'Even with ashtanga, the ultimate objective of the yogi should be to enhance inner, spiritual strength. Classical practitioners of yoga are very spindly, or even a bit fuller-figured. That's how the teachers in India look. Their focus isn't on their visible external physique, but on developing their core energy. In India you see these very ordinary-looking people who can do the most amazing things with their bodies. You'd never guess to look at them.'

I didn't know what to say; I looked at her in silence. Outside, London was passing by; it was a bright, beautiful day. The car's air conditioning was excellent; the air inside tasted clean and unpolluted.

'If I'm boring you,' she said, 'I am sorry.'

'Not at all.'

'Yoga's very important to me. I've got a demanding job and yoga helps me meet those demands.'

'You're a lawyer, aren't you?'

'Yes, I am.'

'What sort of law do you practise?'

'Commercial. I work for a firm called Haine Abbott Wilson, in St Paul's.'

'Been there long?'

'I've been there since I finished studying. Nearly five years now.'

'Good fun?'

'I wouldn't say *fun* . . . But it's engrossing, very intellectually challenging.'

'How so?'

'We promote free enterprise. We help governments break up state monopolies and introduce reforms, opening markets to foreign and private investment. We present them with a format, a legal framework for a competitive business environment.' She slowed the car down; a delivery boy carrying pizzas on a moped overtook us on the outside. 'It can be enthralling,' she said. 'I can see the things I work on making a real difference in the real world. It's very detailed, analytical work. That's why yoga's so important to me, it helps me to concentrate.'

'What sort of monopolies do you break up?'

'I work on energy sectors. Currently I'm working with the Turkish government. I'm helping them formulate a model for a privatised electricity network.'

I watched her driving her car – an M-series coupé with a cream leather interior and rosewood finish – and listened to her speak about her work. Some people operate expertly in this world; they understand the protocols, negotiate them perfectly.

'I get to travel a lot, too,' she added. 'I'm going to Ankara on Monday.'

'You're lucky. It's good to have work that stimulates you.'

'I am lucky,' she nodded. 'I love my job. I've learnt so much through it. It helps me with my pet projects as well.'

'What are they?'

'I help manage a venture capital fund for my dad and his friends. We've created it to invest in young Asian entrepreneurs. It's called Indravest. We're hoping to fund some MBAs and bursaries.'

'You've got a lot on your plate.'

'I like to stay active.' The traffic slowed down again; we were on Piccadilly. 'Duncan does charity work, too. He's an economist, he's got a big interest in third-world development. That's partly why we were in Kenya last month – he's involved in a scheme there.'

'What sort?'

'Microcredit. Lending people money for small-scale businesses, cottage industries. It doesn't seem much, but if people can afford basic tools they can work and feed their families, send their children to school.'

'Sounds good.'

'It is.' Sarupa pressed a button on her steering wheel that switched on the radio; a piano concerto was playing on Radio 3. 'Sophie told me you're a journalist. What's that like?'

'It's okay.'

'Who do you write for?'

'Anyone. I'm a freelancer. I do pieces for men's magazines, and sometimes for newspapers.'

'What do you write about?'

'Bullshit.'

Sarupa looked me; there was an edgy silence.

'I write a lot of lifestyle features,' I explained. 'I've somehow carved myself a niche writing about men's grooming. The last piece I did was about having my back and chest waxed. That was for the *Standard*.'

Sarupa laughed. 'Did it hurt?'

'Yeah, it fucking hurt . . .' I shook my head. 'The things I'll do for £300.'

'Is that what they paid you?'

'The piece was only 400 words long.'

'What did your friends think,' she giggled, 'when they read it?'

'It wasn't published. They didn't use it in the end.'

'Well, at least you got an idea of what it's like to be a woman. You should try a Brazilian wax.'

'Is that what you have?'

She smiled. 'Only when it's called for.'

The thought of her pussy made my cock twitch; I imagined a jet-black triangle of down, wet lips and a hot, tangy smell. I gritted my teeth in longing.

81

'Sophie says you're writing a novel.'

'Sort of,' I replied.

'What do you mean?'

'To say I'm writing a novel makes it sound as if I'm putting time and effort into it. I just work on this story from time to time.' I rummaged through my pockets and found my cigarettes. 'Do you want one?'

'No. But you go ahead, just open the window first.'

I opened the window and lit a cigarette.

'What's your book about?'

'Not a great deal. It's a run-of-the-mill, boy-meets-girl kind of thing.'

'Do you intend to have it published?'

'Yeah, if anyone's dumb enough to buy it.'

'How much have you written?'

'Around 20,000 words.'

'Have you submitted anything to a publisher?'

'I've been sending what I've written to agents . . . I'd love to get a deal.'

'Any luck?'

'The rejection letters are getting politer. I guess that's some progress.'

'What do they say?'

'They usually say there isn't a market for it. That's the trouble with this country, everything has to have a fucking market. If I lived in France, I'd get any crap published and get a grant for writing it.'

'Why isn't there a market for it?'

'Well . . .' I turned my head to blow smoke out of the window. 'It's not very good . . . But when did quality count for anything? It's no worse than the other junk that's out there.'

'So what will you do now? Give up on it?'

'No, I'll keep going . . . Fail again, fail better.'

Sarupa smiled. 'Fail again, fail better . . . That's a nice phrase. Did you coin it?'

'Yes,' I lied. 'I sometimes wish I'd done other things with myself. I should've got involved in business.'

'Really?'

'I've got a couple of ideas which could be a big hit, but they're a bit out of the ordinary. You could put up some venture capital if you like . . . I could be a young Asian entrepreneur.'

'What are they?'

'I play a lot of video games. I've had a couple of game ideas.'

'Okay.' Sarupa looked at me; she was paying attention.

'The first one's called *Holocaust Denial*.' I sucked the last of my cigarette and tossed the butt out the window. 'It's a strategy game, probably for a PC format. The central character is a right-wing academic, who has to outwit Mossad, the CIA and the liberal media, to get hold of and decipher documents that refute the Holocaust and undermine the state of Israel. He has to knit a patchwork alliance of neo-Nazis, Christian militias and Islamo-fascists to help him. He also gets tacit support from within the Wasp establishment.'

Sarupa stared at the road ahead.

'There's a million cranks who'd buy that shit,' I said. 'The world's full of these pricks. We'd make a fucking fortune. But we'd have to keep it a secret that the game was invented by some wog. We can get a honky to front the project.'

Sarupa laughed.

'My other idea,' I said, 'is a straightforward action game, probably for a Playstation format. It's called *Urban Race War*. The character this time is a militant black activist who assassinates police officers and starts riots in South London and Bradford. We could add other locations, like Los Angeles and Paris . . . White kids would love it! Think of all those middle-class wiggers, fighting the power in the comfort of their bedroom . . . Video games are the way forward.'

We'd driven past Cheapside and were moving through Threadneedle Street towards Bishopsgate; the traffic had slowed to a crawl. It was cool inside our car; people in less luxurious vehicles were becoming agitated. Two frustrated children in the back seat of the car in front picked a fight with each other. A van crept alongside us, the driver staring hungrily at Sarupa. She ignored him.

'Your ideas work,' she said. 'As concepts they do work. They have an appeal for distinct groups, there's certainly money to be made from them. But we wouldn't back you. Not in a million years. I don't think any company would. They'd have to consider their CSR.'

'What's that?'

'Corporate Social Responsibility. Businesses don't operate in a moral vacuum.'

'They don't?' This was news to me.

'Of course not. They're intrinsic to the world we live in. They have a vested interest in the well-being of society . . . Society, after all, is an amalgam of labour and customers. Businesses have to be moral stakeholders, if only to secure their own interests.'

Her sincerity amused me. 'I'm sorry you won't back my ideas. I thought I'd spotted viable gaps in the market.' We were now on Bishopsgate, but the traffic was still slow. I was surprised; normally EC1 wasn't this busy at weekends. I looked at the bustle on the pavement. 'I just wanted to book a seat,' I said, 'on the free market roller coaster. I'm a big fan of it.'

'Are you?'

'Yeah . . . It's the best socio-economic system mankind's ever had. No other system is as congruent with human nature as this one.'

'You know, that's just what I think.' Sarupa looked at me with approval. 'It expresses human dynamism, creativity and resourcefulness on a grand scale. That's why it succeeds.'

'It does express humanity on a grand scale, but those weren't the qualities I had in mind.'

'What did you have in mind?'

'Mediocrity and paranoia,' I said. 'They're the basic

84

principles of the human condition, and the base principles of consumerism. That's why I like capitalism . . . There's an integrity to the whole thing.'

Sarupa slowed the car down and steered it alongside the kerb; we were outside Liverpool Street Station. 'You have a strange take on things, Bhupinder.' She looked into her rear-view mirror and reversed the car a little, straightened up and parked. 'If that's how you feel about it, I don't see how you're a fan. You don't think capitalism is actually good for people.'

'I don't think people are good for people.'

'So what is good for them? What do you think can be done that *is* good for them?'

'I'm not interested in that question.'

'Why not?' Sarupa lifted her sunglasses and rested them on her forehead. 'You're intelligent, you have opinions. Why aren't you interested?'

'I'd have to feel I was relevant to the world in order to care about it. I don't.'

'So you're not a socialist, or an anarchist or anti-globalist, even though you think capitalism is mediocre and paranoid?'

'No.'

'What are you, then?'

I bit my lip and thought about it. I looked at the tumult of people moving in and out of the station, the huddle of bodies standing around a Starbuck's coffee stand. 'I'm a tourist,' I said. 'I'm just a fucking tourist . . . I just look at the view.' I took off the sunglasses; made by Burberry, they were rimless with elegant silver arms. 'Nice shades,' I said. 'You should keep them safe. You got a case for them?'

'It's in the glove compartment.' Sarupa was smiling; her brown eyes were beautiful.

I took the box out of the compartment; it was covered in fabric bearing the chequered Burberry design. I carefully put the glasses inside and closed it.

'If you like them,' she said, 'you can keep them.'

'No.' I was surprised, touched by her generosity. 'I can't take these, they must've cost you a bomb.'

'Don't worry, I've got lots of pairs. Way more than I need. Besides,' she said, 'you look cute in them.' She unclipped her seat belt, leaned over the gearbox and kissed my cheek. 'It's been an interesting chat, Puppy. Take care.'

I felt an unexpected sense of peace. This was the moment to cup her face in my hands, press my mouth against hers – but the raging force wasn't there. I felt calm, warm. I opened the passenger door. 'Thanks,' I said. 'We should do it again sometime.' I looked into her eyes, smiled, and got out of the car. I closed the door and watched her check her mirrors; she turned and gave me a wave. I waved back. She edged into the road, joined the flow of traffic and disappeared around a corner. I stood on the pavement, the afternoon sun pounding the top of my head, holding my box of Burberry shades with both hands.

I was almost asleep. I came to with a start and realised I had an erection. Thinking of Sarupa made me feel strange: aroused, eviscerated and lost. I wondered if she was the real cause of this malaise, or a guise for a deeper, more complex problem. Would fucking her solve anything? Would I get the chance?

I was alone in the steam room; Rory had been away for a while. I wondered how much longer he'd be gone: long enough for me to masturbate? I rubbed my cock through my towel, then slipped my hand underneath and slid my foreskin back and forth over my glans. I glanced around the room to see if there was a security camera hidden in the walls or ceiling, but couldn't see any. If there was one, so what? Men no doubt masturbated in here all the time, even fucked each other. Sex acts occur in every conceivable space; any venue devoted to men, especially when in a state of undress, would see far more than most. Men masturbate everywhere. I've jerked off at the back of a bus, behind my desk during a lecture, and with my schoolmates on a field trip to the New Forest (we stood

86

about in a clearing in the woods, wanking over pages from a dirty magazine we'd torn up and shared among us, desperately trying not to look at one another). In every job I've had, I could measure my boredom by the number of times a day I masturbated in the toilet.

I thought of Rory arriving unannounced, finding me cock-in-hand; I didn't want to give him the wrong idea. My erection collapsed.

Over the years I'd known him, I'd grown fond of Rory; he regarded me as a friend – possibly his only one. I was going to meet his boyfriend today. Rory had finally met someone who took him seriously, who wasn't just taking him for a ride. Rory had kept him hidden from me until he was sure about him; he didn't want to jinx anything. Shamir was successful in his own right, managing a string of restaurants on behalf of his family. His latest venture, Cuisine Kashmir, was in Clerkenwell; Fay Maschler had reviewed it in the *Standard* and been much impressed. I'd read a feature on him a while ago, in a food supplement that came with a Sunday newspaper. In the photo he wore a sleek Oswald Boateng suit, his black mane swept back over his head. He glowered at the camera and had razor sharp, extremely Pathan features; his cheekbones were too high, his eyes were like slits. He looked like a man who thought a lot of himself: the pouting young lion of the London restaurant world, yet another clean-cut Asian with the Midas touch. Rory spoke incessantly about him. He was in love. He really was; in the five months since he'd met Shamir, he'd shown more sanity, wit and kindness than ever. Before, he'd been a sad and cynical queen. Short, fat and not at all pretty, Rory was the runt of the scene; he fucked a lot of men he didn't like, who didn't like him. He was on a carousel of cold and soulless, ephemeral sex. Wonderful as that was, he wanted something more: he wanted to be cherished. And why not? Being gay – despite the lunacy of grown men burning scented candles and giving each other foot rubs – is no bar to happiness. My own life was no vindication of heterosexuality.

The plastic bench was torturous; I'd been sat there for an age, and my buttocks had numbed. I wanted to get up and leave, have a cold shower and come to life again, but couldn't move. I'd been steamed into a trance; my limbs weren't mine anymore. The sign outside the door told the clientele not to spend more than fifteen minutes at a time in the steam room, to punctuate its use with a cold shower or a drink of water. I'd been in there, I felt, for an hour and was dehydrated, my body having sweated out its fluids and minerals. This, I supposed, is the way to die: a painless, lethargic acquiescence. I made myself reach down and pick up my bottle of exclusive Next Level mineral water; I opened it and drank the lot.

The thought of meeting Shamir bored me. I was in no shape for conversation, for the effervescence you have to muster when you first meet people, especially a friend's partner. Rory was keen for us to meet; he thought we'd have a lot in common. Though I hadn't met him, I didn't like Shamir; I didn't like the idea of him. The feature I'd read on him bathed him in a neon light: he'd spoken of his ambition and his dedication to his family, the debt he owed his immigrant father and uncle, who founded the business he now ran. Ambition and families are the things I distrust most; both have been a rod for my back. I saw the fault line running through his words: how would he square this loyalty to his family with his love of cock? I didn't mention this issue to Rory; it was none of my business. I wouldn't piss on his parade. But it would all end in tears. I knew it.

I heard voices outside the door. I sat up, adjusted my towel and tried to seem more awake. Rory walked in; he wore bathing trunks, and his hair was wet. His face glowed, he looked delighted.

'Oh, Puppy!' he said. 'I'm really sorry hon, but we went swimming for a bit, and I forgot all about you.'

'Don't worry,' I said. 'I've been relaxing.'

Rory lingered in the doorway, embarrassed. A pair of thin, hairy brown hands appeared on his hips, kneading his love handles. I saw a head of black hair behind Rory's shoulder, and a pair of dark narrow eyes. Rory walked into the steam room, leading his boyfriend by the wrist.

'This is Puppy, babes,' said Rory. 'I've been dying for you to meet.'

His boyfriend stood before me: his nose was far longer than it had looked in the magazine; the photographer had done a great job. He had a slim swimmer's physique, and wore tight orange trunks. His hair was slicked back; there was a burst of fur in the centre of his chest which trailed in a line down his abdomen, into his trunks. He held out his hand. 'Hi,' he said. 'I'm Sham.'

'Yes.' I stood up to greet him. 'You are.'

6

MY FINGERNAILS HAD been chewed away, exposing the raw flesh beneath; I'd bitten off the cuticles and begun to flay the tips of my fingers. I've bitten my nails since I was a child; whenever I'm at a loose end, I invariably chew my nails. I'd always wanted neat, square-cut nails, not the frayed and ragged ones I now stared at. I took up smoking partly as an antidote, something to do in my downtime other than strip my fingers of necessary tissue. Lately I'd felt an ache in the back of my chest; I was scared, so was trying to quit smoking. My fingers now stung like hell; I could barely hold a pen. I looked at my notepad; apart from a few useless doodles, the pages were blank. I hadn't written a word all morning, and the shoot was now almost over. This was the biggest commission I'd had in a while and I didn't want to blow it. I walked over to the make-up artist.

'Can I have a fag?'

'Sure.' She nodded at a packet of Camel Lights on the table beside her. She didn't look at me; she was curling Mia's eyelashes. Mia was facing the ceiling; her chestnut hair spilled over the back of her chair. I picked up the box, helped myself to a cigarette, then walked over to Val and asked him for a light. He fumbled in his pocket and handed me a box of matches. I smoked the Camel Light; the nicotine calmed me. Val was staring at Sophie who was sat on the suede armchair, hiking her gingham skirt around her waist. She spread her legs, showing the crotch of her white cotton panties, then lay back against the vast satin cushion, turning her face to one side and sucking her thumb.

'That's it, dahlin',' said the photographer. 'Jus' like that.' He wanted to create images of highbrow Lolita-chic; all morning he'd made Sophie and Mia sully themselves in sordid, gormless poses. 'Pull ya knees up a bit,' he said in his practised mockney. 'Beau'iful. Now spread ya legs, but wiv ya ankles closer togever. Look innocent. That's it.' He squinted behind the camera, then pressed a button that initiated a frenzy of exposures. 'Lahvely.'

He said his name was Ricardo; I was sure he was lying. He was in his late-thirties, had a crew cut to disguise his hair loss, and wore jeans and a 1966-style England shirt with RICKY printed on the back. His dour face and parched complexion he'd achieved through hard drinking and a million cigarettes. He arrived at his studio late carrying a football, which he kicked back and forth against a wall while his minion set up the equipment. Like many thirtysomething men, he used football to assert his manhood; like most thirty-something men, he had no talent for it. He often miscontrolled the ball or kicked it so hard against the wall that it cannoned around the room. He tired after a short time and stood panting, with one foot on the ball, surveying the situation. His stare lingered on Sophie and Mia; the girls were then wearing gossamer lilac dresses in readiness for the shoot, their scanty black underwear clearly visible beneath. The football display had been for them; he'd tried to project a sort of boyish charm, a carefree joie de vivre, so his inevitable passes at them might not register as just another debauched, mid-life penchant for young women. Eventually he nodded at me; I smiled and asked him to let me kick the ball. He rolled it to me; I flicked it into the air with my toe, juggled it a dozen or so times with both feet, then lobbed it back to him. Clumsily trying to control the ball on his chest, he lost balance and almost fell over. I laughed, and his face puckered; he gave me a crabby look. He didn't like me. I introduced myself and told him I was Sophie's boyfriend. He liked me even less.

I stared again at my blank notepad and thought about what to write. Should I take notes on the decor and ambience of the room to add colour to the piece? Should I ask the models how the clothes felt on them? Should I get Valeron to comment on his designs? There were a million ways to shape this piece; with a little imagination I could write an original and interesting feature. But I was flummoxed as to how to start. I stared at the notepad and scratched a circle in blue ink on the page; I drew over the shape so many times that the pen nib broke through the paper and onto the page beneath. I sighed, closed the notepad and put it in my pocket. I wouldn't take any notes. I would regurgitate the press releases Valeron had already sent me, and not bother finding new angles for the story. I'd fretted away the morning on the stupid hope of doing a good job; I now remembered that I *never* did a good job. Creativity, attention to detail, fastidiousness and initiative – the things that go into doing a good job – are things I don't have. I wondered why I'd taken this feature so seriously, then remembered I'd been trying to quit smoking: my displaced desire for a cigarette had revealed itself as an agitation about work. I walked over to the make-up artist and took another of her Camel Lights.

I'd been commissioned to write about Valeron Da Silva's latest range of clothing by a magazine called *Blasé*. Similar to *Dazed & Confused*, the magazine focused on fashion and 'urban culture'. Valeron was well respected among the cognoscenti of 'urban culture' (i.e. nerdy white kids who move to London, change their hairstyles every year and believe the shit they read in style magazines), and *Blasé* was keen for him to appear in its final summer issue. Because Sophie was Valeron's friend, and because she was modelling his clothes for free, Valeron demanded that I be the journalist who wrote the piece. Bullying the people at *Blasé* made him feel important, and the idiots at *Blasé* thought he genuinely was, so an enthusiastic young woman called Holly rang me to arrange the details.

She said I'd be paid £500 and I could invoice her for expenses. I had a couple of blank receipts a cab driver had once given me and was going to fill them out for maybe a hundred pounds each. I'd already concocted a story about having to travel to London from the bedside of my sick mother, who I said lived in Luton.

Holly spent almost an hour on the phone with me, stressing how 'virile' and 'edgy' the feature should be, how the achingly cool readers of *Blasé* suffered no fools in their quest for the highest sense of taste and style. I told her I was an experienced journalist, with a long track record of writing about 'urban culture', and she could see my work on the internet.

I wrote music reviews for some men's magazines, short pieces only a hundred or so words long; I'd been writing them for nearly two years. Every month dozens of preview CDs arrived at my flat in official music company envelopes; I'd choose ten or twelve to review, then rewrite their accompanying press releases in a less adulatory tone. These were my music reviews. Each review earned me about forty pounds. I then took the CDs – all unheard, still sealed in plastic – to a record store and sold them. My rent was paid with an afternoon's work each month. Those music reviews were a model for all my work: concise and submitted on time. Unlike writers who take pride in their work, I filed only the minimum number of words required; the editors spent no time cutting my features down to size, trying to distil some abstruse argument into a couple of sentences. My pieces were clear, moronically simple; editors loved me – I gave them so little work to do – and my career thrived. Holly read my reviews on the internet and liked them, so rubber-stamped my commission for *Blasé*.

It was now nearly twelve o'clock; the shoot would soon be over. Mia was being photographed lying on her back on the stone floor, wearing a backless, black crêpe de Chine evening dress. The skirt was deliberately frayed along the hem, and split on the left side almost to the waist; Mia's meagre white leg poked out of it, at almost ninety degrees to her body – the limb hadn't a trace of muscle. Her foot was bare, a red satin G-string was strung over her ankle; a Manolo Blahnik lay beside her head, the other one on her right foot, tangled in the skirt. She was open-mouthed, staring emptily at the space above Ricardo's head; the swelling around her left eye kept the eyelid firmly shut.

Valeron was hysterical when he saw the bruise; he screamed at Mia, asking if her boyfriend had done this, as usual, because he wanted money for drugs. Mia didn't reply. The make-up artist spent an age trying to mask it, though not very well. Luckily, Ricardo said he could 'work with it', incorporate it into his ideas; the result was a series of poses – such as the one she lay in now – that I could only describe as 'raped debutante'. I later saw the photos; the airbrushed images of Mia lying on the floor, looking stupid and abused, had a certain erotic force. Ricardo was a genius.

Sophie came and stood by me. She'd wiped the make-up from her skin; her face was bright and elfin. She now wore her jeans and one of my T-shirts; now that I lived with her, she wore my clothes all the time. It was an ostentatious statement of our coupling. I felt colonised; I rarely had anything clean to wear. We watched Mia pose for the last of Ricardo's shots. I was in a good mood; in a few minutes I could go and enjoy myself in the sunshine, my morning's work done. I reached out and took Sophie's hand. She stepped closer to me, and I put my arm around her shoulder. She wrapped her arms around my waist, resting her cheek against mine.

'Sophie . . .'

'Mm-hmm?'

'. . . I'd never beat you up for drugs.'

'Aaaw.' She hugged me tightly. 'I know, sweetheart. You're lovely.'

We held each other in silence.

'Max is a bastard,' she murmured.

'Who?'

'Mia's boyfriend. He's *so* druggy. He loses his head if he hasn't had any. They deserve each other, she's been off her face since she got here.'

'I didn't see any marks on her arms.'

'She injects it between her toes.'

Valeron and Ricardo walked towards us. Val wore camouflage-print combat trousers, tucked into tasselled cowboy boots. His torso was shrouded in a beige pashmina, his long hair tied in a bun on top of his head. He was elated; the shoot had gone well. 'You were great,' he said, kissing Sophie's cheek. 'You looked amazing. The pictures are going to be terrific.'

Sophie was almost crying, moved by the praise as if the shoot had required effort or talent on her part. She clutched his hand: 'You know I love working with you, Val.'

The three of them – Sophie, Ricardo, Valeron – chatted among themselves. I stared past them, at Ricardo's lackey who was packing away the equipment, and at Mia who, changing out of her evening dress, bared her concave chest: her breasts were pale and weary. Her body was longer than Sophie's, and thinner; she had a large dark-red birthmark on her stomach, like a splash of burgundy, and when she wasn't posing she stooped listlessly. She'd said almost nothing all morning. She finished dressing – into a pair of jeans and a sweatshirt – and came and stood with us.

We walked in a group towards the front door – Ricardo left his minion to tidy the studio – and stepped out into the sunshine. Valeron said he had a busy schedule; he kissed us all on both cheeks, hailed a cab and left. Ricardo started crossing the road, and the girls began to follow him.

Sophie stopped and turned around. 'Aren't you coming?'

'Where?'

'To the pub, to watch the football.'

I'd forgotten all about it. I watched Ricardo leading

Mia across the street, his hand cupping her buttock. 'No,' I said. 'I've got a lot to do. I've got to write up this piece.'

She walked up to me and frowned. 'When will I see you then?'

'Tonight.' I touched her cheek. 'At *home*.'

She smiled; she liked it when I used that word. She put her hands on my shoulders and kissed me on the lips. She stared into my eyes and whispered, '*I love you*.'

'Okay.' I squeezed her elbow. 'I'll see you later.'

She turned around and walked across the street. Ricardo and Mia were standing outside the pub, underneath an enormous flag of St George draped over the balcony above them. He was casually holding Mia's waist; he was going to fuck her. I saw it panning out: he'd buy her drinks, grope her while they watched the game; they'd go back to his studio for some cocaine, then sodomy. He was smiling; he had it all figured. Sophie joined them, and they walked inside, Ricardo guiding her through the doors with his hand on the small of her back. Maybe Sophie would join in: she could fellate him while he watched Mia masturbate. I wished Ricardo luck. Someone in this world ought to be enjoying himself.

I walked up the street and around a few corners. I came across a small Bangladeshi tea house and decided to have some lunch. It was cool inside. The dull decor, the metal water jugs and beakers on the table, reminded me of my mother's house. I watched the artisans and fashionistas of Brick Lane walking past outside, on their way to a bar to watch the football. In a few minutes England would play their first game of the World Cup, against Sweden in Japan.

Like the Germans, the Japanese have sublimated their bloodlust into a taste for sport and consumer goods, and were co-hosting the tournament with Korea. Fuji, Sony and McDonald's were among the many firms whose goods were official Fifa-endorsed products. I had no desire to watch a game between England and Sweden, two of the whitest teams in the competition. Watching white guys play football is like watching them dance: they do it with such gauche and inept gusto. No doubt they fuck just as badly. I'd decided only to watch the games featuring Brazil.

As a boy, I'd loved football; now it had little appeal. I watched the occasional match, but paid no attention to league rankings and other competitions: watching a contest involving twenty-two young millionaires, it's hard to care about the result. I looked at the old men sat around me; football meant nothing to them. It was good to have found this niche, oblivious to the world around it. I sat in the tea room, listening to the men speak in Bengali; I didn't understand a word. I took out my notepad and ordered a cold drink and a plate of samosas. The waiter brought me a chilled can of Coke; it bore an official World Cup logo – Coca-Cola was another 'proud sponsor'. I got out my pen and began writing. I was working on a business idea that had recently come to me. I had vague hopes of making money; more importantly, I wanted a reason to contact Sarupa. My idea was nonetheless a serious one that wouldn't compromise her sense of Corporate Social Responsibility. I wanted to clarify it on paper before I phoned her up to apply for Indravest funding, and asked her to lunch.

The idea was for a tour operation, called BigFun Holidays. BigFun would provide package holidays exclusively to fat people. Obesity is a rising fact of Western life; mankind has made excellent progress and there are now more fat people alive than there are people starving – many live in Britain. The fat have the same right to happiness as anyone; BigFun would help them find it. They needed holidays away from the sneering, contemptuous gazes of the slim. They needed an environment with no beautiful people – the sight of which makes them hate themselves even more – and restaurants where they could gorge themselves unashamedly, beaches where their blubber could be bared and tanned, not hidden under a

T-shirt nor wrapped in a sarong. They needed freedom; freedom is found only among one's own, so even the staff would be fat. I also had an idea for a singles venture, BigFun Xtra, catering for fat swingers and the perverts who fuck them. Based on Club 18–30, it would be an intense rota of near-orgies, fuelled by an abundance of alcohol and simple carbohydrates – cream cakes, nachos, whatever they wanted – with the staff urging them to new depths of prurience, turning a blind eye to the high jinks that ensued.

I finished drafting my proposal. I was proud of my work; it fit snugly into 1,000 words, and was a blatant money-spinner. I was surprised the idea hadn't been conceived before by more commercial minds than mine: in America, it no doubt already had, but I'd never heard of a British equivalent.

I wrote up the proposal using Sophie's computer, a sleek blue iMac. I looked up some articles on the internet about the holiday industry and copied some passages into my business plan, along with a few graphs; they were of tangential relevance, but they added a gloss of authority. I phoned directory enquiries to get a number for Haine Abbott Wilson, then called the firm. I hadn't the courage to speak to Sarupa, so asked the receptionist for Sarupa's email address. I wrote her an email – the subject heading was, 'Proposal For Indravest Funding' – with a brief message telling her I had an idea of some entre-preneurial value, and once she'd read the attached proposal I'd be only too glad to have a lunch meeting with her to discuss it.

It was just past seven o'clock; Sophie wasn't yet home. I hadn't heard a word from her since lunchtime. Maybe she was now on all fours, eating Mia's pussy while Ricardo fucked her from behind. This thought aroused me, and I decided to look at some internet porn.

I looked for sites featuring Indian women. Despite being among the most online people on earth – India is the world's largest source of high-tech labour – Indian women are rare in the web's ocean of porn stars. Sites such as indiafuck.com and sins-of-india.net were a fraud; they palmed visitors off with poorly shot images of obviously mulatto and Hispanic women. I downloaded an MPEG involving someone called 'Neelam'; I watched several seconds of her squatting on a fat cock, bellowing, 'Fuck that ass! Fuck that ass!' in a Californian accent. In another scene, a patently German woman, wearing a red *bindhi*, kept her eyes screwed shut as an erection exploded in her face; the ejaculate was grey and gummy, and clung to her face in globules.

One or two sites showed genuine Indian women: amateur sites created by Western sex travellers, they showed skinny white men copulating with hookers they'd picked up on a Keralan beach. The women were sweet, gentle-looking; they didn't give the camera the hard stare that professional porn stars do. They had leathery black nipples and gnarled feet; their crotches, thick with hair, were like pads of wire wool. I thought of the pennies they earned for their work, and how many bowls of rice it bought.

I surfed around for a site showing women from India's diaspora – in Canada, the United States or Great Britain – where the women had access to beauty treatments, where the rewards for porn weren't so bleak. I didn't find any, so I looked at my usual ones instead. One site had film clips provided by blacksonblondes.com; viewers could download brief MPEGs, teasers to coax them into giving their credit card details, to gain full access to 'The World's Largest *All-Interracial* Website'. The product on offer was excellent: the actors were generally good-looking, with well-crafted bodies, the dialogue was exciting and the actresses, if not actually having a good time, made a good job of impersonating it. I downloaded an MPEG of two handsome black men 'double-penetrating' a young white woman. She was beautiful, with fine straight hair and a taut dancer's physique. She sat astride the man who fucked her pussy, facing him, and leant forward so the man behind could get inside her anus. They fucked her roughly; she was panting and her cheeks were red, possibly due to the heat of the studio lamps. The men wore nothing but gold chains and garish basketball shoes, their muscular bodies were oiled and gleaming. Both had razor-thin, manicured goatees. They paid no attention to the girl; they looked over her shoulder, into each other's faces, making conversation – 'Ain't dis da bomb motherfucker!' – and giving one another a high-five. I watched the men holding hands, sweating and smiling at each other, and was struck by how utterly *homosexual* they were. The woman was simply a proxy, a medium by which the two men fucked *each other*: no doubt each could feel his cock jostling with the other's, through the lining between her rectum and her genital passage.

I heard the front door door being unlocked and footsteps on the landing.

'Hello!' It was Sophie.

'Hi!'

'Sorry I've been gone so long.' I heard her walking towards the lounge. 'What are you doing?'

'I'm looking at porn.'

'Really? Oh, let me have a look!' Sophie came into the room and squinted at the screen. 'You're such a monkey! You're *so* naughty.' She rummaged through her purse for her spectacles; she hadn't worn her contacts that day. As she put them on, I brought up the MPEG I downloaded earlier of the German wearing a *bindhi*. Sophie leant over me and peered at the erection, its huge bulbous end being rubbed by its owner. 'Eeurgh,' she said. 'What's that?'

'It's a cock.' I looked at the organ, twitching on the point of climax.

'What's wrong with it?'

I laughed; Sophie was funny when she wanted to be. She laughed too, and sat on my lap. She smelt of cigarettes and alcohol. I nuzzled her neck, trying to smell something else – a hint of Ricardo. She rubbed her face against mine; I kissed her cheek.

'Did you miss me?' she said.

'Loads . . . I was so lonely I had to look at porn for comfort.' I moved the screen cursor and clicked on the MPEG from blacksonblondes.com. 'What do you think of this?'

She stared at the two men and cried, 'Look at their shoes! They're *so* eighties!'

I laughed out loud.

She watched them high-fiving each other. 'Oh my God, that's so funny! What's that silly bitch doing with them? I wouldn't let them buy me coffee.'

I laughed again, and grabbed her waist. We tussled in a moment of mock-wrestling, then fell still, looking at each other.

'Did you miss me, too?' I asked.

'Of course . . .' Sophie cupped my face and brushed my hair from my eyes. 'You're my baby.'

'Did you have fun with Ricardo?'

'Yeah.' She looked away, back at the computer screen. 'Yeah, it was fun. We just watched the football, and spent the rest of the day drinking. Mia's so fucking crazy . . .'

'All day? You spent all day in the pub?'

'Yeah,' she said, still looking at the screen. 'Where else would I have been?'

I hugged her and kissed her hair. I didn't mind her lies: what could I do about them? She sank into my chest; I slipped my hand under her T-shirt and rubbed her stomach. She held my arm close against her.

'What's for dinner?'

'Dhal,' I said. 'I made it earlier.'

I leant forward from the couch, picked up the ashtray from the floor and stubbed out the joint. I picked up my glass and the empty bottle of merlot and put them on the coffee table. I was feeling pretty trashed. Sophie had gone to bed exhausted a couple of hours ago. I stayed up watching the television, getting stoned. I watched anything, including an episode of *Yes, Prime Minister* on UK Gold. Jim Hacker is a great character; through him, one sees the effect of worldly success. In *Yes, Minister* he was a nervous buffoon, at the mercy of wily civil servants, sustained only by his fear of failure. Now he was Prime Minister, and was notably tougher. He called the shots. In this episode he consummately destroyed a Foreign Office bureaucrat who belonged to a cabal that had presumed to dictate foreign policy over his head. He was called to the Prime Minister's office and, in front of his colleagues, made an example of. Hacker sent him to manage consular business in Syria. Damascus was apparently the arsehole of the diplomatic world; the stupid jerk's career was finished. Hacker wasn't a man to be fucked with. He knew people count for nothing, that the means always justify the end. That's the fact. I've never held any power, but I've been powerless. The powerful and the powerless are the ones who know the truth; those who live in-between are too candied in sentiment to stomach it.

It was past eleven o'clock. I thought about rolling another joint but decided not to. Smoking dope made me more morbidly introspective than I already was. I changed channel and watched rock videos on MTV2. A three-piece band, Alien Ant Farm, performed a catchy tune. They wore post-grunge, skater-boy outfits – knee-length shorts, hooded tops, sneakers – and jumped excitedly around the set. The lead singer had a crew cut and a mischievous grin; he sang a thrash-metal cover version of Michael Jackson's 'Smooth Criminal'. The song and the video were full of energy and teenage irreverence. Warm tears came to my eyes, and slid down my cheeks. I wasn't young, and this made me cry. My youth, to all intents and purposes, was over. More tragically, I'd never been young, not like them; I never had their easy-going exuberance. They had faith in themselves and the future; they glistened with it. I wasn't yet thirty, and was completely jaded.

Wiping my tears, I rose from the couch; it was a

deep, glove-covered Matthew Hilton creation, with several cigarette burns in it. I switched off the television and was about to turn off the computer, but decided to check my emails. I logged on and found a response from Sarupa, regarding my idea for BigFun Holidays: 'ha ha . . . v. funny . . .' she wrote. 'u obviously have too much time on your hands . . .'

Without thinking, I replied: 'i should take up yoga.' I sat in the chair, looking at the message she'd sent me. I pored over it, trying to glean something of her in those words.

A jingle sounded from the computer; Sarupa had emailed me back: 'yoga might do you some good . . . i think you have a lot of blocked energy. it might help u release it.'

I sat up, thrilled by the contact. 'blocked energy??? blocked colon more likely. why u still at work? moonlighting as a cleaner?'

I waited for her reply, listening to the hum of the computer. But for the static haze of the computer screen, the room was dark and silent.

The jingle sounded again: 'yes i moonlight as a cleaner. you should try it sometime . . . actually i'm working on a new project in the Balkans. it's taking up so much time right now. I have to work through this weekend, so i can have a couple of days off at the end of next week. I want to spend a few days in the country and relax . . . How's sophie? does she know you're up past your bedtime?'

'sophie's in bed,' I answered. 'she's had a busy day. and i can stay up as late as i want. it's not a school night . . . where are you going for your break?'

'the cotswolds. my dad has a house there. i can't wait to get away . . . I've been working so hard lately. i'm absolutely shattered.'

'a weekend with the parents? i've never been to the country. say hello to the cows.'

'never been to the country?!! what are you? some ultra-urban homeboy?!! my parents aren't there this weekend, so we've got the house to ourselves. we're having some friends over.'

Her words crushed me. I couldn't bear to think of her life, her work and friends; it was a world unto itself that didn't include me. 'no i haven't been to the country and it's not cos i'm a homeboy,' I wrote. 'since when do our lot go to the country? i can hang myself at home and save them rednecks the bother . . .'

'v. droll . . .' she replied. 'why don't u and sophie join us? there's plenty of space and there'll be lots of other people there. one of my friends works in publishing. u can tell her about your book. and you can say hello to the cows yourself.'

My fingers hovered above the keyboard. I could hear her voice in my head; my heart was pounding. 'i want to fuck you so much i'm going mad . . .' I typed the words in a spasm; I moved the cursor to the send icon and dared myself to send them. Instead, I highlighted the text and deleted it. I replaced it with, 'that's very kind of you. i'd love to. i'm sure sophie would too.'

'ok. i'll email u the address later, and a map of how to get there. i'm off home now. i'm SO knackered!!!!'

I wanted to reply. I sat at the desk for an hour, reading and re-reading our correspondence. I heard Sophie get out of bed and walk to the toilet. I turned off the computer, walked over to the couch and collapsed onto it. A few seconds later, I was asleep.

Sitting at a table on the pavement, I watched the people walking by. They were the usual Soho crowd: homos, tourists and theatregoers. A gaggle of young Japanese people sat at the next table; they all had dyed hair – blonde, copper, metallic blue – cut into up-to-the-minute styles. They wore a complex array of labels: Evisu, Prada, Duffer of St George. I couldn't read the statement encoded in their meticulously chosen outfits.

The first non-white people to wholly commit to the project known as 'the West', the Japanese have always fascinated me. Among Indians, Rushdie said, the West is repeated as farce; in Japan the West is modified, improved upon and exported back to Europe and the USA. The Japanese are obsessed with Western culture – the people next to me adhered to Western fashion, its code of being cool – and never seem out of place in London, 12,000 miles from home. Indians, even when born here, are rarely so at ease. The West jars with them, and they cocoon themselves within religion, arranged marriages and extended families. The Japanese have an osmotic character; trends bleed into them, capture their imagination. Indians are less permeable.

Rory and Shamir were inside the bar, buying another round of drinks. I smoked a cigarette and finished the last of my beer. It wasn't yet seven o'clock, so there wasn't the daytime crush of bodies, nor the Friday night melee of shrieking poofs and drunks urinating in the doorways. It was a beautiful evening. Rory emerged from the door with a tray of beers. Shamir walked behind him, palming his hair back over his head. He stopped for a moment, to enjoy his reflection in the window.

'Here you are, handsome.' Rory put my beer down and sat beside me; Shamir took the seat on my other side. He adjusted his sunglasses, peered at me over the rim and raised his beer. I touched bottles with him. Shamir liked to observe manly rituals: he'd patted me hard on the back, shaken my hand too firmly when we met, though I leant forward to kiss his cheek, as I'd kissed Rory's. He also toasted each new drink, and made a point of commenting on every girl who walked past, catching my eye.

I stared at a plump, clear-skinned white woman who'd stopped in front of us, looking at her watch.

'Nice tits, huh?' said Shamir.

She overheard and glared at the three of us. I laughed, and she stormed away in disgust. I don't know why he behaved like this: maybe it was because I was Sikh; our macho reputation precedes us. Whatever the reason, I didn't like it. I felt embarrassed for him.

'So, when's your brother getting married?' he said, leaning towards me.

'End of this summer. September, I think.'

'Your brother's younger than you, isn't he?'

'He's nineteen.'

'Doesn't that put a lot of pressure on you to get married? Aren't your family trying to fix you up with someone?'

'No . . . I don't really see my family that much. They pretty much leave me alone.'

He looked surprised. 'Your parents must be happy though, for your brother.'

'My mum is . . . I don't know if my dad knows anything about it.'

'Why's that?'

'He fucked off years ago.'

'How come?!' Shamir was aghast, but checked himself. 'I'm sorry. It's none of my business.'

'Don't be.' I reached for my cigarettes. 'He couldn't handle it. Being a dad, being a husband, making a living . . . He's the kind of guy who finds it hard to give a shit. It's too much for him . . . So he fucked off.'

Shamir stared at me in amazement. My family history was unusual among Asians, my honesty even more so.

'Best thing for us really . . .' I lit my cigarette. 'He was a manic depressive. He'd sometimes stay in bed for weeks.'

'Where's he now?'

'Vancouver, I think. I'm not sure . . . He moves around a lot. He was in London last year.'

'Did you see him?' asked Rory.

'No.'

We said nothing for a while. I looked at the next table; it was empty, the Japanese had gone.

Shamir broke the silence: 'I went to a Sikh wedding last month. At Ascot racecourse. I've never seen so many people drink so much in my life . . . I was completely arse-holed by the end of it.' He smiled to himself and took a swig of beer. 'The food was great. They had the bhangra playing and everyone was dancing ... Fucking great party.' He raised his bottle again: '*Chuk-dhe fateh*!'

'Yeah,' I sighed, and touched bottles with him again. 'Who was your friend?'

'His name's Sukhdev. I knew him at university. Great guy ... He's a dentist now, lives in Surrey.'

'Is he gay?'

'No.' Shamir looked at me. 'Why do you ask?'

'A lot of arranged marriages are lavender numbers ... Was it arranged?'

'Yes.'

Rory sat back in his chair, amused. 'A lot of them are lavender?'

'It goes on,' I said. 'It stands to reason that some queen will hook up with a dykey friend, or some silly hag who's in love with him. Then he can do his thing, with no hassle ... A lot of chicks probably want a gay husband. Someone who'll keep the house tidy and won't kick the shit out of them.'

'Is that what you're going to do, Shammy?' asked Rory, touching his boyfriend's hand. 'Marry a lesbian?'

Shamir tried to laugh.

'If you do, make sure she's pretty.' Rory squeezed his wrist. 'I won't share you with some fat bitch, whose 'tache stinks of fanny.'

Shamir looked away; he didn't like the teasing.

I patted Rory's arm: 'Did I ever tell you about my driving instructor?'

'The creepy one? You have, but tell Shammy.' He looked at Shamir: 'Listen to this, you'll love it.'

I dropped out of university in January 1995. For more than eighteen months I lived at my mum's. I had no thoughts of what to do with myself; I played video games and lounged behind the till in the shop. After a year of doing this, I decided to be more constructive: I took driving lessons.

Learning to drive was the dullest, most arduous experience of my life, and very expensive. The instructor was a clown, so I ended up taking far more lessons than is the norm. His name was Mr Bains. He was recommended to my mother by her friend; he was an *apna* ('one of ours', i.e. Sikh and of the Jat caste), and sure to do a good job. He picked me up outside the shop every Sunday morning in a white Nissan Micra. I'd drive around Southall for two hours, trying to remember what the road signs meant and which gear to change into.

Mr Bains didn't wear a turban; he had a business-like haircut and was clean-shaven. Composed of metabolised red meat and whisky, he had a hard, patchy complexion. He grimaced constantly, suppressing belches in his throat; he had gastric problems. Like many Punjabis, his idea of an alcoholic was a man who was too drunk to work; I'd always smell liquor on his skin. He worked seven days a week, most of them for sixteen hours. Charging me twelve pounds per hour, he also owned an HGV, and taught lorry-driving for double that rate. He never declared the payments he got in cash; he was raking it in. We spoke almost exclusively in Punjabi; he worked and lived in Southall, so had little use for English. When he did speak it, he did so in a camp nasal accent, like a fawning colonial manservant.

He was known to my mother's friends, so I was on my best behaviour in his company: I addressed him using *dhussi* rather than *dhu* (like the French use *vous* instead of *tu*); I always suffixed my replies with *jhi*; I even called him *uncle*. I was too ashamed to admit I was a dropout. I told him I was taking a sabbatical from studying to help my mum with the running of the shop. In his eyes, I was sensible and polite, the perfect Punjabi son. We'd stop at his house, midway through the lesson, and have tea. He'd sit me next to his ten-year-old boy, hoping I'd be an example to him. His son was addicted to watching televised wrestling, so wasn't very bright. The TV seemed always to be on, showing hulking American brutes pretending to fight each other. His middle-aged wife – lean, attractive, with jet-black hair – wore a *salwar-kameez* and walked around the house barefoot. I'd stare down at her sexy feet when she brought us a plate of biscuits; this added to their notion that I was coy and well brought up.

When I was a boy, Indian girls didn't excite me. They were drab and sexless, had thick plaits and traipsed submissively behind their parents. By the time I was twenty-one, they were far more daring. Wearing denim miniskirts, hair tinted with henna, they'd strut around Southall in high heels, tossing their hair and pouting at the catcalls from the boys who drove past. They turned me on. Mr Bains would catch me looking at them; he'd put his hand on my thigh and remark on my youth, how hot-blooded I was beneath my shy exterior. He urged me to get a girlfriend, to milk my lust. He often asked me whether I'd found one. Eventually, I lied and said I was laying a Pakistani called Shazia. He was delighted. Pakistani girls are a Sikh fetish; fucking one is a triumph, of sorts, over the old enemy. His talk then turned to Shazia. What was the shape and size of her arse? What noises did she make? Did I lick her pussy? What did it taste like? . . .

'You fuck her like this?' He bounced an imaginary body on his lap, and pawed at invisible breasts. He took an unhealthy interest in my sex life. Then, one day, he talked about gays: 'Disgusting, *hunnah*?' He frowned and shook his head. Gays didn't bother me, I said. I'd met some at university – they were as boring as anyone else. He told me there was an old queer who'd cruised Southall for over twenty years; his name was John, and he sucked a lot of cock ('*landh bodh choosdha*!'). Mr Bains asked me if I wanted to go and see him; he said John always loitered at a spot in Old Southall, we could see him there. I was intrigued, and said okay.

He gave me directions as I drove through Southall, past the Somali cafés on South Road, past the *gurdwara* on Havelock Road, towards Cranford. He stopped me at a busy parade of shops, and pointed at a man in a black overcoat, eating *pakoras* from a paper bag: John, London's original curry-queen. He was grey and balding; other than being the only white man in sight, he was anonymous. I looked at the old man, standing by a postbox at the side of the road, and asked whose cocks he sucked.

'Everybody's.' Mr Bains looked at John, shook his head and sighed: '*Landh bodh choosdha* . . .' He smiled to himself, lost in private thoughts.

I asked him to name someone who'd been with John. Mr Bains told me to start the engine and start driving. We drove out of Southall into Osterley, through leafy suburban streets with large detached houses. Mr Bains was silent; he didn't upbraid me for elementary mistakes, and just pointed at the turns he wanted me to take. Heading back through Southall, on my way home, he started talking. He told me about when he was young and newly arrived in Britain. He had a friend who owned a van, and they and some other pals killed time driving it around. John was well known even then; the group decided to go and have a look at him standing, as always, by the postbox. They offered John one of the beers they carried, and joked with him; after a chat in pidgin English, John got in the van and they took him for a ride. Mr Bains laughed describing his friends, young Punjabi tearaways, looking for a good time. And a good time was had by all, as they each gave John a seeing to in the back of the van. One friend, said Mr Bains, choking with laughter, fucked John so hard his turban fell off; he finished the job with his hair flailing everywhere. I listened in awe, amazed by Mr Bains' candour. He continued chuckling long after his story ended. He missed his youth, the good old days.

I was gobsmacked: 'I didn't know you were gay.'

'Gay?!' Mr Bains turned to me in a fury. 'I'm not fucking gay!'

'You had sex with a man.'

'Listen *bittah* . . .' He put his hand on my thigh; this time it didn't feel so avuncular. '. . . Just because you having sex with the man, it does not mean you gay.'

I stared at him in disbelief.

He tutted at my reaction. '*Bittah*, you are young man,' he said. 'You are healthy. If he say to you, "Come on let's do the sex," you say yes, *hunnah*?'

'No,' I said. 'Because I'm not gay.'

Mr Bains didn't press the point and left the conversation there. It was a fortnight until my test; he didn't broach the topic again and we concentrated on my driving. On the test date he gave me an intensive lesson, then drove me to the test centre. Fifteen minutes into it, I failed. I'd never got the hang of reverse parking. I tried learning again, years later when I lived in Hackney. I took a course from the British School of Motoring, and passed after twenty lessons.

Shamir was overjoyed by the story of Mr Bains; it broke ice between us. He'd been uncertain of me; now he relaxed. The three of us enjoyed a few more rounds of beer at our pavement table. The revellers had appeared and the other tables were crowded as people lubricated their evening with alcohol and chatter.

'What are you doing tonight?' asked Rory. It was nearly eleven o'clock and he was anxious to move the entertainment on elsewhere. 'Fancy coming along with Sham and I?' He was going to a new gay club, the Plug, in Farringdon. Danny Rampling and Judge Jules were among that night's DJs and Will Young – winner of *Pop Idol*, the televised karaoke contest – was performing songs from his debut album.

'I can't do clubs anymore,' I said. 'Not unless I'm loaded.'

'Get loaded then!' Shamir slapped me on the back. 'We've got plenty of drugs, haven't we, babe?' He swapped smiles with Rory. 'Come on! You can do your bhangra moves.' Shamir held his face aloft, raised his arms and shook insanely – the basics of Punjabi dancing.

'You're very good at that,' I told him. 'But I should go home. I'm very tired.'

111

Rory gave me an accusing stare. 'Liar . . . I know why you don't want to go clubbing.' He turned to Shamir: 'Puppy doesn't like gay clubs. He doesn't like all those men sweating on each other, and pinching each other's nipples. That's the real reason, isn't it, Puppy?'

'Yeah. That's about right.' I took one of Shamir's cigarettes. 'It stinks like shit in those places.'

Rory looped his arm through mine. 'Puppy doesn't like the smell of men on heat.' He smiled at me. 'I don't blame you. It is pretty awful . . . But hey, when you're out of your head, who cares?'

'I do have a lot on this weekend,' I said. 'I'm going to the country with Sophie tomorrow.'

'Dirty weekend?'

'Not that dirty. We're staying at her mate Sarupa's place.'

'Whereabouts are you going?' asked Shamir.

'The Cotswolds. Some place called Chipping Campden.'

'Sarupa Shah!' Shamir clicked his fingers in recognition. 'You're going to Sarupa Shah's place?'

'Yeah. How do you know?'

'There's not many people called Sarupa with houses in the Cotswolds. I know her family. They're big people . . . How do you know them?'

'My girlfriend is her fiancé's cousin.'

'Duncan! I know him too.' He raised his eyebrows; he was impressed. 'You're going places, if you're hanging out with them.'

'How do you mean?'

'Her dad, Sodhilal, he's a magnate. He's friendly with Tony Blair.' He leant forward and lit my cigarette. 'I saw her and her old man a few months ago, at the Asian Business Awards. They were sitting next to the Blairs on the platform, you could see them chatting away.'

My heart beat faster; the weekend now felt like a frightening prospect. 'How do you know Sarupa?' I asked.

'We're always bumping into each other at these award ceremonies . . . I've had lunch with her, too. She's got me

112

involved with this Asian investment fund she's started.' He gave me a cheeky grin. 'She's very sexy. I bet you fancy her.' He kept his eyes on me; I didn't return his gaze.

I picked up my beer. 'She's a good-looking girl.'

'You'll have a lovely time this weekend,' he said. 'I'm sure the house is beautiful.'

'I hope so.'

We finished our beers and stood by the kerb, waiting to hail a taxi. I kissed the boys goodnight and watched them get into a cab and head eastwards. Rory looked at me through the rear window, and made salacious gestures with his tongue. I showed him my middle finger and he laughed. I was drunk and sleepy; I wanted to get a taxi myself. I went to a cashpoint, looked at my balance and withdrew my card. I walked towards Trafalgar Square. I was getting the bus.

7

I SAT ON the window ledge overlooking Dalston Lane and sifted through the letters. I hadn't informed the companies I worked with of my new address in West London, so I'd returned to Hackney to get my mail. My landlord was happy for me to pop by every week or so; I could keep an eye on the place until he found new tenants. He didn't want the flat being overrun by the dealers downstairs; they'd let junkies stop there to smoke coke and suck their cocks in lieu of money. I made a point of walking past them as they stood outside the bookie's, hoping they'd get the impression I was still around.

I'd been sent some preview CDs and a few samples of male beauty products. I opened a package from Kilfoyle PR, a leading cosmetics public relations firm; they'd sent me a tube of Azure, a new facial scrub for men. Azure, said the press release, was a 'moisture-enriched exfoliant'; it was 'an ideal pre-shave face wash', that contained 'essential meta-proteins, for a unique hydration experience your skin won't forget'. It looked like pretty good stuff and I liked the packaging – the tube came in a transparent box that was chic and expensively designed. I now had several such samples, enough to write an overview of the men's facial wash scene. I'd pitch the idea to GQ, or maybe *Men's Health*.

It wasn't yet midday, so the street was quiet. I looked across it, at the almost deserted council houses on the opposite side. The tenements were being evacuated in the prelude to their destruction; but for a remaining few, the inhabitants had been rehoused. The houses were now dilapidated shells; two of them had been gutted by fire. Some Arsenal flags fluttered from the windows: Arsenal were a great team and had won the Premier League and the FA Cup; the people around here were happy. From one of the houses came the quick, dull beat of a speed-garage radio station. I sat looking at the houses, smoking a cigarette, thanking God I didn't live here anymore.

Across the street I saw a group of boys – white-trash, fourteen or so years old – at the corner of the road. Adolescent boys are strange; puberty strikes them at random, and some were shaped like men, while others were patently still children. They were crowded around an old Ford Escort; one of them was lying on the floor so he could see beneath it. I thought they were going to vandalise the car, or steal it. Something fluttered out from behind a wheel then immediately jumped back behind it: a pigeon. City pigeons aren't very scared of people; instead of flying away, this bird went beneath the car as the boys walked towards it. The boys had spotted it and now it was trapped. The cruelty and imbecility of the working class is limitless: the pigeon tried to make its escape, and one of the boys kicked it before it could take flight. It hobbled a few feet, dragging a broken wing. The boys laughed in delight. One of the larger boys kicked it again, this time against the side of a Transit van. The pigeon slid to the floor, dead. Again they laughed; it was such fun.

I hate poor white people. No one is more stupid or useless. They made my life hell when I was a child. At school every Asian was habitually called a Paki, but I was given special treatment. My *joodha* – or 'top-knot' or 'bobble-head' as they called it – made me the focus of relentless abuse. I'd be pushed around the playground, slapped and taunted; they'd descend on me like harpies, trying to knock it off my head. I'd walk, sobbing, to the nurse's office, holding the hankie my mother had wrapped it in, as they tugged at my hair which now fell over my face and shoulders. I was ten years old. My last two years at primary school were impossible. Before then, no one had noticed me. I had no friends, apart from Asaf, and he wasn't a friend, just another 'stani' who'd been ostracised from the herd. We spent our break periods together, sharing our loneliness; for this we were labelled 'gaylords' by those who made pariahs of us in the first place. The other Asian kids ignored my suffering; they were glad I was taking the heat and not them. The blacks were only too happy to join in; in fact, black boys were among my worst tormentors.

Blacks are forever angry. In America – vexed by their own enduring mediocrity and inability to progress – they vent their spleen at Koreans or Jews, or whoever else happens to own the local corner store. In Greenford they hated Indians. There might have been a strategy to their actions; by helping the white boys to bait me, maybe they were deflecting attention from themselves. If so, it was a smart move. I never saw a black kid bullied once.

Girls sometimes came to my rescue. Their intervention was a blessing, and also humiliating. A black girl called Debby would walk me to the nurse's office and help tie my *joodha* back in place. I'd let her tie my hair into plaits, even pigtails, so she could see how it looked. I was so grateful for her company. I loved her so much.

In time I learnt to sympathise with black people, not judge them for their failures. They'd been fucked by slavery: plantations don't foster an ethos of erudition, commerce and deferred gratification. Poor white people, I can never pity. I've no concern for their class struggle – the bourgeoisie didn't shove turds through our letterbox. The decline of the working class in what is, after all, their own country, only proves their stupidity. My mother barely spoke English, but was a competent, shop-owning microcapitalist: if she can prosper in Great Britain, then it's only the truly fucking dumb who can't.

I smiled remembering Sean and David, two of the boys who tortured me at school. David was in my class; Sean, his younger brother, was in the year below. Sean was white, while David's father was Jamaican; their mother was a filthy Irish crone, who bought Rothmans by the hundred from our shop. Her fingers were brown with nicotine, her teeth were broken, stained and useless. Her sons had permanently bruised arms and legs. Itinerant men drifted through her life and disappeared, leaving their children to be dressed in rags and reared on white bread and baked beans, while the social security money went on cigarettes and tins of Special Brew. Every day she was in our shop fidgeting, striving to explain how many cigarettes and cans of lager she needed. Her peasant Irish brogue made little sense to Mum's Indian peasant ears. Taking a carrier bag of these supplies, she'd walk out the shop muttering, 'Dirty heathen bastards . . .'

Sean and David led bitter hopeless lives, for which I was made to pay. The beatings I took from them weren't the most physically painful, but they lasted the whole day. They beat me each break-time, then followed me home, kicking my legs from under me when I tried to outrun them. I hated them more than anyone. They came into the shop and insulted my mother and sister and Hari, who was then just an infant. We took their money nonetheless: we'd had our window broken when we'd thrown another kid out of the shop and didn't want them doing the same. I never told Mum about what I went through at school. I was her eldest child, I was supposed to make her life easier. I was almost twelve years old when I finally got them off my back: I sold them lighter fuel. Mum sold cigarettes to any child who asked for them, but was scrupulous about never selling chemicals to the underage. Sean and David turned to me for help. I stole tins of butane from the shop, handing them over during the morning break. They'd vanish for the rest of the day, getting wasted. Soon they appeared outside the shop in the morning, sometimes before it opened. They'd push their money through the letterbox, and I'd throw the tins out the bathroom window into the alley where they picked them up. It wasn't long before I just left the tins in the alley before I went to bed, so I wouldn't have to wake up so early. When I started high school I was confident I'd avoid running into them in the open, and my part in their solvent abuse ended. When I last saw the brothers, I was in my mid-teens. I was then big enough to take care of myself, and they were annihilated wrecks, unable even to recognise me.

I sat on that window ledge in Hackney and wondered what became of those two. Hopefully they'd graduated from lighter fuel onto heroin, lived as rent boys then died of syphilis, or maybe starvation. I finished my cigarette, dropped the butt into the street below. I shuffled the letters into some kind of order and tucked them inside my jacket. I had a quick scout around the flat, to check there was nothing untoward, then left. I double-locked the front door, gave it a little push to check it was secure, then walked out of the building. Sophie's car was parked immediately in front, gleaming in the sunshine. It was a glossy black Mini Cooper, only a few months old. Every conceivable extra had been fitted: tinted windows; CD multiplayer; satellite navigation system; exquisite, beige leather upholstery. It was an automatic, easy to drive, and it had a cute metropolitan chic about it. I loved it. Driving it through London that morning, I wore the Burberry sunglasses Sarupa had given me. I cut quite a dash; I could've been mistaken for an up-and-coming designer, or a young dance music impresario.

The car made a high-pitched beep as I switched off its alarm. I got inside, took the shades out of my pocket and put them on. The clock on the dashboard said it was a quarter past eleven; I'd be back at Sophie's by noon. She was at home, packing a suitcase for our weekend in the Cotswolds; she was excited, and had bought me some new T-shirts and a pair of bathing trunks. When I got to Holland Park, I'd relax and Sophie would drive us to the country – I get nervous driving on motorways. I checked my reflection in the rear-view mirror: I looked good. The cocaine flunkies stood in the doorway of the betting shop, staring at me in my new wheels. I nodded at them and they nodded back. For the first time in a long time, I felt confident. I started the engine.

The drive to Chipping Campden began slowly; the traffic leaving London was heavy, so it took over an hour to get to the M40 and onto the A44 leading to Gloucestershire and the Cotswolds. Once we were on the A44, the traffic thinned and the driving was easy. Leaving the city behind, I smelt the pollution diminish and opened the sunroof. I was on my way to see a bit of real England and was looking forward to it. We smoked a joint and listened to the Red Hot Chili Peppers' *Californication* album. I'm a fan of this band: Anthony Kiedis has a lovely, plaintive voice; their songs have great melodies. They're one of the few bands who improve with the years and, for a bunch of white guys with guitars, they managed to look cool and manly. Sophie bobbed her head to the beat of languorous West Coast rock, her mood hidden behind her Gucci shades. She liked driving her car; driving an automatic is child's play. I watched her sleek hands on the steering wheel. I unclipped my seat belt and shifted onto my side so I could face her. Her hair was waxed flat against her skull; she was dressed in a light-blue, chiffon summer dress that ended well above her knees. She'd taken off her shoes and put them on the back seat; I looked at her clean white feet resting on the pedals, her nails painted in a dark, lascivious red. I put my hand on her leg and brushed the hem upwards, revealing her crotch, snug inside a silk white thong. She parted her legs, and I stroked her bare thigh. Pushing the thong to one side, I slipped a finger between her labia. I slid it upwards to her clitoris, teasing it between my thumb and forefinger. I raised my fingertips to my nose and smelt her cunt on my skin. Sophie smiled; she took her left hand off the steering wheel, put it between my legs and rubbed my cock through my jeans. I sat back against my seat, un-fastened my belt and pulled out my erection. She slipped my foreskin back; the head was swollen, a drop of fluid leaked from its slit. She dipped her fingertip in it, smeared it around my glans, then lifted her hand and licked it from her finger. She held her palm against her tongue, lubricating it with saliva. Keeping her eyes on the road, she wrapped my cock in her tight wet fist and masturbated me. I closed my eyes and listened to the Red Hot Chili Peppers: 'Dream of Californication,' he sang. 'Dream of Californication . . .'

The A44 passes through quiet English villages where couples walk about wearing matching fleeces and bicycle clips on their ankles. The villages are tidy and spacious; they have stone buildings and cobbled paths, and names such as Yarnton and Begbroke. I liked the country. Even from the car I could see that life here was quiet, easy and predictable. We drove past the walls of the Blenheim estate, Churchill's ancestral home. I peered out the window as we went past the gates; I wanted to see the palace, but saw only trees. We drove through two more villages – Moreton-in-Marsh and Bourton-on-the-Hill – and came to Chipping Campden. We parked the car in the town square, in front of a hotel, and went for a stroll.

England is a beautiful country and Chipping Campden is the epitome of English rural beauty. The buildings are historic artefacts, protected by law; shops and offices are located in pristine honey-coloured terraces, built with lime-rich Cotswold stone – many have their original doors and wood fittings. The High Street is an historical medley: Elizabethan, Georgian, Jacobean, Regency and Victorian architecture is crammed into a hundred yards. Founded in Saxon times, the earliest reference to the town is in the Domesday Book; it then had the Saxon name Campedene, meaning 'valley with fields', and was part of a province owned by King Harold. In 1185 the town received its charter as a borough; a market was established in what is now the High Street, and the town became Cepynge Campedene – 'Market Campden' – which then corrupted into Chipping Campden. I learnt all this information, and more, doing a websearch the day before; I was now more than au fait with the history and culture of the Cotswolds.

The atmosphere here was of complete tranquillity. People walked quietly about their business; unlike in London, they were generally older and unhurried. There was plenty of money here: our car was parked among Volvos, Mercedes and Range Rovers – a shining silver TVR sat, imperious, outside a post office. Walking past an estate agent, I stopped and looked in the window. Nothing around here sold for less than £300,000.

Sophie went into a shop to buy cigarettes and a few bottles of wine while I waited outside. An old couple in Barbours walked past me: the man was bearded and wore a baseball cap, the woman had a beatific smile, the type one sees in a lot of older women. Was it the smile of a life lived well? I looked at her sullen husband, trudging in his Clarks shoes, and guessed that it wasn't. It was an always-look-on-the-bright-side sort of smile that helps one through marriage and its monotonies. I watched them walk down the street, their Border collie trotting between them.

We stopped in the Noel Arms for a late lunch. I had a cheese and pickle sandwich and a pint of the local beer. Sophie ate a packet of crisps. The inn had been owned by the Earl of Gainsborough in the nineteenth century. In 1651, Charles II – newly crowned – had rested there after the royal army's defeat at Worcester. All this history seemed set in the walls; it leaked from the stone, into my thoughts. The aura of these buildings impressed me, and I tried sharing my new knowledge with Sophie. I made some comments and she smiled sweetly, then went back to eating her crisps and reading the latest copy of *Glamour*. Afterwards we got back into the car and carefully followed Sarupa's directions.

The house was outside the village, down one of Gloucestershire's many nameless roads. Sophie and I turned off a B-road and drove past hedgerows, behind which were quiet grazing sheep and bleating lambs. The sky was a clear, endless blue; sunshine passed through the pollenised air and warmed my cheek. My head was light and my lungs worked slowly: I felt good. I could smell the country – a healthy gust of cut grass, flowers and dung – and relished it. It reminded me of India: there I smelt animals everywhere, at all hours of the day – the oaky smell of clay stoves burning dried cowpats. After a mile or two, we drove over a hill and I saw the house, cosseted among trees, behind pale fencing. I could see the roof of the barn and the upper storey of the main house. Sophie stopped the car in front of the iron gates; I got out and pressed the button on the intercom. No one replied, but the gadget buzzed and the gates opened. She drove into the courtyard, which was gravelled and enormous. I followed behind on foot. There was a central circle of neatly trimmed grass, bearing an immaculate pink rose bush. The white gravel crunched underfoot; it glared in the sunlight, stinging my eyes. On one side was a shed; the doors were open and some cars were parked inside. In front of us was the house, mid-nineteenth-century, built for the landowning gentry, made of ashen West Country stone. Another building had been added to the side; it was modern, walled with green opaque glass – an indoor swimming pool. A set of beach chairs stood outside the panelled doors, which had been slid open; behind them two white bodies moved through the water. I heard barking. A Labrador bounded out from the open front door of the main building. It ran straight past me towards Sophie, who was emerging from the car. Crouching down on its front legs, it stared at her face, wagging its tail.

'Hello, Stan!' she squealed. The dog jumped up and ran in circles around her. 'Hello, darling!' She patted his rump. 'How's my beautiful boy?' The dog barked excitedly; he knew Sophie and was happy to see her. I watched Sophie and Stan; she enjoyed a real chemistry with him – the dog clearly loved her. He leapt at her hands, giving them playful nips. He was a great dog, full of life and very loving. She walked over to me, the dog running alongside her. I love dogs and bent down to rub his head. He licked my hand. He had a thick flaxen coat and deep brown eyes. I fell for him instantly. Sophie told me Stan belonged to her aunt, Duncan's mother. Sophie and Stan spent many summers together; she insisted on looking after him whenever her aunt was on holiday. Stan's presence made the prospect of the weekend delightful. I imagined a long Sunday morning stroll with him through the surrounding country, across fields and over brooks. He leapt up and put his paws on my thigh. Kneeling down, I leant my face toward him and he licked it. I cupped his jaw in my hands and kissed his glistening nose.

'Hellooo!' A tall, slender Asian man waved at us from the open door. He loped towards us in wide, lazy strides. Dressed in chinos and a half-open denim shirt, he was barefoot and held what looked like a vodka and tonic. He stopped in front of us and stood smiling. His chest was hairless; a small Hindu totem hung from a caste thread tied around his throat. He had a handsome, angular face, and a wildly overgrown public school short back and sides; he looked like a young, brown and dishevelled Michael Heseltine. He brushed the hair from his face and smiled broadly; his teeth were crooked, with a slight overbite. 'Hi,' he said. 'Guests of Shah Palace are you?'

'Yes. I'm Sophie.' She shook his hand. 'I'm Duncan's cousin. This is Puppy.' She held my arm. 'My boyfriend.'

'I'm Ash,' he nodded. 'I'm a friend of Super's'

'Super?' said Sophie.

'That's Sarupa's nickname. That's what we called her at university. Super.' He pronounced it 'soup-ah', the way upper-middle-class people would. He smiled and stared at us for a while, shuffling his feet to hold his balance: he was drunk.

'Is she around?' I asked.

'No.' He gave us a boozy leer. 'She's gone into the village, to get some cigarettes. You probably drove past her, she left a minute ago.'

'We should've called ahead,' I said. 'We've just bought a hundred.'

'Good stuff!' he said. 'The smokers here are starting to climb the walls.'

I couldn't stop eyeing his drink; I fancied one myself. 'Is that a vodka?'

'Of sorts.' He looked at the tumbler in his hand. 'Have you got any bags? I'll give you a hand with them.'

Sophie was about to point to the car, but I told her to leave our bag in the boot; I didn't want to unpack just yet. Inspired by Ash, I wanted to kick off my shoes and have a stiff drink. I looked at my watch: it was nearly five o'clock, and the sun was still bright. The chalky gravel basked in the courtyard; I could feel its warmth through the soles of my shoes. I felt the sweat collect in my armpit and roll down my side; drops formed on my forehead and clung to my hairline. It was an extraordinarily hot day; hotter than I'd realised inside the air-conditioned Mini Cooper. I took my cigarettes from my jacket pocket and offered one to Ash; he grabbed it quickly and I lit us both. We walked towards the house, Stan skipping along with us. I felt light-headed. Though Sarupa wasn't there, I was entering the envelope of her life; something shivered in my guts as I walked through the door.

We entered a huge kitchen with a gleaming parquet floor, a black Aga sat hunched in the corner. The kitchen units were modern and turquoise, with worktops made of yellow wood; above them pristine knives and cooking utensils hung from hooks on the wall. There was another oven on one side, a conventional one made of stainless steel; a stainless steel fridge complemented it on the opposite wall. There were windows everywhere, giving an impression of enormous space and freedom; light poured into the room, and danced with the gentle colours and shining metal.

'This is a beautiful kitchen,' I said.

'It is, isn't it?' nodded Ash. His long brown feet were distinct against the sand-coloured parquetry. His toenails were neatly cut, his feet smooth and uncalloused; he obviously enjoyed the occasional pedicure. In his loose clothing, his hair frenzied, a vodka in one hand and a cigarette in the other, he seemed the louche wayward son of Mumbai high society. There was no trace of India in his voice; he'd been raised and, at much expense, educated in England.

'It's a bit formulaic,' I said, looking at the room. 'But it's lovely.'

'Formulaic!' he laughed. 'Super's going to love hearing that. She'll kick you in the nuts if she hears you saying that. She designed it herself, it's her creation. The place needed a woman's touch. Everywhere else is filled with her dad's stuff.' He touched my forearm with a slim, long-fingered hand; a ring on his index finger, made of dark Indian gold, bore the sign for *Om*. 'The rest of the house is a bit naff,' he grinned. 'Don't get me wrong, the building's beautiful. But her dad's fond of buying crap. The place is full of it.'

Sophie walked past us and into the lounge, through a door at the far side of the room. I heard her greeting someone she knew, probably Duncan, and lots of polite, excited laughter.

'Where can I get one of those?' I asked, pointing at Ash's drink.

'Over here.' He went to the fridge, opened it and pulled out a jug, its mouth sealed with baking foil. 'If you're serious about boozing, you don't want to fuck around mixing a drink every ten minutes. So I made up a batch first thing, when I got up.'

'When was that?'

'About an hour ago.' He sucked a vast lungful from his cigarette; the tip glowed for an age, then faded, disappearing in a billow of smoke he exhaled through his nostrils. 'I was so fucking hammered last night, they thought I was going to die.'

'Who did?'

'Sarupa, Duncan . . . everyone. I was lying right here on the floor, and wouldn't move.' He stared pensively at the wooden tiles and smiled. 'I've apologised to everyone today, but what can I do? That's what I call fun. It's my hobby.' He poured me a glass. 'People are so puritanical these days. It gets lonely for an honest-to-God drinker like me.'

We raised our glasses. I took a sip and rolled the taste around my tongue; he mixed a good drink.

'Everything in there's been measured to the millilitre,' he said, noticing my approval. 'I should get a fucking medal for it.'

We sat at the kitchen table and finished our drinks. The table was oval, made of dark, roughly carved wood, circled with equally rustic wooden chairs. We smoked a couple more cigarettes and made pleasant chit-chat. I was in no rush to join the others, and neither was he. He was good company: warm, gently cynical and good humoured. We were going to get along fine.

After thirty minutes or so, we decided to go into the lounge; our absence seemed rude, especially as I hadn't yet introduced myself. The lounge was at the end of a short corridor, lined with shelves crammed with books. The rich buy books by the yard when they furnish their houses. When she redesigned the interior of her home, Luca's mother paid someone to buy hundreds of well-chosen books. I wasn't sure if Sodhilal Shah had done the same, there was too much garbage on the shelves – Harold Robbins, Tom Clancy, John Grisham, Jeffrey Archer. Amid them were self-help books; one was by Antony Robins, entitled *Unlimited Power*; another was called *Think and Grow Rich*. There was also the self-improvement classic, *How to Win Friends and Influence People* by Dale Carnegie; the book was a paperback, almost thumbed to shreds, and held together by brittle, faded Sellotape. There were books on management theory, business dynamics, and numerous biographies of statesmen, sporting figures and corporate titans. Sodhilal Shah didn't fuck around; he was only interested in those who cut the mustard.

We walked into the lounge, which was even bigger than the kitchen; the floor was black stone, with a patterned Eastern rug in its centre. Placed on the rug was a three-foot-high carved Indian elephant set on a wooden platform with casters beneath. It was decorated with gold leaf, its tusks hewn from ivory. I later learnt that it was an antique, looted from Lucknow during the 1857 mutiny when the British sacked the city, making the locals lick the blood of their slaughtered women from the palace floor. At the far end of the room was a refurbished Queen Anne fireplace; on the marble mantelpiece above stood a blue-skinned Krishna figurine, chubby and sensuous. Behind Krishna was a tall, gilded Napoleonic mirror, in perfect condition; Sodhilal, having the pompous taste of a self-made multimillionaire, loved such things. The walls were painted white and the ceiling was high; I was surprised to see no chandelier. By the wall, under the window, was a plump, dark purple, leather chesterfield couch: it was a monstrosity, a huge shining aubergine that monopolised an entire wall. Sophie had kicked off her shoes, and was sat on the couch, sharing a joint with Duncan. The glass coffee table before them was strewn with drugs and related paraphernalia: cigarette papers, bits of silver foil and a glass pipe were scattered about, dusted with the residue of profligate cocaine use. A block of cannabis resin, the size of a matchbox and wrapped in cellophane, sat in the middle of the table. Odd bits of resin were littered amid the rest of the rubbish.

Sophie looked up at me; the near-finished joint glowed against her lips. 'Hey, babe,' she smiled. She'd taken off her shades; her blue eyes, glazing with each lungful, were beautiful. She looked serene; she loved smoking hash. Duncan was collapsed against the sofa, his eyelids barely open. He smiled, raised his hand and gave me a listless wave: he'd been smoking that shit all day. He was dressed in a loose cotton summer shirt and a pair of jeans, his hair a messy sprawl. His sunburn had healed, and he was now browned by the good weather we'd been having. Stan was lying at his feet, resting his head on his paws, eyes closed. Ash and I sat on the two matching aubergine chairs; he'd brought his jug of vodka and tonic, and gave me a refill. This room was also lined with bookshelves – a complete set of the *Encyclopaedia Britannica* occupied one whole wall. There were plenty of other complete works here, hefty oeuvres by W.H. Auden, Shakespeare, Jane Austen, and other predictable names. In one corner of the room was a doorway that led to a vestibule, where there were the doors to a ground-floor bedroom, a bathroom, and a stairway to the top of the house. I heard a baby's cry and a woman's voice coming from there. Stan heard it too; he opened an eye and cocked his ear.

Ash saw me gazing in the direction of the crying. 'That's Ghislaine's little girl,' he said. 'Ghislaine's a friend of Sarupa's. She's here with her husband and their baby.'

'What's the baby's name?'

'Olivia.'

'She's such a sweet baby,' said Sophie. 'You have to see her.' She reached over to the ashtray and stubbed out the finished joint. She picked up a cigarette paper and began rolling another.

'What did you say your name was again?' Ash asked me. 'It sounded unusual.'

'Puppy.'

'What's your real name?'

'Puppy.'

'No it's not. That's just a nickname.'

'My proper name's Bhupinder.'

'What's your surname?'

'Johal.'

'So your full name is Bhupinder Singh Johal?'

'Yeah.'

'How did you know what his middle name was?' said

Sophie. She raised the completed joint to her mouth and bit off the end; I heard the click of her teeth colliding.

'Sikh men always have the name Singh,' said Ash. 'And he's obviously Sikh.'

'Not to me he isn't,' she said. 'How did you know?'

'Well, he looks very Sikh. And Bhupinder's a very Sikh name . . . And he's wearing the bangle, that's a give-away.'

'Is that why you wear that?' Sophie lit the joint and stared at my wrist, at the thick steel band my mother bought for me in Amritsar. 'You wear it because you're Sikh?'

'Yeah.'

Sophie nodded with interest. 'What else do Sikhs do? Are there any special things you have to do? You know, like how Catholics take communion?'

'We're supposed to grow beards and wear turbans.'

'Oh!' Sophie sat up; something had, all of a sudden, been revealed. 'So that man's a Sikh? I thought he was Muslim.'

'Which man?'

'The one who flew that plane into that building. You know, Osama Bin Laden.'

'He's not Sikh. He's Muslim. And he didn't fly any planes.'

'So why has he got a beard and a turban?'

'I don't think that's for theological reasons,' said Ash. 'That's just traditional dress in Afghanistan.'

Sophie looked at me with confusion; she didn't understand the distinction.

'Sikhs wear a very formal turban,' I said. 'It's wrapped very smartly. It's quite snug and neat.'

'And why do they wear them?'

'So they can be clearly identified.'

'What for?'

I sighed; I hate the chore of explaining my background. 'So anyone who wants to kill a Sikh knows where to find him.'

'Who wants to kill Sikhs?'

'No one does right now. But they did . . . The last guru said we should wear beards and turbans to show we're not scared of death.'

'Who killed them?' Sophie was fascinated; we'd never spoken about this before.

'The Moguls.'

'Who were they?'

'They were Muslims,' said Ash. 'They were the Muslim rulers of India.'

Sophie furrowed her brow. 'But Muslims look like Sikhs. And you said Sikhs wore turbans so they could be spotted?' She was addled by this issue, but she had a point. 'If they wanted to look really different, they should've shaved their heads or something.'

'Then they'd look like Buddhists,' laughed Ash. He turned to me: 'The occidental mind grappling with the complex Orient. Poor girl's never going to get it.'

Sophie stared at me; she wanted me to solve the riddle. I couldn't be bothered. I stood up, walked over to her and took the joint from her hand. I took a draught and winced: it was heavy stuff. I looked at Duncan, slumped against the arm of the couch, asleep.

'So why don't you wear a turban?' she asked. 'Because you don't want to be killed by Muslims?'

'Yeah,' I said, walking back to my seat with the joint. 'I chickened out.'

Sophie shook her head in dismay: 'How awful.'

Ash giggled.

'So what are you, Ash?' she asked. 'Are you a Sikh, too?'

'No, I'm Hindu.'

'Oh, fuck . . .' I said. 'Don't start explaining that. We'll be here for ever.' I passed him the joint. 'Let's change the subject. We were talking about names, weren't we? What's your full name, Ash? What's Ash short for?'

'You don't want to know . . .' He sucked on the spliff, raising his eyebrows at the caustic impact on his lungs.

'My name's a fucking albatross.' His voice was hoarse and his eyes watered: that hash was poison.

'Go on.' I was curious. 'Tell me.'

'My name's *Ashit*.' He said it in a Gujarati accent, disguising its English connotation.

I laughed out loud. 'I bet that's not how white people say it.'

'That's not all of it.' He took another drag and passed the joint back to me. 'My surname's Akhtar . . . My name is Ashit Akhtar.'

'A shit actor!' Sophie cried with laughter, and collapsed into the couch. 'Oh my God! Why did your parents call you that?'

'Because they're ignorant fucking bastards. That's why.' He stood up and reached into his back pocket; he took out his wallet, from which he produced a credit card. 'I'm a shit actor. It's official.' He handed me his Mastercard. He wasn't lying, his name really was Ashit Akhtar. 'I shouldn't criticise my folks,' he said, sitting down again. 'They didn't really speak English when they came here, and I was born only a few months later.'

I handed him back his credit card. 'Did your folks come here from Africa or India?'

'India. Gujarat. I know a lot of people from Africa – Kenya, Uganda, Tanzania – but my folks came straight here.'

'Sarupa's family's from Kenya, aren't they?' said Sophie.

'No,' said Ash. 'They have businesses and property there, but they're originally from Uganda. They had a lot going for them there, before they got kicked out.'

'Why was that?' said Sophie. 'What did they do?'

I shifted in my seat; I was embarrassed by her lack of general knowledge.

'They did nothing' he explained. 'It was Idi Amin, this nutcase dictator. He wanted Africa to be for the Africans, so he kicked out all the Indians. It totally fucked up the economy. Uganda's just another bullshit African country now. They're trying to get some of the Indians to go back, but there's no chance.' Ash sipped his drink. 'Sodhilal even speaks Swahili.'

Sophie listened intently, her hands clasped under her chin. 'I never knew that about Sarupa's family,' she said. 'I thought they just came here, like people do. I didn't know it was such a big deal.'

'It was a big fucking deal,' said Ash. 'They came here with nothing, just what they could get into a suitcase. And look at what that family's done since . . . They're amazing.'

Duncan mumbled in his sleep; we all looked at him, expecting him to speak. Instead, he rolled onto his side and lay down against the cushions, his eyes shut.

'He's having a great time,' I said. 'I'm jealous.' I took another lungful of the joint. 'I ought to catch up.'

'The guy works at least eighty hours a week,' said Ash. 'He even sleeps in the office. After a week like that, you need to get wasted.'

Duncan's head rested against Sophie's knee; she was stroking his hair. 'Poor Dunky,' she said. She patted the cushion on her other side, encouraging Stan to sit with her. The dog leapt onto his feet and jumped beside her. She gently scratched the top of his head; he curled up against her thigh and closed his eyes.

I heard footsteps coming from the corridor leading from the kitchen; I thought it was Sarupa returning from her outing and sat up, adjusting my collar, trying to seem less casual. A pair of teenage girls walked into the lounge. They wore damp two-piece bikinis, and their hair was wet. They were the people I'd seen swimming in the pool; their skins were clean and bright, their cheeks ruddy from exercise. One was tall, lean and blonde, her hair tied in a plait that fell halfway down her spine. She had high cheekbones and cool Scandinavian eyes; she looked like Sophie. Also like Sophie, she had a toned flat abdomen and no tits; a jewelled stud glinted on her jutting navel. But her arse was pert, full of life; her small buttocks jigged as she walked through the room. The fabric of her bikini bottom had gathered in the centre; the crack of her butt peeked out like a sniper.

'Hi, Cecily!' cried Sophie. She rose to her feet and opened her arms.

'Sophie!' squealed the blonde. She ran into Sophie's embrace. The two greeted each other in a fluster of hugs and kisses, a buzz of compliments and queries: 'How are you?'; 'I love what you've done with your hair!'; 'You look *so* great in that bikini!'; 'Where did you get that dress? It's fantastic!' This process was a ritual among highborn, West London daughters; I'd seen Sophie perform it many times – largely with people she hardly knew.

Cecily's friend stood nervously in the centre of the room, clasping her hands and staring at the floor. She was rounder, with wide hips and plump thighs; she was altogether more nubile and sexier than her friend. She had curly brown hair, warm brown eyes, and a touch of acne on her forehead and the bridge of her nose. She flashed a sweet smile at me in embarrassment. She wasn't overweight, but was conscious of her body which, unlike Cecily's, wasn't honed by vomiting and Pilates. This girl paid less attention to her figure and was more attractive for it. I stared at her ripe belly, at the bristles of her untrimmed crotch, visible in outline against her bikini.

Cecily beckoned her friend towards her and introduced her to Sophie. 'This is Ruth,' she said. Ruth politely stepped forward and shook Sophie's hand.

Sophie gestured at me and the girls turned around. 'Puppy, this is Duncan's sister Cecily.'

I stood up and walked over to them. 'Hello Cecily. Lovely to meet you.' I kissed her cheek; I could smell the chlorine on her. Her shoulders and sternum were dotted with freckles, tiny clots of melanin disrupting the chalk-white surface of her skin. She was tall, like Sophie, and gangling; her nipples were hidden under two scraps of pink Lycra which made up her bikini top. Like Sophie, her thighs didn't touch even as she stood with her ankles together; I could see the curve of her pudenda. I turned to her friend and nodded: 'Hi, Ruth.' The two girls looked at me with wide eyes and said nothing. I made small talk: 'Have you two been swimming?'

'Yeah,' said the girls in unison, still staring at me.

'The pool looks great. I think I'll jump in there later.'

'Yeah,' they said.

'Have your summer holidays started now?'

'Yeah.'

'Have you had any exams?'

'Yeah.'

Their monosyllabic double act was impossible; I guessed they were shy around grown men. 'What exams did you take?' I tried affecting an adult concern for their education; I didn't know what else to say. 'A levels?'

'Yeah,' they said again.

I stood there like an idiot, waiting for them to say more.

'I took my last exam on Thursday,' said Cecily.

'What subjects did you take?'

'Drama and Media Studies.'

'How do you think they went?' I didn't believe I was having this conversation; I was boring myself.

'I've done okay, I think.'

'What are you going to do now?' asked Sophie. 'Are you going to university?'

'No, I don't want to go to university. I'm really committed to my music. I want to work on that.'

'What music's that?' I asked.

'I'm working with this really great producer. We're making good pop music. You know, *really* good pop music. There's none of it around right now. There's Kylie, but that's about it.'

'That's great!' said Sophie. 'Are you making a record?'

'This guy's helping me to make a demo tape,' she said. 'I was in LA at New Year, and I met him at a party. I'm going back there in a few weeks. I can't wait to go, everyone my age is making it there right now.'

'Everyone your age is making it there?' I kept my laughter to myself. I'd met a lot of rich white kids who were set on acting, modelling or music; Cecily would no more become a singer than Sophie had become a model. When a rich white kid tells you they're acting, modelling or making music, it means they're doing fuck all. I asked Ruth if she'd done any A levels.

'Yes,' she said. 'I did French, Spanish and History.'

I looked at her, standing bashfully in her prudent brown bikini, and asked, 'Are you going to be a pop star too?'

'No.' She shook her head. 'I'm going to teach English in Chile for a few months. Then I'm going to university the year after next.' She was a bright girl; she wasn't full of shit.

'Which one?'

'Sussex. I'm going to study Art History.'

'Good for you.' I glanced at her breasts; they were small and well shaped, her nipples were hard under the wet Lycra. I liked her; she had an easy, unaffected femininity – she'd be a lot of fun in bed. Sadly, it would be some spotty middle-class pune who'd break her in – no doubt he already had.

I continued making polite and pointless conversation, but I was stoned and tired; I wanted some sleep. I asked if I could have a lie down, and Cecily led me to the bedroom Sophie and I would be sharing. We walked up a spiral staircase, past the bedroom where the baby was kept. She was still crying; I could hear the parents arguing inside, trying to keep their voices low. The bedroom was on the top floor and had an en suite bathroom. The room was small, the beamed ceiling was low, but it was cosy and had a window that overlooked fields full of ewes and fluffy lambs: I could hear their bleats, smell their dung. I looked at the view, at the lambs walking shakily beside their mothers, and at the rolling hills in the distance. The air was calming, delicious to breathe. I sat on the bed and thanked Cecily for showing me to my room; I watched her feisty young butt bounce through the doorway and out of sight.

The bed was close to the floor, but wide; it had firm

gigantic white pillows and a thin quilt, over which was spread a diaphanous Indian fabric. I lay down; the mattress was deep and comfy, but my urge for sleep was gone. Talking to the girls had tired me; now that I was alone, I was wide awake. On the bedside table was a pile of books: the New Testament, the Bhagavad-Gita, and the Koran. Sodhilal Shah, I learnt, kept a copy of each book in every bedroom of his many homes. He was a deeply religious man, who was open to all faiths. I opened the Koran; I'd meant to read it since 9/11, and now was my chance. I couldn't make sense of it, so gave up after twenty pages. I didn't bother with the Bible, I'd heard that Jesus stuff before; instead, I read some of the Bhagavad-Gita. It was less opaque and had a conventional structure, and consisted of a speech by God (played here by Krishna) to some guy called Arjuna. God insisted Arjuna go into battle against his kin because it was his caste duty, that he shouldn't let his love for them interfere with his *dharma*; he ought to 'renounce the fruits of one's actions' and concentrate on the spiritual obligation at hand. I could discern the argument in this book, but felt no better for it. I don't understand the appeal of God: why should we jump through His stupid hoops – *karma, dharma*, fasting, prayer, sexual probity – before He stops treating us like dirt? If He had an inkling of pity, He'd magic away AIDS, hunger, work, poverty, paedophilia etc, in an instant. But He doesn't even spare us migraines, or piles. Either God doesn't exist, or considers us with stony indifference: worship is basically useless.

I lay there looking at the ceiling, listening to the lambs outside. I'd been raised according to scripture; I'd been baptised in infancy, and had my name chosen using the Guru Granth Sahib – the Sikh holy book. The priest opened the book at random; the first letter of the first word on that page was the letter that began my name. I never had a haircut, was a vegetarian and had been warned off using cigarettes and alcohol. Every Sunday I sat in the *gurdwara*, cross-legged beside my mother, listening to an interminable service that I didn't understand. Afterwards we ate *langar* standing up in the communal canteen, our meals served on prison-issue metal trays. Then came two hours of Punjabi lessons. The temple provided them for free; like other immigrants, Sikhs were desperate to retain their customs in a foreign land. I attended the lessons for years. I had no enthusiasm for my mother tongue and the lessons bored me to death. I learnt nothing I would later remember. I hated Sundays; all I could think of was that I was missing the televised football and that week's edition of *The Smurfs*. Dad had the right idea; he closed the shop early and spent the day with a bottle of Bacardi and a whore, or some slut he'd sweet-talked from behind the till. He often spent it with a lurid Chinese woman who worked at the nearby takeaway. She wore Woolworth's flip-flops, too much make-up, and black leggings over her lumpy misshapen backside. Once, he took me with him into her shop, called Mr Han's. I stood there quietly, while my dad made sex-talk with her and showed off his son, confirmation of his potent seed.

When Dad stopped pretending to be a father and a husband and finally fucked off, Mum's spiritual fervour reached its peak. The beatings and constant humiliations were forgotten; she did all she could to get him back. She was hysterical and visited a series of mystics who milked a small fortune from her; in return they recited bullshit incantations and gave her tatty little jujus. She had great respect for the Hindu religion; Sikhism is, in essence, an outgrowth of it, and we'd always kept Hindu pictures in our home. A priest at the *mandhar*, at no expense and in good faith, told her of a ritual that might help her. He wrote down the chants to be spoken and what was to be done on a piece of paper, and gave her an astrologically auspicious date on which to perform it.

The ritual consisted of a sequence of prayers, punctuated by the throwing of sanctified coconuts into flowing water. The closest thing to flowing water near our house was the Grand Union Canal. It didn't actually flow, but it looked like a river and for Mum, that was enough. On the day of the ritual, Mum made me take the day off school and join her. We went to a place in Northolt, where the canal flowed under a bridge and past an industrial estate (the canal also runs through Southall, but Mum didn't want to do it there in case anyone we knew saw us). I sat on a wooden bench, dejected by the sight of my mother standing by the bank in her *salwar-kameez*, bowing and moaning imprecations, stopping every few minutes to lob a sacred coconut into the water. Each coconut had a holy thread tied around it; I watched them splash into the canal, amid the broken bicycles, the prams and the other junk dumped in there, then rise and bob on the oily surface alongside the empty crisp packets and cigarette ends. It was lunchtime, and a group of white men were taking a break from the industrial estate; they stood on the bridge eating their sandwiches and staring.

'What the fucking bollocks is she doing?' said one. They were too polite to say anything more, but their faces showed their bewilderment at these two wogs and their inscrutable ways.

I wilted in shame. I wanted to drag Mum away from the bank, scream at her to finish this nonsense. Instead, I put my face in my hands and silently cried. The tears welled against my palms and rolled down my wrists, into my sleeves. I cried for my desperate, backward and abandoned mother, and for my desperate no-good bastard father. Most of all, I cried for me, the desperate first-born son who'd now have to pick up the tab, but couldn't afford the bill. I was fourteen years old, and I knew then that religion was for suckers. There was no God. If there was, He was a shit and not to be trusted.

I took a shower; the bathroom was small and clean. The water was hot, the soap smelt beautiful. I stood under the water and washed the smell of sweat and cigarettes from my skin. Sodhilal liked his guests to be taken care of; everything I might need was here: disposable shower caps, toothpaste and throwaway toothbrushes, shampoos, conditioners, and all sorts of lotions. I opened a tube of shaving cream and lathered my cheeks, still red from the hot shower. I opened a packet of razors that sat on a ledge above the sink, took one out and began shaving. I had over a week's growth of facial hair. Punjabis are a hairy people, and I now had a full beard. I shaved in short downwards strokes; this is the best method for preventing cuts and razor burns. Once the beard was gone, I splashed warm water on my face and lathered myself again. I cleaned the razor under the tap and shaved once more; this time I used short upward strokes, to get a close shave and smooth finish. I washed off the foam and dowsed my face in cold water. I opened a tube of moisturiser; the cream had a manly scent, and I applied it liberally. I looked in the mirror and ruffled my hair; I'd had a crew cut more than a month ago and now had a soft fuzz around my head. I was a good-looking guy.

The Punjab overlaps India's border with Pakistan, and was the historic gateway for migration in and out of the subcontinent: Greeks, Persians, Afghans, Moguls and Aryans have all entered the region through the Punjab. It was also a staging post on the silk route, a link in the tenuous communication chain between China and Europe. I looked at myself in the mirror, tracing the ethnicities in my face: thick Eurasian eyebrows; a round Tatar face; fine black oriental hair; a Mediterranean nose; full Indic lips and wide Asiatic eyes. My parents weren't attractive people; somehow, in the collision of DNA at my conception, their genes combined in a harmonious sequence. I was grateful I wasn't ugly; I didn't have to strive for wealth to avoid a life of substandard sexual partners. Despite their protests otherwise, women find beauty far more compelling than charisma and intelligence. Any man who is good-looking, dull but basically harmless, can never fail with women. A woman senses trouble when a handsome man expresses his intellect; she knows he's aware of his qualities and will eventually bore of her, possibly fuck her best friend. I make inane conversation with them. I find a topic they're interested in and let them babble at length, asking pertinent questions and making observations. Women love to talk, and mistake this ruse as genuine interest on my part.

I walked into the bedroom. The window was open; air blew inside and chilled my wet skin. I didn't towel myself off; the hot shower had made me sweat, and I wanted to cool down against this breeze. If I dressed now, I'd only sweat into my fresh clothes. I sat naked on the bed, enjoying the silence and the lethargy of my warm limbs. It was nearly eight o'clock. The sheep were quiet, the light had softened, and the room was now quite dark. I'd dozed off while thinking about religion. I woke thinking I could smell the incense Mum burned throughout our home, and hear the lull of Sikh hymns she played on a tape recorder. I looked at the beams above me, remembered where I was, and was disappointed. I hadn't spoken to my mother for over a month; I felt guilty and made a mental note to phone her in the next week.

I shivered at the breeze. I didn't want to catch a cold, so put on a clean pair of jeans and a T-shirt that Sophie had bought me. It was too big; it fell midway down my thighs. I didn't put my shoes on, preferring the sensation of the cold floor against my feet. I walked out of the room barefoot, feeling unsure. Sarupa would now be back among the others and I was certain to meet her. I slowly made my way downstairs. The room with the baby was silent; she was probably asleep. I hovered in the vestibule, hearing voices in the lounge, on the other side of the door. I pushed it open and walked into the room.

'You're back!' said Ash, turning away from a chat he was having with Duncan. 'Back in the land of the living. Rest well?'

'Yes, thanks.' I walked into the room. I smiled at Duncan, who was now awake; he smiled back and raised his glass. He asked me if I wanted some wine. I did, but his bottle was empty. He got off the couch and walked to the kitchen to fetch another. I sat down beside Ash; he offered me a cigarette, and I took it. His skin was greasy and his eyes had dimmed; he'd been drinking a lot. A white couple, in their mid-thirties, were sat on the aubergine chairs; they'd pushed the furniture together, to sit close to one another. We were the only people in the room. I gave them a wave: 'Hi.'

'Hi,' smiled the woman. 'I'm Ghislaine. This is my husband, Ben.' She gestured to the man beside her. She was petite, dark-haired and dark-skinned – very attractive. She had sharp, almost severe features: a short nose and sleek chin, a small tight mouth and thin lips. But she smiled warmly; her dark eyes were gentle. Her husband was dark-haired, too, boyishly handsome, tall and broad-shouldered. Diffident and bespectacled, he seemed ashamed of his size and sat with his hands on his knees, hunched forward, trying to diminish his bulk. For a man of his size, Ben had little masculine presence. His wife, sat upright and meeting my gaze, projected far more authority. She was clearly in charge.

'Was that your baby I heard earlier?' I asked.

'You heard her crying?' she said. 'I am sorry.'

'Don't be. That's what babies do.' I looked at them and smiled. They were a few years older than me, but their faces were hardened by lack of sleep and constant worry: people age so much faster once they've had children. Ghislaine wore a knee-length black dress. I looked at her slim stockinged calves, her tidy little ankles, and asked what she did for a living. She was a director at a publishing house; she read submitted manuscripts, decided which might be developed, and helped shape ideas with their existing writers. Ben wore black trousers, an unironed shirt and scuffed black shoes; he was a teacher at a state comprehensive in Lambeth.

'Those South London kids are wild,' I said. 'They must give you a hard time.'

'Some do,' he said.

'Have you always been a teacher?'

'No. I worked in advertising before. But it was very fake, very pressured. I'm much happier now that I do a job helping people.' He smiled. He was a nice guy, the caring type.

'Do you ever put your foot down with the kids?' I asked. 'Or are you more touchy-feely?'

'I guess I'm the touchy-feely sort,' he nodded. 'I haven't got it in me to rant at them and lay down the law. There are always kids who won't behave, or haven't any interest in being taught. But you get the odd one who's got a chance of getting ahead. I focus on helping those ones, rather than fighting battles with the rest.' Ghislaine put her hand on his knee and gave him a loving smile; she was proud of him. 'It is a cliché,' he said, 'but I've had a good upbringing. I wanted to do something for people that haven't. A lot of them don't want help, but someone's got to provide it all the same . . .' He raised his eyebrows and sighed. His hair was overlong and tousled, his outfit shabby. He couldn't look me in the eye when he spoke. Those Lambeth kids gave him hell every day; it was obvious.

'Do you live in South London?' I asked.

'No,' he said. 'We've got a house in Parliament Hill.'

'That's a lovely area. You lived there long?'

'We bought it a year ago,' said his wife, 'when I was pregnant. We wanted a house with a garden and at least three bedrooms. We plan to stay there a long time. We want to keep things stable for Olivia.' She was smiling, happy about the way her life was going.

'How do you know Sarupa and Duncan?' I asked.

'Sarupa and I did yoga at the same club in West London,' she said. 'I lived in Swiss Cottage then. I've known her for about four years.'

'You still do yoga?'

'Yes. But I do a different style now, I do ashtanga. I have one-to-one lessons at my instructor's house three or four times a week, before work. I can't fit in much more.'

'Because of the baby?'

'We have a nanny . . .'

'Of course.'

'With the job I'm in right now, I hardly have any spare time. But the nanny's very good, and Ben always gets home early. He cooks dinner and puts Olivia to bed . . . Don't you, darling?' She looked at Ben, who stared at his hands resting on his knees. I liked Ghislaine. She epitomised the values of modern women: a careerist and mother, she took care of her figure and was married to a feminised invertebrate who was easy to push around. Women like her would rule the world.

Duncan walked back into the room, holding a bottle of red wine. He poured me a glass. It was a good Beaujolais, and it went down well.

'There's food in the kitchen,' he said. 'Why don't you all come through and have some?'

We got up – Ash, Ben, Ghislaine and I – and followed Duncan into the kitchen. Bowls of food were laid on the table: samosas, tandoori chicken, lamb bhuna, spinach and paneer, chickpeas and cauliflower. It was almost a banquet.

'We had a caterer deliver it,' said Duncan. 'They laid the table as well. Good job, don't you think?'

'It looks great,' I said. I picked up a plate and began loading it with vegetables and small, warm nan breads that smelt of butter. From the corner of my eye, I saw Sophie speaking animatedly to Ruth and Cecily; they held plates, and stood in a huddle in the middle of the parquet floor. Sarupa was with them. I couldn't look in her direction and kept my eyes fixed on the food before me.

Ash was drunk and ate messily, bits of rice falling from his lips onto his shirt. He was talking to Duncan, Ben and Ghislaine about his work. He was a lawyer for the Crown Prosecution Service; he dealt with a lot of cases at Southwark Crown Court. He turned to me and said, 'You're pretty streetwise, aren't you?'

'Why do you ask?'

143

'Have you ever heard the expression "blood-clot"? It's a West Indian term of abuse. I heard it in court the other day.'

'It's not pronounced like that.'

'How's it pronounced?'

I mimicked a Jamaican voice and said, '*Blerdclaaht.*'

'Good accent,' giggled Ghislaine. 'What does it mean?'

'It's a reference to a menstrual rag. You can also call someone the anal equivalent, which is *raasclaaht.*'

'Excellent!' laughed Ash. 'I love your pronunciation. But I prefer how I heard it in court, in the clipped Etonian vowels of a grey-haired barrister. It was exquisite.' He imitated the barrister's voice: '"The defendant called the victim a blood-clot, m'lud, then belaboured her about the head with a hammer."' Ash laughed and gulped the last of his drink. 'It's the finest word I've ever heard. In fact, I'll be using it for the rest of the evening.' He raised his glass. 'Duncan, you blood-clot . . . I need some more wine.' Duncan laughed, and refilled his glass.

'Talking of swear words,' I said, 'you've reminded me of a kid I knew at school. He was called Barry. He was this trampy white kid who didn't brush his teeth and looked like shit. All the white kids at my school looked like shit.'

'How come?' asked Ash.

'There were loads of immigrants at my school. The smart white people got their act together and sent their kids somewhere else. It was just the trash that got left behind.' I looked at the four of them, staring at me in silence.

'Anyway,' I continued, 'we had this Sikh chemistry teacher, called Mr Dhillon, and Barry wanted to curse him in Punjabi. So we taught him to say *merhi mha dhi pudhi.* But the actual phrase is *dheri mha dhi pudhi,* which means "your mother's pussy". We'd get Barry to run up to Mr Dhillon in the playground, and shout "*my* mother's pussy" instead.'

'Brilliant!' cried Ash. The other three laughed as well.

'It was great,' I said. 'He'd stand there doing some stupid Bollywood dance, shouting "my mother's pussy! my mother's pussy!". We loved it. So did Mr Dhillon.'

'Where did you go to school?' asked Ben.

'I went to high school in Ealing.'

'And the children were mainly Punjabi?'

'A lot of them were. A lot of them were black as well. A lot were refugees. I knew boys who fought in the Iran-Iraq war, they'd killed people.' I asked Ben where he'd been to school.

'Godolphin and Latymer,' he said. 'It's a public school in West London. Lots of good little Jewish boys like me went there.' When he said that Ghislaine smiled, and looped her arm through his.

I turned to Ash: 'Where did you go to school?'

'St Paul's. It was a super-competitive public school. I hated it. Duncan went there, too, but he's a few years older than me.'

Duncan nodded. 'It was very high pressure. But it stood me in good stead.'

I looked over his shoulder at Sarupa, who was still talking to Sophie and the two girls. I drained my wine glass and walked past them on my way to the kitchen counter, where the booze was laid out. I poured myself a glass of orange juice and splashed it with vodka; I took a big gulp, then topped the glass with vodka again. Sophie and Sarupa were behind me. I could feel their eyes on me, but didn't turn to say hello. I was being aloof and obviously strange, but could do nothing about it. Sophie walked over to me and put her hands on my waist; I turned around to face her.

'Hello, sleepy,' she said, touching my cheek. 'You've been gone for ages. Did you have a good rest?'

'I feel a lot better now.' I kissed Sophie and looked into her eyes. In my peripheral vision I saw Sarupa looking at us.

Sophie rested her head on my shoulder and nuzzled my neck. 'You smell lovely. Are you wearing cologne?'

'I used the moisturiser in the bathroom.'

'And you've shaved.' She stroked my chin. 'You look ever so sexy.'

'Do I?'

'All the girls think so. Cecily and Ruth think you're gorgeous.'

'They're just kids.'

'So does Sarupa.'

'She does?' I felt myself grow an inch or two taller.

'It's your eyelashes,' she said. 'They're so extravagant . . . Boys always have the nicest eyelashes, it's not fair.'

I looked over Sophie's shoulder at the young women talking to Sarupa. The two girls wore denim hipsters and off-the-shoulder tops. Cecily had restyled her hair for the evening; she had ironed it flat, and wore it straight and loose. Sarupa wore a floor-length satin dress, gun-metal grey and cut on the bias. It curved around her copious figure; the fabric shone against her dark skin. Her black hair was voluminous and still had its sunbleached tint; it cascaded over her shoulders and the side of her face. I looked at her plump bare arms, and wanted to bite at the brown skin: she was luscious and amazing. A simple platinum chain hung around her neck; a matching bracelet was on her left hand. For the first time, I looked at her engagement ring. The stone was modest, exquisite, and shone with a blue light; she'd obviously chosen it herself. She looked at me and smiled. Raising her skirt with both hands, not wanting to tread on it, she walked towards me. She wore black, high-heeled, open-toed sandals; she'd had a French pedicure, her nails tipped with translucent white polish. I looked at the floor. I didn't want my gaze taken by her décolletage, her dark fat cleavage.

'Hello, Puppy.' She put her hand on my elbow and leant forward to kiss me. 'You're awake at last.' She wore little make-up, but I could smell the perfume rising from her neck. Her beauty desolated me. I felt crushed, completely defeated. I tried to keep my feelings hidden.

146

'I'm sorry,' I said. 'I got stoned and had to lie down.'

'He's such a lightweight,' said Sophie. 'Aren't you, darling?' She kissed my jaw.

'Don't be sorry,' said Sarupa. She tucked her black hair behind her ear and smiled; her brown eyes glowed with good humour and forgiveness. 'You're our guest. I invited you here to relax and do what you want. If you want to crash out, go ahead.' She looked at the plate of food I was holding. 'Why don't you try the lamb? It's amazing.'

'I don't eat meat,' I said.

'Oh?' She seemed a little surprised. 'Any particular reason?'

'I like animals,' I said. 'I wouldn't kill one, so I don't feel right about eating them.' I looked at Sarupa; she was looking at me with interest, stroking the length of her champagne flute. 'It's a lovely house,' I said, suddenly feeling awkward. I nodded to the room.

'Thanks for saying so. But there's a lot that needs doing. I'm taking my time with getting things done, but I'll get there.'

'Doesn't your dad mind you changing things?' asked Sophie.

Sarupa leant closer to us. 'I haven't told anyone else here,' she whispered, 'because I don't want to jinx anything. But the house is mine. My dad gave it to me as an engagement present. I can do what I like with it.'

'When is the wedding?' I asked.

'Next summer. You'll come, won't you?'

'Yeah, if Sophie hasn't bored of me by then.'

'Of course I won't,' said Sophie, clutching my waist. She looked at Sarupa: 'So you're going to live here when you're married?'

'At weekends, definitely. Duncan's promised to scale down his work, so we can spend time here. And when we have children . . .' She raised her champagne; I watched her throat palpitate as she sipped it. 'When we have children, I'd rather not raise them in London. In London you have to keep them inside all the time, here they can have more freedom. There are some wonderful schools near here, too.'

'It'll make a lovely home,' I said.

'Have you seen the rest of the house?' she asked.

'No. I've only seen the lounge and our bedroom.'

'No one's given you a tour?'

'No. But I'd love one.'

'Why don't you let me show you the rest of what's downstairs.' Sarupa held my wrist and turned to Sophie: 'Do you mind if I borrow him for five minutes?'

'As long as you don't shag him,' joked Sophie. 'Keep your hands to yourself, Sarupa Shah. He's all mine.'

Sarupa looked at her in mock open-mouthed dismay, and laughed.

'I don't want you using Puppy for a last hurrah,' said Sophie, 'a final fling before marriage. Behave yourself.'

Sarupa held my wrist in both hands. 'Puppy's too nice to be led astray. Aren't you, Puppy?'

I didn't reply and could only look at the floor in embarrassment. The girls laughed as I blushed. Sarupa led me away to the far side of the kitchen, to a door leading to the unexplored part of the house. She led me through it into another lounge, bigger than the other. It had a stone floor and a high ceiling; black leather couches sat either side of a thick Eastern rug, upon which was a glass-topped coffee table. I slowed down and let Sarupa walk ahead; I wanted to see the sway of her hips, her sumptuous buttocks shifting beneath the satin. I stood beside her as she introduced me to the room. Above us was a gross, coruscating chandelier; Mogul and Hindu art were hung on the walls, mostly pictures of turbaned men on horseback hunting deer. She spoke about the various ornaments in the room. I didn't listen to a word. She guided me around showing me various pieces, but I was lost in the sight and the smell of her. I watched her lips mouth words I didn't hear, her beautiful hands gesture to things I didn't see. Did Duncan have any idea of what he had? Did he have any sense of the woman he was marrying? The gentle smell of her perfume stirred an awful mix of feelings: desire, pain, rage, sadness . . .

Sarupa led me to the swimming pool through a glass-walled anteroom full of exercise equipment. The pool was fifty feet long and six feet deep. The walls were tiled with aqueous green enamel; the bottom of the pool had been tiled the same. The still water looked like a sheet of jade. One whole wall was made of green opaque glass and faced the courtyard; at the far side of the pool was the door to a steam room.

She took me back into the lounge and through a side door; we were now in her father's office. At its centre was a huge mahogany desk and a tall black leather chair, behind which was a window that looked onto the garden. Outside was a patio filled with statues and sculpted shrubs. The walls were lined with shelves full of documents; there were framed photographs placed alongside them. I walked along the sides of the room and looked at the pictures. Sodhilal was in all of them, posing with the great and the good. He was a gaunt man, bald and bespectacled, with a thin nose and a dour mouth. His eyes faded by work and responsibility, he looked pained and exhausted. He stood beside some of the wealthiest Asians in Britain; Lord Alli and the industrialist Lord Paul were among them. In another picture he stood with Sir Edward Heath, both wearing dinner suits and black ties. In other photos he smiled alongside Bollywood stars, including Amitabh Bachchan, Madhuri Dixit and Hrithik Roshan. In others he was with cricketers, such as Sachin Tendulkar and Mohammed Azharuddin; in another he was with John Major – both wore cricket whites and held bats. I walked to the desk and picked up a frame; it held a photograph of Sarupa and her father standing with Tony and Cherie Blair. Sodhilal wore a white Nehru suit; his daughter wore a lustrous ivory sari, trimmed with gold. Tony's outfit was like Sodhilal's, but was black and had its cuffs edged with silver. Cherie wore a blue and silver sari that hung awkwardly on her, and a matching *bindhi*; she gurned at the camera with a nervous smile. The Blairs, keen on rich Indians, were only too happy to dress up for them. Money is the most cosmopolitan thing in the world.

'That was taken at the Asian Business Awards,' said Sarupa. 'I helped organise the event. They're lovely people. Cherie's a fantastic woman, and very intelligent.'

'I think they're kind of weird,' I said.

'Why's that?' Sarupa sounded offended. She knew the Blairs personally and was fond of them.

'Well . . .' I put the frame back on the desk. 'They're always fucking for a start. People in their position should have better things to do.'

She crossed her arms and stared at me: 'What are you talking about?'

'She's been pregnant twice since he took office, hasn't she? At her age, either she's on hormones, or they're fucking all the time. They shouldn't be doing that.'

'It's lovely that they still have sex after being married so long. It's sweet. It shows how much they love each other.'

'At his age, and in his position,' I said, 'Tony should be fucking someone else . . . Why strive for success, if you're just going to fuck your own wife?'

'Shut up, you idiot,' she said. 'You're being stupid. You're trying to annoy me. I know what you're like.' She watched me warily; I'd pissed her off.

I pulled the chair away from the desk and sat in her father's seat, to piss her off some more. There was another photo on the desk: Sodhilal stood shaking hands with Baroness Thatcher. She looked lively and distinguished; the picture had been taken some time in the mid-1980s.

I held up the frame. 'Your dad's friends with Mrs Thatcher?'

'He's met her a few times. They've supported a lot of the same issues.'

'What's she like?' I looked at the photo: Thatcher was smiling at Sodhilal, and wore her hair in that trademark bouffant.

'She's amazing,' said Sarupa. 'She's the best thing that ever happened to this country. She was Britain's first Indian Prime Minister.'

'What do you mean?'

'Think about it. She was the child of a shopkeeper, who made it to Cambridge, then to the top of her career. Her life and values are totally consistent with ours . . . She believed in hard work and ambition, and created an economic environment in which people with those values could flourish.' Sarupa took the frame from my hand and stared at it; she smiled at the sight of her father bowing to her heroine. 'Thatcherism did attract a vulgar nationalism, but its essence always resonated with Indians. Tony Blair has a lot of support among Asians, because he's a Thatcherite without racial prejudices.' She placed the frame carefully back on the desk. Her face had hardened; she was impassioned. 'The left held us back. Dad couldn't get decent work when he came here, because the unions didn't want jobs going to immigrants. He had to start out as a cleaner. Then he started his business, with my brothers helping him, and the rest is history. We'd have got nowhere, working for other people.'

Sitting in Sodhilal's seat, I felt a frisson of chauvinistic hauteur. I belonged to a remarkable people; this made me proud. My own failings were an anomaly entirely of my own making. If I'd lived by the ethos of my race, my life would've been different, so much better. I stared at the desk, at the slim black laptop that lay open before me. I thought of how I'd betrayed my mother and siblings, how I'd neglected my responsibilities and let my life drift, rather than taking destiny by the throat like so many others had.

'What are you thinking?' said Sarupa. 'You look glum.'

'I was thinking about how great it must feel to be successful. It must feel great to have money and no fears.'

'Money isn't everything.' She put her hand on my shoulder. 'It's more important to be happy.'

'No it isn't. And you know it isn't.' I swivelled the chair round and faced her. 'Happiness is overrated. It's bullshit.'

151

I took her wrist from my shoulder and held it with both hands. 'It's contingent and transient. But money . . .' I stared at her elegant fingers, at the diamond shining on her ring. 'Money is *always* money. It doesn't fuck you around. You know where you stand with money.' I looked up at Sarupa; she had a smirk on her face. 'Why are you laughing at me?'

'You're a funny boy, Puppy. You can be quite intense.' She placed her right hand on my head. 'I wouldn't worry too much about money. You'll be a success. I think you'll be very successful.'

'Yeah, right.'

'You will. You can tell with some people.' She rubbed the top of my head in circles; it felt delicious, soothing. 'Haven't you got lovely hair,' she said. 'It's so soft. Short hair suits you. You look like a Japanese schoolboy.'

I smiled at the compliment; I leant forward, resting my head against her stomach. Holding her wrist in one hand, I put my other hand in the small of her back and pulled her close. The movement of her fingers slowed down. I shut my eyes, lulled by the stroking of my scalp, the warmth of her body, the rhythm of her breathing pressing on my face. I wanted to stay here, like this; I wanted her to stroke me into sleep that lasted for ever. A tear rose in my eye. I pushed my face into her belly and wiped it against her dress. I inhaled deeply, quelling the emotion, and rose to my feet. I kept my face from her and walked to the door, my eyes wet. 'We should get back to the others,' I said. I walked through the door, back towards the kitchen.

Resting my arms along the side, I floated in the water. My toes poked out through the surface, the skin white and crinkled. The heat was well regulated; it never dropped more than a degree or two below body temperature. I looked at the Tag Heuer watch Sophie had given me: it was eight-thirty in the morning. I was hungover, and hadn't slept at all. I'd stared into the darkness, listening to Sophie breathing beside me. I'd got out of bed and made myself coffee in the kitchen, then sat on a bench in the garden to watch the sun rise. I'd smoked cigarettes and listened to the emerging birdsong, smelt the rising morning scent of the flowers. After a while, I'd decided to try out the pool. I went back to the bedroom and changed into my new beach shorts, then came and lay here, face up in the water like a sea otter.

I'd spent most of the evening playing with Stan and making bawdy conversation with Ash. He was a fine drinker; we'd had a great time. He finally fell unconscious on the lounge floor at around three. I was left to finish the last of the malt whisky alone; everyone else had gone to bed. I even started reading some of Sodhilal's books. I love reading books; I have less time to fret about my life when I'm reading. But I couldn't read much last night; I was too drunk to concentrate. So I lay next to Sophie, my eyes open in the pitch blackness.

The door swung open behind me; I turned my head and saw Ghislaine and Ben walk along the side of the pool in their swimming costumes. Ben was holding his baby daughter; she had inflatable plastic rings around her chubby arms.

'Good morning,' said Ghislaine. She wore a black one-piece bathing suit and was in fantastic shape. She had a flat abdomen, square shoulders and muscular buttocks; the muscles in her thighs and calves rippled as she walked. A man could have strenuous, grappling sex with a woman like that. I said hello and nodded to Ben, who looked like most men on the slide to middle age: his skin was blanched and his legs were skinny; his shoulders were slumped and his chest, though broad, was shapeless and flabby; love-handles bulged above his hips. He had a handsome face, and looked as if he might have once been into sport, possibly rugby – but the body succumbs quickly to the harassment of work, fatherhood and marriage. I wondered whether Ghislaine ever held his physique against him. I watched him cradle his daughter lovingly in his arms: a beautiful child, she had her mother's dark hair and her father's blue eyes. Ben was great dad material; Ghislaine could easily disregard his fading physical appeal in favour of his paternal qualities. She could always find excitement elsewhere: maybe she fucked her yoga instructor. I wondered if Sarupa had the same pragmatic attitude to Duncan.

Ghislaine dived expertly into the water and began swimming gracefully and at speed: she was a very strong swimmer, had probably swum for her school. I watched her glide back and forth through the pool in a front crawl; her technique was flawless. Ben sat on a plastic chair and played with Olivia; he gave the child his little finger to hold and play with. Olivia squealed with joy and gave her father a toothless grin. He was having a lot of fun with her; she was the apple of his eye. Ghislaine finished her swim and climbed out of the pool. She sat next to her husband and took the baby from him; this upset him, as he'd been enjoying himself. Ghislaine made a great display of faces for her child, and loud baby-talk; she wanted to make a big show of what a good mum she was. She made eye contact with me, the way people with children do. As you do on these occasions, I made the obligatory comment on how cute her baby was, then relaxed in the water again. I didn't want to speak to Ghislaine; she'd annoyed me the night before: she'd booed me off the karaoke machine for singing so badly. The whole point of karaoke is to sing badly, but Ghislaine was a bossy cow; she wanted to get back on the machine and perform her Blondie routines. I'm no fan of karaoke, but I took offence at having scorn poured upon me while trying to do my best.

I listened to the inane pointless crap she was speaking to her baby, and wondered why people went out of their way to have children. The few occasions I'd spent with my nephews left me underwhelmed. Children are just people, only smaller and dumber. I looked at Ben rapt with the sight of his child; she was the centre of his world. Kids do have a use: they give you something to do with your life, an effective prophylactic against suicide and alcoholism. I thought of the beautiful mixed-race children Sarupa would have with Duncan. They'd live here, in the tranquillity of the Cotswolds, in an antique house redesigned by their mother.

I pulled myself out of the water and towelled myself dry. I waved to Ben, Ghislaine and Olivia, and said goodbye. It was nine; I wanted to leave before everyone was awake. I didn't want to be here. I didn't want to see Sarupa at the breakfast table, didn't need the torment. I wanted to be in London on my own, or maybe in a bar with Michael, drinking beer and talking about football and pussy. I'd borrow Sophie's car and drive home on my own. There wouldn't be much traffic on the motorway on a Sunday morning – I'd be okay. Sophie wouldn't mind; she'd hitch a lift back with her cousin. I walked back into the house to get my things. Stan was awake; he ran from under a table and leapt up at me. I knelt down, kissed his nose and rubbed his head. I was going to miss him.

8

WE WATCHED THE television in a state of lethargy. It was
ferociously hot and the flat wasn't air-conditioned; the
heat sapped what energy we had. It's no fun, smoking
dope in such heat. Smoking dope hadn't been fun in years,
but I smoked it anyway: what else was there to do? I
looked at the television screen: David Attenborough was
narrating a documentary series on life in Antarctica. I'd
seen this episode before; it was about elephant seals. Two
alpha males were fighting, ripping open bloody flaps in
each other's hides. It was the mating season and they were
competing over a harem of cows.

'Look at them killing each other,' sighed Michael. 'Over
what? Pussy.' He offered me the joint; I waved it away,
and he smoked it himself. 'Pussy's a fucking con,' he said.
'Motherfuckers kill each other for it, and what do we get
in return? Nothing.' We watched the two bulls fighting.
They crushed baby seals beneath them as they fought;
oblivious to everything around them, they didn't see the
younger males sneaking onto the beach to quickly fuck
the nearest cow. 'See that?' said Michael. 'That's what
pussy does. It makes a fucking fool of you.'

We sat on Evie's couch and watched the rest of the show
in silence. I hadn't seen Michael since he'd moved into her
flat, until today. Evie didn't like me. Michael regressed into
his natural state in my company; she didn't like that. She
was away this week, at an exhibition of her work in
Hamburg. Michael and I were free to make mischief.

'Let's go get some food,' I said.

*   *   *

We ate at Lemonia, an excellent Greek restaurant near Primrose Hill, a five-minute walk from Evie's flat. Her work was appreciating in value fast, and she'd been able to buy a small second-floor apartment. A few months ago she'd appeared in a feature in *Guardian Weekend*; she'd been named as one of a new batch of Young British Artists, set for stardom. She was thirty-three years old, six years younger than Michael. Her white mother had given her up for adoption when she was born. She'd been raised in Richmond by an affluent Scottish couple who'd christened her Evie and given her their surname. Her natural father was Afro-Caribbean; she knew nothing about him and was determined to reconnect with her lost roots. Having Michael's baby was central to this project. Michael was happy to be her black paterfamilias; it put a roof over his head.

I broke a warm pitta bread and dipped it into a bowl of hummus. We ate at a table on the pavement and watched beautiful women walking to and from Primrose Hill: upper-class women look the best, their genes refined by generations of monied men marrying attractive women. It was hot and they wore very little as they sashayed past, pretending not to notice to us. We watched them swinging their behinds and their designer shopping bags.

Michael told me about Evie's show in Hamburg. She was in demand on the Continent and in New York, where she would exhibit in October. Evie had exploded into prominence last year; her work had featured in *Cunt!*, a radical post-feminist exhibition at the ICA. Like Charles Saatchi's *Sensation* exhibition, it was a coup de main on the British cultural sensibility: hundreds of column inches had been written on it in the broadsheet press; embittered traditionalists and other reactionaries had vandalised several of the works on display. Intimidation always fails against the avant-garde: one's attitude to *Cunt!* now defined where one stood in this society; only those who celebrated it belonged to the cognoscenti of contemporary Britain. Evie now moved in the highest circles and counted

157

Tracey Emin, Damon Albarn and Kate Moss among her personal friends.

Evie was in Hamburg overseeing the installation of one of her sculptures in a museum there. One of the pieces shown at the ICA, it was a six-metre-high white mug made of bone china, filled with hundreds of litres of English breakfast tea. Entitled *Milk and Two Sugars*, it was, according to *Weekend*, 'a heartfelt meditation on the British condition'. Two four-feet-tall sugar cubes were custom made, costing many thousands of pounds, which Evie – in a fit of postmodern brilliance – had *dissolved* into the tea. This, said *Weekend*, made the work 'a profound contemplation upon notions of assimilation and the shifting nature of our modern identity, now as fluid as the light-brown liquid within this masterpiece'. A lot of highly educated white people, wearing black spectacles and Helmut Lang, agreed with this assessment. Evie's success was assured. There was even talk that Charles Saatchi would buy the piece.

Identity was a hot topic in today's society and Michael was keen to jump on the bandwagon. With Evie's help, he'd taken his first steps towards becoming a contemporary artist. 'I got £10,000 funding,' said Michael. 'Can you believe that?' He smiled broadly. 'The thing isn't going to cost anywhere near that much to make. I can just pocket the rest.' He filled his mouth with another forkful of haloumi, and watched a high-class diva strut past; she was a tanned brunette wearing Versace hot pants. Michael's idea for an artwork had been commissioned and lottery money was being fed to him through a funding body. His concept was for a multi-screen video installation: called *Niggers*, it involved images of everyday white people – plumbers, bank clerks, taxi drivers – dancing the running-man to Vanilla Ice's 1990 hit single, 'Ice Ice Baby'. Michael's journalistic career had been undistinguished, poorly paid and marginally more successful than mine: modern art presented a new opportunity. 'I just gave them a load of crap,' he said, talking about the application process. 'I wrote about how this idea deals with the white paradigm, and its appropriation of the black subject.'

'What does that mean?'

'Fuck knows. Evie told me to write it. But they fell for it. Can you fucking believe that?' Michael put down his fork, and unwrapped a packet of cigarettes; he gave me one, and lit us both. 'I was just fucking around when I came up with that shit. I was drunk. I think I was trying to piss Evie off. But she thought it was a good idea and told me to put some work into it. And now I'm a fucking artist!' Michael laughed out loud, smoke pouring from his mouth and nostrils. 'White people are mad,' he said. 'You've got to tap into their madness, if you want to get anywhere. It's taken me a long time to learn that, but I'm getting there.'

'Good. I hope it works out for you.'

'Thanks.' Michael sucked his cigarette and stared into the street. 'It's like that sculptor, Anish Kapoor. He's got the hang of these freaks. He gives these twisted honkies what they want, and they pay him a fortune. He must be a millionaire by now. I saw some of his stuff last year, and didn't know what the fuck it was . . . It was this huge, shiny fucking shit . . . I couldn't see what the deal was. But crackers can, and that's why the guy's loaded.' Michael slumped into his seat and stared pensively into the street. His life had changed direction, and this made him reflective. 'That's the key to making it in this country,' he said. 'Knowing what white people want.' He smoked his cigarette and tapped his fingers quietly on the table. 'But they're fucking nuts . . . And it's hard to stop yourself going nuts with them.'

I sat quietly, nodding at his words.

We finished our lunch and walked to Primrose Hill; it was a sunny day, and we wanted to sit in the park. We stopped in a shop and bought a few cans of beer. There were plenty of people in the park, but there was lots of space; we picked a spot halfway up the hill, overlooking the Edwardian houses opposite. In front of us, sat on a picnic blanket, were a middle-aged couple and their two children; the son was aged about five, the daughter a toddler. Michael stared at them. I followed his gaze and watched them too. The couple reminded me of Ben and Ghislaine: both wore billowy cotton slacks and sandals, expensive sunglasses and loose summer shirts. The man had his son on his lap, and was spooning food into his mouth. Their children were healthy, clean and well presented; the daughter wore a white lace bonnet. Michael stared at them in silence. Evie was seven months pregnant and it was playing on his mind.

'What's wrong?' I asked.

'Nothing.'

'Tell me,' I said. 'What's bothering you?'

'I'm looking at that guy with his kids.' He lit another cigarette, and stared at him. 'You see a lot of guys like him these days . . . You know, these Nick Hornby types, who think they're great because they look after their kids and do the laundry. It's a crock of shit.'

'What do you mean?'

'It's fucking crap. That's what I mean.' He sucked his cigarette between tight pursed lips. 'You know why they do it, don't you?'

'I don't know,' I said. 'Feminism?'

'Immigration,' said Michael. 'Mass immigration. That's what turned these white boys into a bunch of pussies.'

I raised my eyebrows; I didn't know what he was talking about.

'White chicks love dark cock,' he said. 'Even Princess Diana was crazy for it. When the spades, the Pakis, and the rest of them got off the boat with their big dicks and their beautiful faces, the white boys shit themselves. That's why they bring their women cups of tea in bed, and listen to their bullshit. It's the only way they can get laid.' He sipped his beer and smiled. 'Niggers don't have to do that.'

I said nothing; I had nothing to say. I watched the

people in the park. There were a lot of them: young couples frolicked in the grass; old folk walked hand in hand; families kicked footballs and tossed frisbees among themselves. Michael watched the couple playing with their children; he had a fifteen-year-old son himself. The boy lived with his mother in Lewisham; she bore Michael a terrible grudge, and they argued whenever they spoke. Michael saw his kid maybe once every other month, if that. Looking at the couple and their children, he became withdrawn and silent; he knew he'd fail at fatherhood again. I saw no reason for him to feel bad. There's nothing wrong with being a shit parent. There's nothing wrong with being shit at anything.

'No one raises their kids properly,' said Michael.

'What do you mean?'

'Look at those two.' He gestured at the couple on the picnic blanket. 'They look like good people. They look like they earn good money. They'll send their kids to good schools and take them on nice holidays. But they'll still fuck them up.'

'How's that?'

'Because no one tells their kids the truth about life.' He finished his cigarette and flicked the butt into the grass beside him. 'People like that fill their kids' heads with trash. They feed them this crap about morality, responsibility, careers and sex within the context of a loving relationship . . . They don't tell them the truth.'

'Which is?'

'That life is shit. Life is short and it's full of shit.' He looked at me and smiled. 'So you might as well do what the fuck you want, all the fucking time . . . What else is there to do?'

'Nothing,' I said. 'There's nothing else to do.'

'People like that . . .' Michael nodded at the couple. 'They can't handle the truth, so they can't tell it to their kids. That's why this country's full of middle-class weaklings, hooked on Prozac. People don't realise what the

161

world is like until it's too late, then they have a fucking breakdown.' He lay on the grass and closed his eyes against the sunshine. 'That's why our dads are such great men. In their own shit way, they're great men. They just do what the fuck they want all the fucking time. They don't give a fuck about anyone.'

'Yeah. My dad's a fucking hero.'

'I'm serious,' said Michael. 'Your old man did you a favour. Me and you know the world is shit, and it's full of cunts. That gives us strength in life. We won't flake out like these other chumps. We know what the score is.'

I didn't reply. I sat on the grass, looking at the couple playing with their two beautiful children, and past them at the tall Edwardian houses that border the park; behind them, hidden in the distance, was the bustle and stink of Camden on a Saturday afternoon. I could hear Michael continue speaking, airing another of his grievances with the world; I didn't listen to him. I lay on the grass and stared into the blue sky above me. I listened to the laughter and shouts of people playing in the park, and thought about Sarupa. I closed my eyes and saw her face. The image exhausted me. Nothing I've ever wanted has come true; I was tired of being let down. I was tired of my lingering, lifelong sense of incompletion. I'm a man of few talents; the one skill I have is the acceptance of disappointment. Nonetheless, I lay there feeling drained and beaten. I hadn't wanted much from life: love, safety, a sense of belonging to somewhere or someone. Instead, I had nothing. I listened to the people around me laughing and joking with one another: was anyone happy, or was everything a shroud, hiding one's mediocrity and sadness?

Luca and I sat on deckchairs on his terrace, and looked across the rooftops of Belgravia. I hadn't seen my friends for weeks so spent the weekend catching up with them. It was Sunday evening; Luca and I drank coffee and caught up with one another's goings on. He told me his mother was in London having her latest cycle of chemotherapy. She had breast cancer; the cancer had spread elsewhere, and she was very sick. If it didn't respond to this treatment, she'd die within weeks. Luca had tried to visit her that afternoon.

Kate was in her mid-fifties; she was an ex-model. She'd struggled without her tight-fisted ex-husband's support to raise Luca and his elder sister in the manner they'd been born into. When their wheeler-dealing wop father ran off to live in Majorca with another ex-model (much younger, but less pretty), she'd refused to fight him for child maintenance; she didn't want money from a man who begrudged his own children. She started a business on her own – casting models – and put her children into good boarding schools. Against many odds, the business was a success. For over twenty years she worked twelve hours a day, six days a week, to give her children everything they wanted (skiing holidays, horses, cars and first-class music tuition). As a result, her looks faded, though never vanished. Her standards were high and her work was hard; she needed two bottles of red wine to get to sleep each night. In twenty years, she'd had only one boyfriend; she fell in love with him three years ago, having realised that her children barely knew her, having spent school terms boarding, and holidays abroad with their friends. Her efforts had been for nothing. Her son was an overindulged alcoholic, incapable of relating to women – especially her. The daughter, Sara, was a would-be photographer, who'd never exhibited – and never would – who was bent on marrying the same kind of arsehole her mother had. She was always on the arm of some flash, self-satisfied retard who loved being at casinos with Sara beside him, looking beautiful and being ignored. Sara was thirty-four. Luca was my age, twenty-nine. Both still depended on their mother, and the money she'd invested for them. Kate was now retired and spent all her time with her boyfriend – a kind, septuagenarian former theatrical agent – at his home in the Algarve, where they drank heavily and tried to laugh as much as possible. She was a stunning and remarkable woman who'd achieved everything but what she'd really wanted. And soon she'd be dead.

Sitting on the veranda, I heard evening birdsong in the trees below us. I listened to Luca recount the events of that afternoon. He was dressed in a green army-surplus jacket, dirty jeans and a pair of shabby sneakers; his hair was greasy and unwashed. He'd done a lot of drugs the night before; his brown skin was dry and pasty, his lips cracked from constant smoking. His gaze flitted around, never settling for more than a few seconds. I looked at his dirty fingernails; he hadn't bathed in days.

After clubbing all through the night before, he'd gone for a late breakfast at a pub in East London. He'd drunk an enormous amount during the night, and now he drank a good deal more. He'd been with a group of fellow DJs who, like him, were abject failures. They spoke at length about the records they'd played: DJs are, in essence, children's entertainers, but speak about their work as if it has substance and value in the world. Luca had seen his mother only once since she'd returned to London, more than a week ago. She was staying in a private room at the Royal Marsden Hospital; she was too ill to be at home.

After several rounds of beer, Luca lost his mind. He wailed about his mother's plight and screamed his love for her. He'd never spoken about his feelings before; now the words gushed forth in a flood of psychological incontinence. He was in a fit of tears when his friends bundled him into a taxi: no one had the stomach to hear talk of death; they wanted to speak about the club nights they'd be playing in Ibiza. Luca made the driver take him to Chelsea. Desperate to see Kate, he was terrified that she'd already be dead. He'd been a poor son; he wanted to beg forgiveness, tell her he'd always loved her, despite the gulf between them. He had a vague recollection of the ward she was in and made his way there. He climbed several flights of stairs and arrived panting, sweating with fear and exertion. He remembered that the door to her room had a window with a purple curtain inside it. He found a door with a window and a purple curtain, and peered through the glass at the cadaverous figure lying propped up on the bed: her skin was yellow with sickness, her face withered almost to the skull. Luca pushed open the door and walked to the bed. He kissed her cold cheek: she smelt awful, like stale vomit. He put his ear to her mouth, but couldn't hear her breathe. Luca's heart pounded in horror; his limbs weakened and he grabbed her shoulders to support himself. He shook the body, wanting to rouse it; he looked at the ceiling, blinded with tears, and shrieked. Nurses rushed into the room and grappled him to the floor; they'd been alerted by the panic button the patient held in her hand, to summon them whenever she'd soiled herself. It wasn't his mother; he'd been too drunk to notice. He'd molested and terrorised an old woman with liver failure: two storeys below, Kate lost another day to cancer, in agony and alone.

Luca was escorted from the building by a security guard and dumped onto the pavement. Too embarrassed to visit the hospital again, he never asked his mother's forgiveness. Weeks later, his sister – with whom he also rarely spoke – would send him a text message saying Kate had died. He'd be on his knees at the time, in a toilet cubicle of the 333 club, snorting cocaine off the seat.

I stood over the sink and splashed my face with water. It was a hot evening. Despite the coffee I'd been drinking, I was feeling tired. The cleaner had been to the house only two days ago, and the bathroom was already a shambles. A crust of shaving foam, speckled with facial hair, had dried against the sink enamel; the toilet was spattered with the debris of a spectacular defecation. Luca had no shame about the state in which he kept his home while his mother was away. I looked at myself in the mirror and wondered why I'd decided to visit him. Seeing Luca, listening to what had happened at the hospital, had a great effect on me. For the first time, I understood what a sad, dumb bastard he was.

I left the bathroom and walked along the corridor to the stairs that led back upstairs to the lounge – 'the war room' – and the balcony. I felt my feet sink into the deep, cream carpet, and ran my palm against the luxurious silky wallpaper. Luca lived in a beautiful house. When his mother died, it would be his. Luca was the last person to be trusted with a fortune: he was a fool with no self-control; that money would make a catastrophe of him. I walked upstairs thinking about the conversation he'd made: he spoke about the incident at the hospital as if it were just a drunken escapade, one more comedy mishap to add to his record of idiotic faux pas and mis-behaviour. At times he broke into giggles; he found much of what he'd done hilarious. He had no idea of the precipice on which he stood. I thought of the money he'd inherit, the insects it would attract – sycophants and manipulators – and the excess it would fund.

I entered the lounge. Luca stood by the drinks cabinet draining a tumbler of whisky. He refilled it, poured another and offered it to me. I looked at him and felt disgust. Alcoholism is the coward's alternative to suicide: Luca's cowardice, hidden beneath his tomfoolery and bonhomie, disgusted me. I'd prepared a speech for him while I was in the bathroom, exhorting him to change his ways and save himself. But I said nothing. I took the drink, sat on the couch, and sighed in resignation. A good friend would have taken Luca to task, raged at him to grow up and take charge of his life. I wasn't a good friend. I was a long-standing playmate, a drinking pal. Who was I to criticise him? I thought of Kate dying on her own in hospital.

'How's it going with that girl?' he asked, filling his glass again.

'Sophie? It's going okay,' I said. 'She's in New York right now. She's visiting her dad. He's lives there.'

'What does he do?'

'He's got some kind of business out there. I don't know much about it.' I stared at my drink; conversation with

166

Luca now felt like small talk. I'd known the guy for six years, and had nothing to say to him. He was slouched against the arm of the couch; his shabby green army jacket was falling off his shoulders, his T-shirt stained with beer and sweat. I looked at him and asked, 'Why are you such a fucking lush?'

He raised his eyebrows. 'What do you mean?'

I wanted to know why he was such a loser. He had so much: he was rich and white, handsome and well educated; he spoke several languages. Why was he such a fuck-up? What was his excuse? A minute or so elapsed, and my question was forgotten. I asked Luca if he was seeing anyone.

'Yeah.' He sat up and ruffled his greasy hair. 'I've had this silly bitch on the go for a few weeks now. She's starting to piss me off.'

'Who is she?'

'Her name's Emma. She does PR for a record company. I've known her for a couple of years. We got together at a party last month.'

'What's she like?'

'Well . . . she's a woman.' He sat up and poured the last of his whisky down his throat. 'She's a real pain in the balls.'

'Why's that?'

'She found out that I still shag Kitty. She read my text messages when I was asleep the other night.' Luca had dated Kitty in his teens; they'd been fuck-buddies ever since. She was sassy and learned, and was now an account director at an advertising agency. Whenever she was between relationships, she liked having sex with her beautiful, maladjusted ex-boyfriend. She would have made Luca an excellent wife, but was too smart to waste the time on him. Luca shook his head. 'Emma totally lost it,' he said. 'Went completely fucking mad. She was crying and making an idiot of herself. I've only been screwing her a month, and she was making such a big deal.'

'What did she say?'

'She kept saying how disgusting it was that I could sleep with two women at the same time. That it was disgusting that I could leave one girl's house and go straight to the other's. She couldn't get her head around it.'

'What did you say?'

Luca got up to refill his glass. 'I just told her the truth.' He gulped back half the glass, and immediately topped it up again. 'I told her that I know Kitty very well and get on great with her, as opposed to Emma, who's annoying and not very interesting but has great tits.' He cupped his hands in front of his chest. '*Great* tits. If Kitty was built like that, she'd be perfect.'

'What did Emma say to that?'

'She took it badly. She started crying and ran out of the house.'

'Then what?'

'Nothing.' Luca walked to the couch and collapsed back into his lazy slump. 'Nothing happened. She called me later on, and asked me to her place for dinner.'

'And you went?'

'Yeah. She had those two sweethearts . . .' he cupped his hands in front of him again, '. . . ready and waiting for me.' He closed his eyes and smiled. 'It was fucking lovely.' He sat quietly for a while, lost in pleasant thoughts. He opened an eye, raised his brow and looked at me. 'How's it going with Sarupa?' he asked. 'Now you're with her friend, does that mean you're over your crush? You're not mad about her anymore?'

'No. I'm not mad about her,' I said. 'Not anymore.' I stared past Luca's head and through the doors behind him that opened onto the balcony; I could see the red sun setting on the corner of the city. Several million people were out there, ploughing several million furrows. Barely a handful knew or cared anything about me.

I drove slowly. It was late Sunday evening and the roads were quiet. The drive didn't take long, just a few minutes. While Sophie was away, I made free use of the Mini

168

Cooper. London is a completely different city if one has a nice car; it's no longer a gauntlet of strife and neuroses. A nice car inspires magnanimity: I'd listen to Mahler on the digital radio, relax in the comfort of the leather seat, and bear the rancour of other drivers with grace, forgiving them for knowing not what they did. I drove away from Luca's house, towards the King's Road; I wanted to see the beautiful Italian women having supper with their husbands and boyfriends. They sat at pavement tables and smoked cigarettes; their dark hair tied back, their sunglasses rested on their foreheads. They wore chinos and sleeveless shirts; their sweaters were draped over their shoulders, the arms tied in a knot in front of them. I drove past the cafés and pizzerias, and looked at the couples sat outside. Everyone seemed so chic and contented.

I parked the car and walked around, looking for a convenience store; I wanted to buy some flowers. I went into a couple of shops, but they had nothing. I was about to buy something else – a box of chocolates maybe – when I saw a man hawking roses to the people sat at the tables. The Italians tried to pretend he wasn't there; this only made him pester them more. I crossed the road and hailed him towards me. The roses were selling at two pounds each; they weren't the best I've seen, but they looked and smelt okay. There were about a dozen left in the bucket in which he carried them; I haggled with him, and he sold me them all for twenty pounds. He had a pallid, malnourished complexion; his smile was ugly and gluey with plaque. He told me he was Kurdish; he was delighted to finish work so early. We sat on the kerb together, unwrapping the individual roses to make a single bouquet. I gave him a cigarette and thanked him for the flowers.

It was a lovely evening, warm and breezy. I left the car where I'd parked it, and decided to walk to the hospital. I thought of Luca as I walked there; I'd wanted to bring him with me. I tried broaching the idea of visiting his mother, but he was having drunken phone sex with his new girlfriend at the time. I decided to leave him at home.

I got to the hospital and went in search of Kate's ward. When I found it, I was stopped at the reception by a nurse who said visiting time had ended over an hour ago. She was a sweet, buxom, East African girl; her name, displayed on a badge on her lapel, was Honesty Nkwezi. She was petite and lovely in her nurse's smock, her long braids tied behind her head. She spoke English with text-book precision; educated people from former colonies always do. I told her I'd come to see Kate; compelled by the need to see her, my voice wavered and my throat felt heavy. I was almost crying; I didn't know why. I wanted to see Kate more than anything.

'Visiting time is over,' she said, 'and Mrs Cassani has been very tired today. She has been medicated, too. She is asleep now.'

'Let me see her. Please,' I begged. 'I won't wake her, I promise. I just want to see her, for a minute . . .'

Honesty looked into my face and heard the sincerity in my voice; she saw the flowers in my hand. 'You should call in advance, you know.' She intoned her words slowly. She was humane and very pretty, and took pity on me. 'Alright then,' she said, 'but be very quiet with her. And next time, if you are going to be late, please make a phone call to us first.'

I looked into her lovely brown eyes and thanked her; her teeth were clean and white, her black skin shone with health. I glanced at her full chest, her dainty hands, and made a mental note to talk to her later on: I'd offer to take her out sometime – maybe for a spin in the Mini Cooper. She gave me directions to Kate's room. I walked along the corridor into the ward. I stopped, looked behind and exchanged smiles with her; she blushed and pretended to take an interest in a folder on the desk beside her. She was very cute.

Outside the room, I knocked gently on the door; there was no reply. I pushed the door slowly open and peeked inside. The lights were dimmed. I could see Kate lying on her back, her head resting to one side. I walked into the room and stood by her bed. Translucent tubing snaked out from under her nightdress, and led into a small cylindrical drum set on casters on the floor; this device was plugged into a socket. The drum had a clear plastic lid; inside it was a watery red liquid, like weak blackcurrant cordial, that bubbled every few seconds. I could see more of it in the tubing, being pulled slowly towards the drum; it was being sucked from Kate's body. Kate had secondary cancers in her lungs and her chest had filled with fluid; it was now being drained, to give her some quality of life, a short respite of easy breathing before they filled again. I looked at her lying asleep, and couldn't believe that she could rest with that tube plunged into her side. There was a soft tapping on the door; I turned around and saw Honesty creep into the room holding a vase. She put her finger to her lips, to keep me from talking and waking Kate, and put the vase on the bedside table. She poured some of Kate's drinking water into it and took the roses from me; she quietly unwrapped them, then placed them in the water. We shared another smile as she left the room. I was definitely going to ask her out.

I slid a chair across the floor, next to the bed so I could sit by Kate. I sat down and listened to the rasp in her breath. I could hear the fluid frothing in her lungs. Her skull was bald, pale and blotchy. Her face had shrivelled; the skin was flaccid and empty. Her magnificent bone structure – her heart-shaped face, with its slender chin and high cheeks – was lost under folds of listless meat. I looked at her frail hands; her nails were as immaculate as ever. I reached out and touched her wrist. I sighed. The pain I felt was terrible. I sat holding her hand in silence. A deep ache pulsed slowly through me, but I couldn't cry.

I'd never spoken to this woman for more than a few minutes. She had little regard for me; I was just another loafer her idiot son wasted time with. Having slept on

171

her couch, after a night out with Luca, I'd occasionally bump into her in the kitchen on a Saturday or Sunday morning. She'd pour me a cup of coffee and make perfunctory conversation. Her tone of voice barely concealed her annoyance at the sight of me. She'd ask me if I wanted any breakfast; I'd thank her for the offer and decline, and she'd head for her office at the top of the house and not be seen again.

Holding her hand, I leant forward and kissed her forehead. 'I'm sorry,' I sighed. 'I'm sorry I've never been a good influence on Luca. I'm sorry for the worries I added to your life . . .' She didn't wake; she didn't hear a word and continued rasping in her sleep. I thought about my mother; I hadn't spoken to her in weeks. I wondered what life might have been like if I'd had a mother like Kate. 'I'm sorry . . .'

I gently pulled her hand onto my lap, and sat back in my seat. Kate had never given the impression of being anything but a strong, stoic, deeply saddened woman. Her life was written in the bags beneath her blue eyes, the lines around her often down-turned mouth. She'd married young; she was nineteen when she met Alessandro, and married him when she was twenty. She was an ordinary girl from Putney. Spotted by a photographer while shopping in Covent Garden, she began a short career as a model. She met him at the opening of a club in Soho. He was sixteen years older than her, and had been fucking models for a long time. He knew what to say to these gauche young women, awestruck and privately terrified by their glamorous new lives. He fed Kate the same bullshit he'd fed countless girls; she, of course, fell for it. Somehow they became married. He was in his thirties and it was 1971; people then thought one's thirties was a mature age, and he decided he needed a wife. Nine years later he was gone. Kate was left to raise two children on her own, though she'd never had a proper job in her life.

Kate shifted in her sleep. I held my breath; I didn't want

her to wake and find me holding her hand. She mumbled something, moving her head, and now she faced me; her eyes stayed shut. I looked at her wasted face. She seemed to have aged a century in the past year. The last time I saw her was almost three months ago, in May; she'd been in this same ward, having her lungs drained. I'd accompanied Luca when he brought her a bag of toiletries and a few books. I sat quietly in the corner as they swapped platitudes and clichés; neither wanted to talk about what was at hand. We didn't stay ten minutes. Luca gave his mother a quick hug and I gave her an embarrassed smile, and we left to go and find a prostitute.

On my way out, I looked around for Honesty. I didn't see her, so stopped at the reception desk and waited. A Filipino nurse appeared; he sat at the desk and kept glancing at me as he did his work. After a while my presence began to look odd, so I left. I never saw Kate again. She never knew I'd been there; I hadn't given my name to Honesty, and didn't leave a note with the flowers.

I drove with the radio switched off. I didn't wipe the tears that rolled from my face onto my shirt. My throat ached with sorrow. I drove along Chelsea Embankment; over the water I saw the golden Buddha in Battersea Park. I continued down Millbank, past the Houses of Parliament, and down Victoria Embankment. Across the Thames, illuminated against the South Bank, was the London Eye, its capsules moving imperceptibly. I imagined clusters of people inside them, drinking champagne and gazing over the city. I drove through town pondering my life, my past and my lack of any discernible future. I drove into East London, through Spitalfields and onto Shoreditch. It was Sunday night, but the streets around Hoxton were still crammed with bodies.

When I first moved to Hackney, in 1996, Hoxton was aflame with ambition and ideas. It was the Mecca of 'Cool Britannia'. Artists, designers, musicians, creative

173

people working in every type of media had set themselves up there. Before they arrived, the place was an empty buffer between the City and the immigrant slums of East London. This was its attraction: white people gauge their cool and creativity by the degree they tolerate being in proximity to blacks and Asians. People from across Britain flocked there in the mid-nineties; for a few years the area had a vibrancy I'd never seen before. I'd never seen white people so self-confident and *open*. 1996 was the era of Britpop, and the final year of two decades of Tory government. The idea of what it was to be British was up for grabs; people's vision of things was loose, carefree. People came to London to recreate themselves. They wanted to experience all it had to offer, wogs and all. Michael and I hung out in Hoxton a lot. We lounged in the bars watching the crowd, and occasionally picked up girls. Screwing those white chicks, I felt a sea change in the culture: they weren't fucking me just to get back at their parents. Those girls were inquisitive; they were experimenting with their lives, they wanted to experience different things with different people. And I, for the first time, didn't think white people had an innate distaste for me.

Hoxton was now only a shadow of what it was; little of the old crowd was still here. Those who found success had taken their money and run; the rest, bored of failure, now tried their hand at something new somewhere else. I looked out the window at the young people who lined the street outside the clubs and bars: they were nothing special. These people dressed in accordance with the style press; they had none of their predecessors' originality. Only a few years ago, Hoxton set the trend; it was the foaming vat from which tastes were distilled. The kids I saw now were bland and white, drunk and over excited; they came to wallow in the fading odour of what had been, having got their first jobs in London – probably in marketing or IT. I drove past them, and along Hackney Road; I turned left into Queensbridge

Road, heading towards Dalston Lane and my old flat above the bookie's.

I parked outside the row of shops directly beneath the flat. I unlocked the front door, knelt down and picked up the letters on the doormat. Closing the door behind me, I was trapped in absolute darkness. I walked up the narrow stairway. The bulb at the top of the stairs had gone, so I had to identify the keys with my fingertips. Five minutes later, I was inside. I tried the light switches; none of them worked, and I remembered the electricity had been cut off. The windows hadn't been opened for weeks; the smell of rodent faeces had turned the air sour. I fumbled my way into the lounge. There were no curtains; the room was flooded with the amber light of the street lamp outside. In the middle of the room was the sofa, the shabby velvet relic, its cushions scuffed by the hours Michael I sat there smoking dope and watching television. I walked towards the window and tripped on something; it was soft and heavy. I looked down and saw a fat king rat, dead at my feet. I gently kicked him towards the window, rolled him into a shaft of light and looked at him. He had a fat stomach and fine short fur; his eyes were shut and his mouth was open, showing tiny rat teeth, his little tongue poking between them. He looked serene, sated and at rest. I wondered what had killed him. I hadn't laid out any poison; I love animals and have never killed a thing, not even a spider. He hadn't been killed by a cat; he was still in one piece. He must have had a heart attack, brought on by the tonnes of junk food that litters Hackney. After gorging on pizza crusts and kebab meat, the poor bastard made his way here to die. I was touched by this. I stood there and mourned him in the glow of the street lamp.

I opened the window to let in some air, and looked at the letters in my hand. Two of them were mobile phone bills; I used the stiff envelopes to scoop the rat from the floor and drop him into the street below. I tossed the bills out after him. I looked at the other letters; all of them were junk mail apart from the invitation to my brother's wedding. I opened the envelope and held the rectangular card to the light.

You are cordially invited to the
wedding of

Harinder Singh Johal
and
Miss Pardeep Kaur Chadha

September 18th, 2002,
Heston Sports and Community Centre,
Slough, Middx.

The words were embossed in imitation gold leaf. It was the most tasteful thing my family had ever contrived. I sighed and felt hollow in my guts; Hari, I realised, had already been married – in the legal sense, by a registrar – and I had missed the event. This invite was for the religious service and wedding party, the cultural consummation. My mother and sister had phoned several times over the last few weeks. I never returned their calls nor listened to their messages. I rarely spoke to my family; I had so little to say to them. I'd assumed the phone calls were to pester me to get involved in the pre-wedding rituals and had ignored them. I'd assumed, God knows why, that when it came to the important stuff, I'd be hauled into line. I hadn't. I'd missed the marriage of my only brother, and someone else had been his best man.

There was no handwriting on the invite, no personal words from Hari or my mother. The card expressed how little they wanted me to be there. They'd sent it to me to let me know it was happening, that I'd failed them once more and worse than ever. I sloped over to the couch and collapsed onto it. '*I'm such a fucking prick,*' I sighed. Then I wept for the second time that night.

I walked across the street to the dingy café and got myself some breakfast. Sitting at a collapsible table by the window,

I drank a cup of weak tea and ate a slice of toast. The place stank of cooking oil and cigarettes; dour scruffy men sat around reading the *Sun*, getting ready for another godforsaken week in their deadbeat bullshit jobs. They ate charred sausages, chips and deep-fried bread, numbing themselves with starch and saturated fats.

I stared out of the window; I could see the flat. The betting shop was opening its doors for the day. I looked around for the cocaine flunkies, but couldn't see any. I hadn't seen any last night, nor the last couple of times I'd been here. Maybe they'd opened a crack house and moved away. I finished my breakfast, left the café and walked back towards the flat. The sky was overcast; the sunlight, leaking through the clouds, was dull and hazy. The heat was damp and cloying. I stepped over the dead rat I'd thrown onto the pavement, and went into the newsagent to buy cigarettes. Like my mother's shop, it was cramped and overcrowded with produce: the shelves were a mayhem of tins and packets of dried food; the magazine rack was a disordered mess; the floor was strewn with boxes of crisps and other snacks. The shop was next to the bookie's and was owned by a skinny, stoat-like man called Patel. Over the years we'd built a rapport as I listened to his diatribes against the local blacks and Bangladeshis. He was happy to have an Indian to talk to, and he let me run a cigarette tab. He had the stamina of a god: he'd sat behind that till eighteen hours a day, every day, for nearly thirty years, accumulating the daily trickle of money to pay for his children's education. One of his sons was now a solicitor, the other a doctor. Patel was looking forward to a comfortable retirement.

Handing me a packet of Marlboro Lights he told me, 'I'm building house in India. Big house. I'm leaving this bloody fucking country.' He wore a sleeveless cardigan over an old shirt; he had a moustache, and the little hair he had left he draped over his pate in a wispy veil. A couple of black kids came into the shop, wearing hooded tops and talking loudly. Patel eyed them suspiciously: 'Too much bloody rubbish in this country,' he said. One of the kids asked him if he sold anything to drink for fifty pence or less. 'Yes,' he said. 'I give you water from the tap.' The kids took offence at this and began insulting him in patois; I was stood nearby, so they didn't take it further. They walked out of the shop shouting abuse. 'Fuck off!' shouted Patel. '*Kaaleh* bastards!' He looked at me with a grimace: 'These *kaaleh*. Stupid, huh?'

I nodded and paid for my cigarettes, but couldn't leave for ten minutes; Patel made me listen to him rail against Hackney's various people. He was a very angry man. He had two successful sons who'd now take care of him, but he was now well over fifty; the best years of his life had been spent holed up in this dump, serving East London's underclass and trying to stop them stealing from him. He liked to speak at length about the work he'd put into securing his children's future, he liked saying how hard things had been for him in this country. Like my mum, Patel never questioned his life, which was a series of inescapable duties, not choices. Like my mum, he took great pride in having never failed in those duties; like her, he had a constant sense of bitterness and unease.

I walked upstairs to the flat. I went back into the lounge and sat on the old couch. I'd slept fitfully the night before, maybe three hours in all. It was hard to sleep on that couch; the springs had collapsed years ago, and there was nothing to use as a pillow. The floor was littered with cigarette butts. I'd smoked a packet and a half through the night, and my throat was now sore. The top of my lungs felt dry and gritty; my skin itched from lack of sleep and the constant smoke. I hadn't brushed my teeth for twenty-four hours; my mouth felt greasy and my tongue swollen. I sank into the couch, unwrapped my Marlboro Lights and smoked another cigarette. I looked at the room, at the mouldy discoloured wallpaper and the tall elegant windows, and at the chintzy threadbare carpet that was strewn with rat shit. I had no claim on this property anymore. The landlord had found new tenants; he was having the flat fumigated and tidied this week. I was to leave my keys behind when I last came to pick up my post. I was now basically homeless. The only place I could stay was at Sophie's, and I didn't know how much longer I could be with her. She was a nice girl, but she bored me. Fucking her already felt like a chore. I'd even faked the occasional orgasm. I smoked a lot of weed, to loosen up and get into the swing of things, but the underlying discontent was always there. She didn't rock my world.

She loved the sex as much as ever and gave me a lot of head. I'd lie back and watch her mouth on my prick, listen to her moans and wonder what the fuck she got out of it. She'd slurp on the end, suck it so deep she almost gagged. Her spittle ran down the shaft and over my balls. Coming up for air, she gave me hungry, almost vengeful looks – the look of a bitch in season – and told me how much she loved doing it. '*It makes my cunt ache*,' she groaned. '*I can't stand it*!' She'd straddle my leg and grind herself against my knee; she often came several times before I did. She was in love; that's how girls are when they flip their lid.

I thought about what I might do when I left Sophie. There weren't many options. Evie didn't like me so I couldn't crash with Michael. Luca was too much of an arsehole, even by my standards. I couldn't ask Mum for help, having fucked things up with Hari's wedding. I'd have to sit it out at Sophie's. The only alternatives were to find another woman who'd go nuts over me – with no guarantee she'd look as good or be any more engaging than Sophie – or rent a room in a shared house or flat. Hackney was one of the few areas I could afford; if I moved back here I'd have to live with strangers just as broke and lonely as I was. The thought made me shudder. Sophie was all I had; I'd stick with her for a while.

I got up and stood by the window. Patel was standing on the pavement below with one of his sons. It was Hanesh, the elder of the two; his blue Volkswagen Passat was parked in front of the shop, beside the Mini Cooper. Hanesh was dressed for work; he was the lawyer, and wore a sensible commonplace suit and haircut. Patel had raised a pair of judicious, conscientious young men. They were cowards and nerds, but smart ones. I'd met them many times, and always made the same tired conversation: we asked after one another's family and work, trading the maxims and homilies of our race. They shared their father's concrete certainty about life and the world, and didn't quite know what to make of me. My shapeless meandering existence was strange and exotic to them; they were amazed and unsettled by my lackadaisy. They'd lived by the tenets of our people; they were cosseted, neurotic and profoundly afraid. I'd talk about my life – what I wrote, what I'd read, the places I'd been and the girls I was seeing – and their eyes would glaze. Any suggestion at a world beyond their jobs, their families and their old man's precepts discomforted them. My life was a dangerous example; it contravened the logic behind their achievements. Bland and assiduous Indians were now the backbone of this country; the NHS, the legal system, the technocracies of commerce and the state were diligently upheld by men like Hanesh. To him I was somewhat outré, and best kept at a distance.

I watched the two men talking on the street; I don't speak Gujarati, so didn't know what they said. Two men walked past wearing Turkish football shirts, animated and cocksure. Turkey had finished third in the World Cup and Turkish people felt they had now taken their place in the world. The atmosphere around here might improve as the Turks behaved themselves for a while, before joining in the general anarchy once more. I turned away from the window and faced the empty room; it was the last time I'd see it. Leaving my letters where they lay on the floor, I left the flat. I locked the front door, walked downstairs and let myself out. I locked the door behind me and posted my keys through the letterbox. I was never going in that flat again; another portion of my life had elapsed. I walked past Hanesh and Patel; they nodded to me and I smiled. They watched me get into the Mini Cooper; they'd never seen me in a car before. I gave them a wave and drove back to Holland Park.

I was exhausted when I got there; my sleep deficit was taking effect, and the drive had been long and tedious. The roads were blocked with traffic and I'd moved at a crawl. There was nothing of interest on the radio; it was a struggle to stay awake at the wheel. Inside the flat, I took off my shoes and my jeans; I walked to the bedroom wearing just my T-shirt, and fell on the bed. I was thirsty and wanted a glass of water, but hadn't the will to go to the kitchen. I thought about Hari and felt ashamed. It crossed my mind to call him, to apologise and make amends. I thought about what I could say. I sifted through a dozen excuses, looking for the right one, and drifted quietly into sleep.

Waking slowly, I floated in a blissful drowse filled with visions of Sarupa. We were naked in one another's arms, but weren't fucking, surrounded in calm white light. I could feel her body against mine, the warmth of her wonderful flesh, the caress of her thick dark nipples against my chest. Her brown eyes looked directly into mine; I could taste her on my lips. There seemed to be so much of her, a luxurious abundance. I felt myself being gently absorbed, her body folding itself around me, our brown skins melding. Her soft hands slid across my back and over my buttocks; I felt her sleek fingers between my legs, stroking my testicles, gently probing my anus. I moaned aloud and opened my eyes; my cock was rock hard and painful. I shut my eyes to see her face again, and saw only blackness. I tried to masturbate, but it felt pathetic – almost sacrilegious – and I stopped. My desire was absolute; all I could feel was a measureless absence, my nerves bared as though I'd been skinned. I had never felt so raw, so abject. I turned and struck the pillow with my fist. '*You fucking bitch!*' I screamed. '*What the fuck have you done to me!*'

*　　*　　*

181

A month before, I'd never been so alive; for a couple of days everything in this world seemed open to me. I was incandescent with happiness; my every breath was sweet, every sound was music. I sat in Sophie's kitchen and thought about those two days, as I drank coffee and smoked my way through a packet of cigarettes. The windows were open; the sky was grey, the air was thick and wet. The weather was a thermal wrap; the city lathered in the oily heat of exhaust fumes and sweating bodies. I got up and switched on the air-conditioning unit that sat in the corner of the kitchen. I made myself another espresso; I'd given up on getting any sleep. I sat on a Jacobsen stool, sipping imported coffee and nursing my thoughts. I contemplated becoming a Buddhist. I was tired of my emotional life. It was better to live in a blank state of equanimity than be cursed with hopes that were always dashed. I thought about that weekend in the Cotswolds and the days that followed; I thought about the gamut of emotions I sped through. I thought of how beautiful Sarupa was, the smell of her skin, how fresh the air had been as we walked across the fields that Sunday morning, anticipating one another's touch and the taste of each other's mouths.

9

IT WAS TEN o'clock. It was a glorious Sunday morning in late June, and the day was already warm. The sun hung above the hills ahead of us; the light was soft and clear. The crisp air was full of birdsong. I stared overhead, at the serene emptiness of the sky. We walked along a dirt track, marked with dried imprints of horse shoes, and scattered with dung. The trees carried the last of the blossom; the smallest breeze brought tides of tiny pink and white flowers that fell on us like snow. Stan leapt excitedly at the falling blossom; he was a wonderful dog. I chased him through the trees and into a field where we fell onto the ground and wrestled. I held him in my arms and kissed his face. I loved him.

'You're very good with him,' said Sarupa, walking towards us. 'Have you got a dog?'

'I had one for years,' I said. 'He was the best friend I ever had.' I put my hand in Stan's mouth, and he pretended to chew it. I lay on my back and rubbed his stomach; he climbed onto me and licked my face.

'What sort of dog did you have?'

'Alsatian cross,' I said. 'I don't know what other breeds he had in him. But he looked very Alsatian.'

'What was his name?'

'Raja.' I sat up and held Stan's face in both hands. I looked into his eyes and he calmed down. He sat beside me, wagging his tail. I remembered Raja, and my chest felt heavy. 'He was an amazing dog,' I said. 'Absolutely amazing.'

'Why's that?' Sarupa stood over me; I looked up at her

gorgeous face framed against the blue sky. I said nothing. Seeing her in this light induced silence. She tapped my leg with her foot. 'Why was your dog amazing?'

'For lots of reasons.' I turned to face Stan. 'He was bilingual, for one.'

'Really?'

'Yeah. I spoke to him in English, and my parents spoke to him in Punjabi. And he understood whatever you told him. He absolutely knew what you were saying. It didn't matter which language you used.' I put my hand on Stan's paw and he rested his head against it, closing his eyes. 'This guy is just beautiful.' I stroked his ear. 'You're *so* handsome, aren't you?' He sat up and began licking my face again.

Sarupa watched us and smiled. 'You really do have a way with him.'

'I love animals,' I said. 'They respond to that. They know I'm not full of shit.'

'I was watching you last night. You spent more time with him than you did with anyone else.'

'I hope you didn't think I was being rude.'

'Not at all.' She crouched down and stroked Stan's back. 'I thought it was lovely. You were very sweet together, like the best of friends.'

'Who wouldn't want to be friends with this guy?' I held up his face and kissed it once more.

'So you do have a soft spot. You're not the complete cynic you pretend to be.'

'I don't pretend to be a cynic.'

'Yes you do.' She looked into my eyes and smiled. 'You have this world-weary pose, as if you've seen and done everything and are now so bored. It's quite amusing.'

'I'm glad you like it.'

'I said it was amusing. I didn't say I liked it.' She sat down on the grass, plucked a dandelion blossom from the ground and twirled it between her fingers. 'I'd have liked it when I was a teenager. Teenage girls like that sort of boy.'

'What sort?'

'Sullen and pretty.'

'So you think I'm pretty?'

She didn't reply. She looked at Stan, who sat between us. 'What was your dog Raja like?' She ran her hand along Stan's tail. 'Was he like him?'

'No. Raja was a lot bigger, and a lot quieter. He was very lazy, but *so* smart. He was the cleverest dog, and the sweetest. My dad bought him to be a guard dog in the shop, but his temperament was too gentle. So he became my best mate instead. He slept in my bed with me. From when he was a puppy, until he died, he slept in my bed with me.'

'What happened to him?'

'He was hit by a car. I was taking him to the park, and this car came from nowhere and hit him.' I stared at the ground and sighed. 'I won't have a dog again. I couldn't stand it when he died . . . No one's ever loved me like he did.' My sadness must have been apparent; Sarupa put her hand on mine and squeezed it.

'How long had you had him?'

'Eleven years. I was seventeen when he died.'

We sat quietly for a while. Sarupa's hand stayed on mine. I looked at it, at her beautiful brown skin and her engagement ring.

'What were you like as a teenager?' she asked. 'Did you have lots of girlfriends?'

'No. I had lots of spots, and a turban.'

'Oh dear.' She stopped herself laughing. 'I can't imagine you in a turban. You don't seem the type.'

'I had this awful beard as well.' I smiled to myself as I remembered it. 'I didn't shave once in my teens, so my beard was all fluffy and patchy. I looked like Rasputin. And I had the most sebaceous adolescence on record. You should've seen my acne. It was fucking awesome.'

'No!' she gasped. She sat cross-legged beside me, staring at me with wide eyes. 'You'd never tell from looking at you.'

'It was like an Old Testament affliction,' I said. 'Even my spots had spots, and I had this permanently shiny face. I thank God I went to a boys' school. I didn't have to watch everyone around me going on dates and getting laid. It would've killed me.'

'That's extraordinary.' She stared at me and shook her head. 'I can't believe you looked like that. I can't believe you were religious.'

'I wasn't. My mum was. She still is.'

'How did she react when you decided to cut your hair?'

'She didn't know about it until it was a fait accompli. I cut it a couple of days before I dropped out of university.' I looked at Sarupa. She sat watching and listening to me. Her hair was tied up, and her loose summer dress fluttered in the breeze. She wore an old beaten-up pair of Converse sneakers; she looked girlish but chic. I smiled at the sight of her.

'Why did you drop out of uni?'

'I was bored. I was doing a business administration course, and I wanted nothing to do with it. I had this gut feeling that if I graduated, I'd be pushing a pen in some drab office for ever. So I dropped out. I figured I'd have more freedom being a total loser, than if I joined the rat race.'

'Where were you studying?'

'De Montfort. It's in Leicester. It's one of those places that used to be a polytechnic.'

'I've heard about it. Lots of Asians go there, don't they?'

'Yeah . . . That's another reason why I left.'

'I'm surprised you went there. You're obviously very bright. I thought you'd have gone somewhere better.'

'I could've . . .' Stan looked up at me, and I ruffled the top of his head. 'I deliberately flunked my A levels. I'd been offered a place at Durham.'

She stared at me open-mouthed. 'Why didn't you go there? Why would you want to screw up and go to De Montfort?'

'Because I didn't want to be a doctor.' I toyed with

186

Stan's lead. 'I was supposed to be a doctor. That was the goal my mum set for me, and it almost happened. I revised my balls off for my A levels. I looked at the questions in the exams, and I knew the answers. I knew all of them, but I could hardly write them down. I just drew stupid doodles instead.' I looked at Sarupa; she was listening intently. 'I wanted to be a failure,' I said. 'I didn't want anything to be expected of me anymore.'

'That's why you failed your A levels?'

'Yeah. And that's why I dropped out of university. I'd had a lot of pressure on me since I was a kid.'

'Lots of parents have high expectations of their children. Mine are the same.'

'This was different,' I said. 'My dad walked out on us when I was a kid, and my mum piled all her neuroses onto me. She wanted me to make up for what a cunt he was.' I paused and looked at Sarupa. I expected her to say something, but she was silent; she wanted me to continue. 'I don't blame her,' I sighed. 'Poor cow . . . She had such a fucking bullshit life.' I reached into my pocket and took out my cigarettes. I lit one and looked out across the field. It had been left fallow and was sparsely covered with short wild grass. 'She came all the way here, to marry someone she'd never met. She had no family over here, knew absolutely no one. And my dad was a cunt . . . such a fucking cunt.' I smoked my cigarette and stared at the trees that lined the field; behind them, in the distance, were the hills. 'He hit her,' I said. 'He'd really knock the shit out of her. He did it pretty regularly.' I heard Sarupa tut and sigh. I could feel her staring at me, but didn't turn to face her. 'She turned all that pain into ambition for me. I was the oldest kid, I was a boy . . . I was supposed to solve everything. And when he left, she couldn't cope. Even though he was a fucking bastard. She couldn't handle not having a husband.' Ahead of me, a stout black crow pecked at something in the ground. 'She wouldn't let me forget what she'd gone through,' I said. 'She laid loads of pressures and guilt trips on me.'

I thought of the time Dad threw her onto the street. She ate and slept at the temple each night for a week; during the day she wandered the streets of Southall, frantic and penniless. I remembered her face, warped and swollen with bruises, trying to smile when she sneaked into the house to visit her children. I remembered how blank, how nulled I was at seeing her. I turned to Sarupa; she was biting her lip, watching me closely. 'I don't know why I'm telling you this. I've never really told anyone before.' I stood up. Stan got on his feet and barked, he was keen to start moving again and ran in circles around my legs. I held out my hand and he jumped up, trying to nip at my fingers which I kept just out of reach. 'He's got so much energy, hasn't he? I bet he needs lots of walking.'

'Loads,' said Sarupa. 'If he's not walked properly, he's hyperactive all day.' She stood up and brushed the dust and grass from her dress. She smiled at me.

'Where shall we take him?'

'That way.' She pointed to a gap in the trees at the far side of the field; it was the opening of a path that led into the woods. 'The village is on the other side,' she said. 'We can walk him there and back.'

We stood for a moment and looked into each other's eyes. She called to Stan, and we began strolling, slowly, side by side, towards the village.

An hour before, I had been ready to go home. I was slumped on the aubergine couch in the lounge, contemplating the two-hour drive back to London and twiddling Sophie's car keys (I'd taken them from her purse while, she was still asleep). I'd thrown on some clothes and stuffed the rest of my belongings into Sophie's travel bag. I'd left the bag in the bedroom; she'd need it to carry her own things. I hadn't written a note. I was going to send her a text as I drove home. I sat slumped on the couch, unable to summon the energy to get up and leave. I was sad and exhausted, hadn't slept all night, and had at last figured I had no chance with Sarupa. She was a brilliant woman with an excellent career;

she was on the cusp of great things. She'd never take an interest in me. It was madness on my part to think she might.

In the centre of the room was the high-tech karaoke machine we'd played with the night before. The machine had an inbuilt CD burner, and we'd recorded ourselves singing. I picked up the remote control, lying on the couch beside me, and played the CD. Ghislaine's bland, drama-schooled voice was the best; no one else could hold a note. I sped through the disc, hearing snatches of everyone's performance. Duncan's singing was barely musical; Sophie was excited and shrill; Sarupa and Ash sang an incoherent duet. Then I heard my own voice, and sat up. I'd never heard my voice objectively before; the sound of it surprised me. It was deep, earthy, nearly monotone; the vowels were sluggish, each consonant landed with a thud. It was an absurd jumble of accents: cockney enunciation and occasional West Indian inflection overlaid a quiet drone from the Punjab. It was from Southall, and was incongruent with the rest. Like the sight of one's face, the sound of one's voice has great power; it situates you and conjures expectations in the minds of others. I was taken aback by how particular I was, how rooted in time and place: everything about me came from the Punjabi suburb of West London. I felt embarrassed. I realised how outlandish my presence here was. Everyone else belonged to a milieu of metropolitan wealth, their differences in colour subsumed within a shared order of money. Their lives were firmly aligned. Mine was experiencing just a glancing encounter with theirs, before I ricocheted back into oblivion.

I looked at my watch: it was almost ten o'clock. I sank into the couch and stared at the ceiling high above me. I had to leave very soon; people would now be getting out of bed, and I didn't want to explain my early departure to them. I heard scratching at the door; it edged open and Stan padded into the room. I patted the couch beside me and he clambered onto it and lay down. I scratched his head and looked into his large dark eyes.

'Morning.' Holding a glass of fruit juice, Sarupa stood

in the doorway. Wearing a long summer dress and pair of sneakers, her hair was tied in a bun; wisps trailed down either side of her face. She wore no make-up; her face was clean and fresh.

I stood up. 'Good morning.'

'Sleep well?'

'Yes,' I lied. 'Very well.'

'Would you like some coffee?' she asked. 'Or some juice?'

'No thanks. I'm okay.'

'You sure? How about some breakfast? I'll make some eggs, if you like.'

'No, I'm fine. Thank you.'

She walked into the room, sipping her drink, and joined me on the couch. Stan sat between us. 'I didn't take you for an early riser,' she said. 'Have you been awake long?'

'A while . . . How long have you been up?'

'A couple of hours. I always wake up early when I'm in the country.' She smiled. 'It's so peaceful here. The air's so fresh. My head always clears when I'm here.' She closed her eyes and sighed. 'London feels so far away.'

'What have you been doing all morning? I haven't seen you anywhere.'

'Yoga. I did my morning practice in one of the rooms upstairs. It gets a lot of light. We've put some mats in there. I'm trying to get Duncan to do some too.'

'Did he join in this morning?'

'No. He's still asleep.'

Listening to her voice, I was acutely aware of the difference between us. Her accent was no different to Duncan's, her pronunciation precise and impeccable. All of Sodhilal's effort and sacrifice was vindicated by that voice. It was the voice of the established. It hummed with confidence. Like Patel, the shopkeeper, Sodhilal had elevated his children into a sphere beyond his own: how satisfied he must feel hearing that voice, its calm authority.

'I ought to take him for a walk,' she said, stroking Stan, 'before everyone's up. Is Sophie still in bed?'

190

'She is.'

'What are you going to do for the rest of the morning?'

I hesitated; I didn't want to say I was leaving.

'Come for a wander with us,' she said, before I could answer. 'It's lovely around here. You won't see countryside like this in London.'

I looked into her kind, intelligent eyes, and didn't know what to say.

'You can stay here, if you like,' she said, mistaking my silence for reluctance. 'You can hang out in the pool, or help yourself to breakfast.'

'No, I'd love to go for a walk. Where were you thinking of going?'

'There's a village a couple of miles from here, we can go there. It has a lovely little tea room. I'll treat you to a cup of real English tea.'

'You have to promise me a scone as well.'

'It's a deal.' She stood up and smiled. 'Shall we go?'

I followed her into the kitchen. She picked up Stan's lead from the counter and opened the front door. I stepped outside after her into the fresh, clean air. The sun was low and bright. I felt a sense of genuine and unexpected happiness. I watched her fasten Stan's lead to his collar. She looked beautiful. We walked to the side of the house; at the end of the garden was a gate that opened onto a narrow lane. I held it open for her as she walked through. 'I'm excited,' I said. 'I've never had a scone before.'

There was a half smile on her lips; she'd been watching me with amusement for some time. I smeared some clotted cream on the remainder of my scone and spooned some jam on top. I raised it to my mouth and licked at it salaciously. I made a lewd moan as I took a bite, and she finally laughed out loud. Her laughter pleased me; I couldn't help laughing, too.

I relaxed into my seat and looked at her across the table. For the first time, I was truly at ease with her. The light in her eyes proved I had nothing to fear. I'd always been tense before, too concerned with what she might think of me; as a result, I was over-cocky. Our walk in the country had opened doors between us. We'd talked and laughed; I'd held her hand as we climbed over gates, stumbled down banks and hopped tentatively from stone to stone to get across a stream. We looked openly into one another's eyes and shared moments of comfortable silence. I knew now that she liked me. I felt secure and unworried; I could simply enjoy her company.

'How have you managed to live nearly thirty years without eating a scone?' she asked, still smiling.

'No one's ever offered me one before.' I glanced around the tea room. 'I don't usually hang out in places like this.' The room was small and tidy; the tables were immaculately laid, the linen was clean and perfectly pressed. The only other customers were a pair of quiet, elderly women wearing cashmere and expensive bouffants; a black dachshund sat in one of their laps. I took another bite of my scone; it was somewhere between sponge cake and shortbread in taste and texture. I enjoyed it immensely. 'This is good,' I said, holding up what remained. 'Very good.'

We'd talked a lot during our walk, mostly about our families. Sarupa was the youngest of three children – she had two brothers – and was the only one born in the UK. She missed the chaos and penury that greeted them when they first got here. She vaguely remembered a bedsit they once lived in. It was incredibly cramped, with suitcases piled in the corner and a washing line hung across the room. Her father did several drudge jobs to pay the bills – cleaning, packing, driving – but was a merchant by caste, with a keen eye for the main chance. He always had plans; he just had to accumulate the capital first. Like every Indian, he saved and bought a house long before Thatcher made it the fashion; he then started a business importing and wholesaling electronics. It was the seventies; the world's insatiable lust for leisure technology had only just begun. What started as a foothold in the burgeoning market for tape recorders and colour TVs accelerated into the mass provision of VCRs and hi-fi units, before moving onto high-speed processors and mobile phones. The business, today called Shah-Tec, now encompassed a portfolio that included satellite broadcasting, biotechnology and internet banking. You had to hand it to Sodhilal Shah; he was a clever cunt.

Sarupa was the baby of the family, adored and indulged by her father and brothers. Her mother was traditional, selfless, dutiful and pious; religion gave her something to do in old age, now the children had been raised and their fortunes made. She spoke limited English, and was Sodhilal's firm and unquestioning ally. Sarupa and the younger of her brothers went to public school as soon as their father could afford it. He'd been to one himself, an old colonial boarding school, on the coast of Lake Victoria. He was an Anglophile who'd studied in London in his twenties; he loved P.G. Wodehouse and Evelyn Waugh. He loved their subtle wit and turn of phrase; he lamented that one now has to go to India to hear English spoken like that.

As often happens, Sarupa's education and subsequent career created a gap in understanding between herself and her mother. They were close nonetheless; Sarupa escorted the old girl to religious ceremonies and cultural events. Her mother bore change well, acquiescing to it with a resigned shrug; she concerned herself with devotional practices and the well-being of her grandson.

Sodhilal was at the centre of Sarupa's life: 'We're best friends,' she told me, 'I speak to him almost every day.' He'd handed the day-to-day running of Shah-Tec to his sons, and was now writing a book, *The Shiva System*. He was formulating a model of corporate and global capital management, based on principles he'd discerned in Vedic scripture. The ancient Hindus, he believed, had an uncanny insight into the dynamic of postmodern political economy. The notion sounded like complete shit to me, but had intrigued Tony Blair; he'd asked Sodhilal to email him a précis.

'So . . .' I said, pouring us both another cup of tea, 'how come you're a lawyer? Why aren't you working for your dad?'

'I might, one day. Right now I want to do other things. I need to branch out on my own and do something for myself.' She leant forward to add milk and a large spoonful of sugar to her cup. 'It can get claustrophobic working with my family. I didn't want to spend every day around them.' She sipped her tea. 'I think it's better for me to develop a separate career. If I do get involved in the business, I'll bring a fresh perspective.'

'Have your brothers ever worked anywhere else?'

'No.' She put down her tea and picked up a scone; she held it delicately in one hand and gently sliced it in two with her knife. Her fingers were slim, her nails perfectly manicured. She did everything so elegantly, scooping small portions of cream onto her scone, rather than one great blob, and dabbing only a smidgen of jam on top. She nibbled at the edge, making sure not to smear her lips.

Watching her, it occurred to me how much she liked her food. She was a big girl; she didn't get like that eating bean sprouts and rice cakes. Cream teas were a pure sensual pleasure she couldn't resist; this was her second helping. I loved the way she looked: lush and sumptuous, she oozed feminine appeal. Yoga helped her maintain an exquisite balance; any less of her would have dimmed her allure, but if she got much bigger she could be considered fat. She had a natural propensity to roundness; in later life she might balloon, especially after childbirth. I watched her enjoy her scone. I imagined she kept a jumbo pack of chocolates in the drawer of her office desk, Maltesers probably; quietly popping one into her mouth every so often, she'd savour them melting against her tongue, as she drafted and proofread contracts and negotiations.

For Asian women, carrying some extra pounds generally isn't a head-fuck; Sarupa dressed to accentuate and complement her shape. Big white girls, their eyes full of shame and sadness, hide themselves under shapeless skirts and long jackets. Devised by pussy-loathing queers in the fashion industry, and disseminated by the shit-head fag hags who work for glossy magazines, the cult of thinness is set in the Western mind. Nothing revolts those fruits more than fat tits and round arses; nothing delights them more than making women look like withered boys. Sophie couldn't bear to be any bigger than she was, though she was a week's fast from being skeletal. Did she really find that image so compelling? Or was it just Anglo-Saxon masochism?

Sarupa finished her scone; she looked at the tray and considered having a third, but then sat back in her chair holding her hands together in her lap. Outside, the sun was burning, the heat warming my neck through the window pane behind me. I turned to look through the glass at Stan, who was tethered to a railing outside, shaded under a tree. He lay patiently, his head resting on his paws. I looked at the clock on the wall: it was eleven forty-five. Nearly two hours had passed since we left the house; the walk back would take another forty or so minutes. Luckily everyone had got trashed the night before, so wouldn't be getting up until now; they'd have no idea how long we'd been gone.

Our conversation had lulled. We sat in our seats, reflecting. I tried to remember when I'd last sat quietly, like this, with a woman. The answer, I guess, was never. I'd never had a meaningful relationship with a woman, certainly not with one I was fucking. Sophie and I always did stuff to make out there was something between us: we got loaded, fucked or watched movies, anything to kill time. We didn't really talk; we didn't have that much to talk about. Only a few moments had to pass in silence before someone put on a CD, or rolled a joint. Quietly being ourselves with each other was something we hadn't tried. She seemed happy enough all the same; she'd never complained. In less than two hours with me, Sarupa had a better idea of who

I was and what I was about than Sophie would ever get. I stared at my hands, clasped on the table before me, and contemplated my loneliness.

After a while, it became clear we had to leave; the others would wonder where we were, and Sarupa wanted to organise lunch. I paid the bill and we left. Stan leapt up, excited as I untied his lead, and we began our way back to the house. The tea room was in a very small, very pretty village. I didn't know its name; I hadn't asked. I watched Sarupa lead the way downhill, along a narrow lane, as Stan ran back and forth between us. I knew quite a lot about her now. I knew she'd studied English at King's College, before converting to Law. I knew she liked tiresome, canonical writers like E.M. Forster and Virginia Woolf, and hip contemporary ones like Haruki Murakami. I'd read something by him once, *The Wind-Up Bird Chronicle*; it was about some guy whose wife was lost in a sort of spirit world. He didn't do a lot about it, other than smoke cigarettes and gaze into his navel – the kind of lame thing I'd do, if that happened to me. The book was complex, its narrative convoluted and taxing; I gave up after a couple of hundred pages. I hated paying good money and being made to feel dumb. Sarupa used the term 'post-colonial' to describe a lot of the books she was into; she thought Toni Morrison was a genius. I said I liked Iceberg Slimm; he was a cool black motherfucker who'd pimped a lot of chicks and been hooked on smack. His books were great. Sarupa listened to me talk about him – she was a good listener – but I got the feeling she would never read him; her taste was shaped by a good university education and the Saturday *Review* section of the *Guardian*.

'Let's cut through there,' she said, pointing at the grounds of an old church at the edge of the village. 'The graveyard backs onto the woods. It'll be quicker.'

Walking through the grounds, I read the dates on the headstones; some of them were from the eighteenth and nineteenth centuries. Though it was almost lunchtime, there didn't seem to be anyone around. Beside the church was a memorial to the men of the village who died in the First World War. For such a small place, it had lost a lot of people – several dozen at least. I mentioned a book I'd read about the war, and the conversation turned to literature again.

'What was the last thing you read?' she asked.

'Something by Bataille,' I said. 'I think it was called *Story of the Eye*. It's a piece of fin de siècle French pornography.'

Sarupa smiled. 'Was it good?'

'Filthy,' I said. 'I loved it.'

She laughed. 'What was the storyline?'

'It's about a couple of kids who go nuts, completely sex crazed. They're at it like monkeys, all the fucking time. They do some very mucky things with a boiled egg.'

'Hmmm . . .' She raised her eyebrow. 'Why aren't I surprised that you'd be reading that?'

'It's more than just filth. It's very fevered, very condensed writing, a bit like Faulkner. You get a real sense of intensity, a sense of those kids just wanting to fuck like hell, all the time. It captures the way teenagers would fuck, if they didn't have any hang-ups. You really sense that energy and madness. It's very sexy.'

She was looking at me carefully, listening to my words; her black hair shone in the sunlight.

'I don't think many teenagers get their rocks off like that.' I smiled. 'I know I didn't. I don't think many people ever do, even as adults. Well, maybe after some hard liquor and a lot of coke.' I almost asked her of she'd ever been laid while on drugs, but held my tongue. I felt my cock thicken; the thought of sex and the sight of her summer dress fluttering against her body made me tense. I breathed a little deeper, trying to relax, and stared into the distance.

We walked to the edge of the graveyard in silence; Sarupa didn't look at me and kept her gaze on the path. I realised what I said might have made her uncomfortable. I felt hot with embarrassment. Stan ran ahead of us to the wall that enclosed the churchyard; wagging his tail, he turned and looked at us and ran back. I clapped my hands and he bounded into my arms. I picked him up and cuddled his body; he didn't mind being held at all. He kept my mind from thinking of what a dick I'd made of myself.

The wall was decayed; a section of it had fallen down, creating a gap that led into the woods. It was a handy shortcut; she obviously knew the area well. There was a pile of crumbling bricks and mortar at the foot of the wall, about two feet high, that we had to walk over.

'After you,' she said, looking away from me.

I walked through the hole; Stan leapt through behind me and ambled into the woods. I stood on hand as Sarupa stepped onto the broken stones; they shifted beneath her feet and she stumbled forwards. I put my hands on her hips to steady her and she leant against my shoulder; I lifted her and carried her through the hole. I bent my knees to gird myself; she was pretty heavy. I put her down, and she fidgeted with her dress, straightening it, keeping her gaze firmly away from me. Her unease was tangible. Had I really been such a prick? Could she actually be that touchy?

'This way,' she said, turning to the woods.

In that moment, somehow, I knew she wasn't annoyed. She began walking and I reached out and took her wrist, stopping her in her tracks. Standing behind her, I put my arm around her waist; letting go of her hand, I brushed the hair from her neck. She held my forearm to her stomach; I gently stroked her cheek and the length of her neck. I kissed her ear, heard her breathing slow, and lowered my head to kiss her nape; she sighed, and I wrapped both arms around her, nuzzling her, smelling the scent in her hair, the salt on her skin. Kissing the side of her face, I unbuttoned the front of her dress; I slipped my hand inside and squeezed her warm belly. She wasn't wearing a bra. I held her breast and she moaned; her nipple hardened against my fingertip. I was now calm, my mind perfectly clear: if life were as easy as fucking, I would have no problems.

I turned her around and held her face in my hands; her stare was wide, almost fearful. I looked into her brown eyes and softly kissed her lips. She didn't respond. I kissed her firmly, sucking her lower lip, and she came alive, opening her mouth, taking my tongue and gripping my shirt. I grabbed her behind with both hands and she groaned, rubbing her face against mine, pushing her big tits against me. She wore a thong underneath; I lifted her skirt and gripped her bare buttocks, my hand between her cheeks. My cock was stiff; I lowered myself to press it against her crotch. Our kisses were fraught and hungry; we left trails of saliva on one another's faces, in each other's mouths. She wound her hips in circles, the itch rising in her cunt.

I pushed her backwards, against the wall, away from the gap and out of possible sight. She said nothing and looked at me with big open eyes. I undid the last buttons; the dress slipped from her shoulders and fell about her feet. I crouched down, held her ankle and lifted her foot out of it. I did the same with the other as she watched, motionless – like a child, being undressed for bed. Folding her dress neatly, I placed it carefully to one side. I looked up at her fat breasts, her nipples dark and swollen. When I kissed her belly, she stiffened expectantly, breathing slow and heavy. I hooked my finger in her G-string and pulled it down; I lifted her feet out of it, and tossed it onto her dress, lying on the ground nearby. Her pussy had only a sliver of soft black hair. I pressed my nose between her thighs; the stink of her cunt was rich and heavy.

I stood up and put my hand between her legs. Looking into her eyes, I slowly fingered her. We kissed, and she grabbed at my erection; I opened my fly and she pulled it out of my jeans. We stood there for an age, kissing and masturbating one another. I felt a glimmer in my loins. I didn't want to come; I lifted her hand from my cock and kissed her palm, then her fingertips. I looked down at her big tits, swaying with each breath; my cock throbbed with blood. I knelt down, facing her breasts; breathing deeply, almost from my guts, I grasped them in each hand and squeezed them hard. I sucked her tits greedily, taking her nipples deep into my mouth, as deep as I could: I'd wanted to suck them for so long.

'*Take it easy, baby*,' she gasped. '*It hurts.*'

I relaxed my grip and continued sucking her tits; she held my head close, and stroked my hair.

'*Come on . . .*' she urged, '*. . . fuck me.*'

I stood up again; I thought of fucking her against the wall, but our difference in height made this awkward. We weren't shaded where we stood; the ground beneath us was hard and dry.

'Get on the floor,' I said.

We sat down together and kissed again; I ran my hands over her warm, brown skin. She unbuttoned my shirt and pulled it off; she stroked my shoulders and kissed my chest. I kicked off my shoes and pulled off my trousers. She bent forward and began sucking my cock. I lay down flat, pleasure coursing through me.

'Sit on my face.'

Straddling me, she sucked my cock slow and deep, her mouth as tight as possible. I winced, my limbs tautened; it was too good to bear. She ground her cunt against me while I sucked her clit. Grabbing her fat buttocks, pushing my face into them, I sucked her smooth, clean arsehole. '*Oh God . . .*' she moaned, raising her head. She sat up, grinding herself on me, jerking me off while I tongued her.

I started to come again; I pushed her off me. 'Let's fuck,' I said, rolling her onto her back. Kneeling between her legs, I lifted her calves to pull off her sneakers. I kissed the soles of her feet and sucked her toes; she giggled, watching me. I pushed her ankles back; her limbs were supple and pliant, her knees came to meet her chest. Pressing her legs against her body, I looked at her cunt; I leant down to suck it once more, leaving daubs of saliva. Slowly, I slid my erection back and forth between her wet labia and over her clitoris. She closed her eyes, sighed and smiled, turning her head to one side. I shoved my cock in; she gasped, eyes wide open, and gripped my forearms. I lay down on her, fucking her deep and hard, her ankles on my shoulders. Cheeks reddening, she grimaced, knotting her brow, and stared into my eyes. Her pussy was sweet and hot; I slowed down to enjoy it, fucking her with a strong, steady rhythm. My breath deepened; beads of sweat dripped from my temple onto her face. One fell in her eye, stinging her, making her squint. I felt myself coming; my groin crashing against hers, I fucked as hard as I could, wanting to come deep inside. My balls emptied; my anus dilated, my head lighter than air. My ejaculation sparked her; her moan was guttural, obscene. I kept on fucking her; the sensation was now acute and excruciating. She finished coming; the tension left her brow, her mouth eased into a smile. I slumped on top of her, panting, and kissed her damp forehead. She slipped her legs around my waist, winding her hips. My cock, still inside her, was hard and aching.

'*Jesus Christ . . .*' I sighed.

She giggled.

We stared into one another's faces in silence. She wiped away the sweat rolling down my cheek, and kissed my jaw. '*You're beautiful,*' she whispered. She closed her eyes and hugged me, her face pressed into my chest; sliding her hands over my back, she held my buttocks and pulled me into her. My eyes wide open, I was still out of breath, breathing heavily. I tried to take stock of what had happened; there was no happiness in me, only exhaustion and bewilderment. I had a sudden sense of emptiness, of inevitable looming sorrow. I was scared. A tear came to my eye; I held her close, letting it drain into her hair. Feeling her fingers on my skin, the warmth of her body, I relaxed into her arms; my limbs were tired and heavy. I shut my eyes, trying to forget my fears, and was asleep within seconds.

I woke up feeling cold, a breeze chilling the sweat on my skin. I was alone. The sun was visible through the

cracks in the canopy above me; I could hear the twit-
ter and rustle of birds moving through the leaves. I was
still tired, and my body felt stiff. That fuck had left me
wasted. I sat up; my skin was covered in dirt and twigs
from the forest floor. There was no sign of Stan or
Sarupa. The pile of her clothes had disappeared. It was
now nearly one o'clock; I'd been asleep for maybe an
hour. My head was foggy and unfocused; I didn't know
what to make of finding myself alone. I was hollowed,
disappointed but unsurprised; on some level, I'd
expected it. I'd shot my load, but there was no relief;
it had deepened my sadness, pulled it to the core of me.
I sat there, naked and cross-legged on the hard, dusty
ground, listless and unable to think. I picked up hand-
fuls of dust and dried grass and watched them drift on
the breeze as they sprinkled through my fingers. Nothing
had been resolved; things were as bleak and complicated
as ever.

I sat there for a while, not caring about what the others
back at the house might think about my absence. The
thought of seeing them, the thought of talking to people
and having to muster a semblance of interest in them,
exhausted me. Slowly, I brushed my skin clean, picked up
my clothes, and got dressed. I wandered into the woods
and found the path back to Sarupa's house.

The house came into view as I emerged from the trees.
I trudged across the field towards it, taking my time, not
wanting to get there. It was now extremely bright and
hot; merely walking made me sweat profusely, my shirt
clung to my skin. I realised I'd arrive at the house looking like shit, my clothes damp and dusty; I probably stank
too.

I opened the gate and walked into the garden; at the
far end of the lawn were Ghislaine and her baby. Olivia
lay on a blanket on the ground; Ghislaine knelt over
her, tickling her belly. She didn't notice me, so absorbed
was she in her daughter. They were sharing an intimate,
unspoilt moment; I could hear Olivia's squeals and

laughter. I stopped to watch and listen. Ghislaine's voice was soft and easy; I hadn't heard it like that before. Calm and filled with love, it captivated me. I realised I might one day want to hear a voice like that, speaking to a child of my own. I wanted something beautiful and true, something I could sacrifice my life for, make me forget about myself. I gazed at Olivia; she was so tiny, vulnerable and blameless. My heart ached looking at her.

I walked quietly to the house, making sure I didn't disturb them. Through the window, I could see Ash and Sophie speaking to one another in the kitchen; I sneaked past them, and past the lounge, in which Duncan sat chatting with Cecily and Ruth. The window into the vestibule at the back of the house was open; I climbed through it and headed upstairs to the bedroom. The bed hadn't been made; Sophie's clothes were spread all over it. As usual, she'd made a huge mess getting ready; she made such a big deal out of what she wore. I went to the bathroom and took a shower.

I changed into some fresh clothes and went back downstairs. In the lounge, Cecily and Ruth were sat either side of Duncan on the aubergine couch. He was already stoned; he gave me a wave and a happy, witless smile.

'How's it going?' he drawled.

I was about to reply, but he didn't seem interested; he was preoccupied with rolling a joint. He didn't ask me where I'd been, or anything about Sarupa. He was a pretty dumb, incurious kind of guy. The two girls were in bathing suits, ready for another bout in the pool; they were chatty and pleased to see me.

'What have you been up to?' said Cecily. 'We've not seen you all day.'

'Not a lot.' I couldn't look her in the face and found it difficult to speak. 'I took a long walk.' I wanted to get away from them, but didn't know where to go. If I went to the kitchen, I'd only have to talk to someone else. I sat on one of the chairs and made idle conversation. I couldn't help stealing glances at Duncan; he fascinated me. What did Sarupa see in him? He was odd-looking and uncharismatic, unremarkable in every way. I was sure he was dull in bed, thoroughly mediocre. I thought of him enjoying her body, and felt a rising hatred. The thought of his stubby white prick inside her made me sick. A jerk like him had no right to be anywhere near her. I watched him fumbling with his joint and wanted to punch him, feel his jaw crack against my fist.

The door opened; Sarupa came marching into the room. She was wearing jeans and a white silk top; she was checking the contents of her handbag and didn't see me sitting on the chair. She walked over to Duncan and kissed his cheek.

'I'm going now,' she said, ruffling his hair. 'I'll call you tonight when I'm finished.'

'Okay, babe,' he smiled.

'I hope you feel sorry for me,' she said, 'having to go into the office on my weekend. I work too hard for those wankers.'

'You do,' he nodded. He made a glum, childlike face for her, guaranteed to infuriate me if I was in want of sympathy.

She leant down to kiss Cecily and Ruth. 'Enjoy the rest of your weekend, won't you?'

'What a shame you have to leave early,' said Cecily. 'Do you want a hand with your bags? We're on our way to the pool.'

'Thanks. They're by the door.'

'I'll get them,' I said, standing up.

She turned around and stared at me; she was startled, dumbstruck.

I gestured to Cecily and Ruth to stay put. 'You guys stay there. Allow me.'

'Thank you,' she said, staring into her handbag. 'That's very gallant.'

'Lead the way.'

Sarupa turned and said goodbye to Duncan and the

204

girls again, then walked towards the door. I followed her into the corridor, picked up her bags and went into the kitchen. Ash and Sophie were no longer there; I could hear their voices coming from the direction of the other lounge.

I walked beside her through the courtyard. 'Why are you running away?'

She didn't reply, just stared directly ahead at the shed where her car was parked.

'What did you tell them?'

'I said I had to take a conference call back at the office,' she said. 'I said it was an emergency, and no one else was around to take it.'

'And they bought that?'

'Yeah. It wouldn't be the first time I've gone in at the weekend.'

We got to the shed, a high, spacious building, originally built for horses or cattle. Inside, thick, dark beams of wood stretched across the ceiling; at the back was a hayloft, with a tall wooden ladder leaning against the platform. Her BMW was parked at one end of a row of cars, the Mini Cooper was at the other; Ash's soft top Audi TT and Ghislaine's Volvo estate were sandwiched in-between. Sarupa pressed a button on her key and the boot of her car popped open; I laid the bags inside and closed it. It was parked near the wall of the shed; we stood at the driver's side, unseen to anyone passing the half-open door. We held hands and looked at one another. I didn't know what to say; neither, I guess, did she. Her hair, washed again, was soft, bouncing lightly on her shoulders; her brown eyes and dark skin glowed. I touched her cheek; I took her in my arms, and we held each other silently. I sank my face into her hair and pulled her close, feeling the heat of her body seeping into mine.

'*I love you so much* . . .' I sighed.

Folding her arms tightly around me, she raised her face and kissed me. Her lips lingered against mine. She slipped a hand inside my jeans and held my buttock. 'I'll call you in a couple of days,' she said. She rubbed the tip of her nose against my chin, and smiled. She let me go and opened the car door; I held it for her as she got inside. I pushed open the door of the shed and watched as she started the ignition and backed out; she looked at me as she turned the car around to face the gates. They opened automatically; she drove through them and out of sight. I stood there stock-still, hopeful and elated. Something wonderful, I was sure, was about to happen. Despite what life had taught me, I let that feeling overwhelm me. I walked back to the house, trying not to smile too broadly.

IO

THE DRIVE BACK from the airport was difficult. The rush-hour traffic was gruelling, and Sophie wouldn't stop talking. She was excited; she'd spent the last fortnight hanging out with her father and getting to know her new step-mother – a thirty-year-old, Japanese-American interior designer. Hired to revamp his Manhattan loft apartment, she got a whiff of the old boy's dough and then worked herself under his skin; they'd been married now for nearly a year.

'She's *so* brilliant,' wittered Sophie. 'Everything she does is totally feng shui. You should see Dad's place . . . Just being there balances your energies. I feel completely harmonised now.'

I looked through the windscreen at the traffic, slowly snaking its way ahead. 'How was your flight?' I asked, wanting to change the subject.

'It was okay. I made Dad buy me a business-class return. I won't risk buying an upgrade on the day, in case I get landed in economy.' She shuddered at the thought, then went back to talking about Mika.

I imagined the marriage clearly: an old white man and his young, highly passive-aggressive oriental wife. She probably wangled herself whatever she wanted; in return she'd look good and provide fellatio. That, no doubt, was the sum of their sex life; his heart wouldn't take much more, and she was probably frigid. Women who like getting fucked don't marry old men. I wanted to explore these issues with Sophie, but she was busy singing their praises. She'd got on well with her new mum; they were both self-improvement enthusiasts, and exchanged books and life-affirming anecdotes. The last two weeks, said Sophie, had been a great opportunity to shop and 'do a lot of work on myself'. Whatever the fuck that meant was anyone's guess. Sophie had returned inspired and ebullient; she was irritating the shit out of me. She kept reading me passages she'd underlined in a book Mika gave her, *Happiness Is Free, and It's Easier Than You Think!*. I looked at the title and wished to God it was, humming tunes in my head to make sure I didn't hear a word.

We came to a standstill in a traffic jam; I picked up my cigarettes, gave one to Sophie and then lit myself one. With nothing else to do, I couldn't help but listen to her.

'I've got a whole new take on things,' she said. 'I'm going to change my life, take an entirely new direction.'

'How's that?'

'I'm going to be a healer.'

'Oh yeah?'

'I've got the gift. I'm very intuitive, Mika said so. She's really tuned into people's energy, and she says I'm the same. I can read their auras. So I've decided that's my path, healing people, and I'm going to follow it.'

'How are you going to do that?'

'Essential oils . . . or maybe crystals.' She toyed with a translucent blue stone, hanging from her neck. 'I got this downtown. I don't know what it is, but I know it's special. Mika thinks I've got a feel for these things. I've brought some books back with me.'

I sighed quietly. I'd enjoyed having the flat to myself, spending my evenings alone and in silence. I'd always wanted to live alone, but never been able to afford it. Now Sophie was back, I had to be a nanny once more. I couldn't do it for long.

'Life's about decisions,' she said, leafing through her book. 'You have to choose to be happy. Happiness is basically a choice.'

I looked at her thin white face, at the customised Balenciaga T-shirt she'd picked up in the East Village along with a new handbag. 'It's not a choice,' I said. 'For people like you, sweetheart, it's an obligation.'

The comment passed over her; she continued staring into her book. 'I'm going to be twenty-five soon,' she said. 'I'm not a kid anymore. People can't arse around for ever, can they? You can't just drift along, without any meaning.'

The traffic started moving; I shifted the gearstick and eased my foot off the brake. 'No,' I replied. 'I can't.'

I dropped her home and drove immediately to Ladbroke Grove; Luca was performing at a party there later that night. I hadn't told Sophie I was going to a club; I didn't want her coming with me. I parked several roads away, then walked down the high street. It was almost ten o'clock, but it was still light. The street was busy, but unhurried, as people ambled about their evening business.

I went into an off-licence to buy cigarettes. Ahead of me in the queue were a pair of meaty-faced, white-trash heifers; their fake-blonde hair curled and lacquered, they wore tracksuits and huge, gold-plated sovereign rings. Their frames were burly, their plastic nails long and deadly. Their children were amazing: a gorgeous, brown-skinned trio – two boys and a girl – aged between five and eight. They chased each other down an aisle while their mothers chatted, waiting to be served. Their bodies were lean and their eyes bright; their skins gleamed, their loose black curls seemed soft as down. The magic of miscegenation: genes alchemised by a slap of the tar brush, even the ugliest honky can have enchanting offspring. This, I thought, is why white women go out of their way to have mixed-race babies, especially the poorest. If you've got fuck all, having beautiful kids is a great way to feel less shit about yourself.

I paid for the cigarettes and made my way downhill, towards the club where Luca was performing. Michael, Rory and Shamir would be there too. We were having a boys' night out, of sorts. At the door, the bouncer checked my name against the guest list and let me in. I spotted Rory and Shamir and went over to them. Rory wore a tight white T-shirt over his tubby frame, and a pair of denim hipsters. He'd changed his hairstyle; he'd worn a sort of ginger mop before, and now he had a Beckham-style mohawk.

I sat down with them. 'Looking good,' I smiled.

'Thanks!' said Rory. He started a speech about what made him change his hair, but the music was too loud to hear it. Shamir sat between us, nodding to the rhythm.

The party was being held by Luca's record label to showcase the talent on its books. One act it was hoping to break in the UK was KinQ – pronounced 'kink' – an openly gay gangsta-rapper who was big in Los Angeles underground clubs. Rory and Shamir were fans, so I invited them along. Posters for his forthcoming album, *Watch Yo' Ass*, were plastered over the walls. Behind the DJ's booth was a huge screen, showing the video of his debut single, 'Pussy Ain't Shit 2 Me'. Overlaying the music from Gloria Gaynor's 1979 dance classic, 'I Will Survive', his voice blared from the speakers, making it impossible to hear much else:

> *Puuusseeey!*
> *Ain't shit to me!*
> *Dat's right baby, pussy just ain't shit to me.*
> *I got too much life to live . . .*

It was a catchy tune, and its sentiments were clear; KinQ sought to present a new, muscular and assertive queer identity. He was a brawny, swarthy Latino, with dollar signs embossed on his gold teeth; the video showed him turning his nose up at curvaceous, bikini-clad women, choosing to take a foaming bubble bath with two svelte, gamine young men instead. He snarled at the camera and growled his lyrics; one boy soaped his chest, while the other sucked wantonly on the barrel of an assault rifle KinQ pointed in his mouth. KinQ was from the mean streets of South Central LA; he was no sissy. The same couldn't be said of the pansies mincing to him on the dance floor. The club was full of faggamuffins and homey-sexuals – gay men who appropriate the dress, attitude and vernacular of reggae and hip hop – who moved daintily to the music, while trying to seem sour-faced and macho. It was inevitable that gay culture should fuse with that of rap music; they had so much in common: licentiousness, conspicuous consumption, misogyny and body fascism. KinQ had got there first; he was going to be a star.

Michael was on the dance floor, too, trying to ignore the dinge queens who kept bumping into him, wanting to make contact. He was dancing with a tall, dark-haired white woman, Carla; she was a partner in the dealership that sold Evie's art. He'd been fucking her for a while. The fairies were giving him a hard time; they jostled around him, knocking him off balance and trying to pretend it was accidental. He was driving them wild; they were desperate to be near him. He was handsome, deeply masculine, and a resolute heterosexual: what more could a fag want? The love homos have for straight guys is the love that dares not speak its name. Like any other girl, the homosexual longs for a *real man*. I looked at Rory and Shamir sitting beside me, sipping cocktails and sizing up the trade: if I only gave the nod, they would've eaten me alive.

Michael and I got to know Rory around three years ago. I then worked for *UK Asian*, a flimsy, stupid weekly paper aimed at 'second-generation British Asians'; I was its entertainment correspondent. Michael was the deputy editor of the *Afro-Caribbean Monitor*, a more politicised publication, with an equally low circulation. Both newspapers belonged to Ethnic News Ltd, owned by a sly Punjabi bastard called Jagdev Mehti. He'd recognised the commercial possibilities offered by a bourgeois, liberal New Labour government, and the fallout to come from the inquiry into the murder of Stephen Lawrence.

211

Quasi-positive discrimination was one obvious sop to quell the ensuing rage, and the jobs the state would provide had to be advertised somewhere. He started *UK Asian* from scratch, and bought the *Monitor* for next to nothing; it was then at near-bankruptcy. When the surge of guilt finally came, after twenty years of Thatcherite repression, Jagdev was onto a winner; he had a guaranteed piece of the action. His two shitty papers turned over a fortune, as local authorities, the NHS, the police and every other public body advertised for ethnic-minority candidates in the medium they considered most apposite – the ethnic press. In his turn, Jagdev paid his staff a pittance and sold his company to the first buyer that came along. That was Magnus Pryke Holdings, a conglomerate that owned regional and niche publications throughout the country. Its chairman and CEO was Magnus Pryke, a tyrant and former RAF officer; the executive charged with overseeing the new acquisition was twenty-six-year-old Rory Magnus Pryke, his fat and cowed, closet-homosexual son.

For Rory, the job was a dream come true; it was a chance to live and work in London, without upsetting his father. The company's HQ was in Norwich; in London, Rory was left pretty much alone – the first real independence he'd ever had. His office was on the top floor of our building in Bethnal Green, and his job was a no-brainer; the public sector just kept on advertising. Jagdev stayed on board as the executive editor, and took Rory to lunch in Brick Lane almost every day. Other staff sometimes joined them, including me.

Rory fell in love with the area and went native; he learnt how to pronounce his favourite dishes, and bought a Talvin Singh CD. He'd hang around my desk, asking questions about the Asian music scene. There was a lot of 'fusion' stuff around, mixing Indian and Western dance music; I got sent albums and lent them to him. DJs were playing it in Hoxton and at bars in Brick Lane; Michael and I would take Rory there for a beer after work. Rory was having his eyes opened; he was on his own in the big city, hanging out with a couple of spooks – it was the coolest time of his life. He got pretty attached to me; I'd broadened his horizons.

He was, to me, obviously gay. He had a tendency to dramatise, and a taste for Bollywood films and other high camp. People are blinkered; no one else at work picked up on it, and his family didn't know. I liked having him around; he made a change from everyone else in the office. My other colleagues, all black and Asian, had a typical, immigrant, one-strike-and-you're-out mentality. They were desperately ambitious and terrified of failure. They didn't treat their work with the contempt it deserved; they were sure it was a stepping stone to something better, bolstering their applications for training programmes with the BBC or the *Sunday Times*. None of the staff was particularly well educated; anyone who was didn't stay long. The stories we produced were boring, humourless and sloppy; the average immigrant's complete ignorance of libel law meant we got sued far less than we deserved.

I had to produce sycophantic reviews of Bollywood films and bhangra boy bands; most of the stuff was too shit to endure and, as usual, I simply rewrote the press releases, not having watched or heard a thing. Bollywood films stupefied me; the scripts were inane, the acting almost pantomime. They were redeemed, however, by the extraordinary beauty of the actresses and the songs which, ingeniously layered and exquisitely sung, would excite a lurking sense of *Indianness* in me. Now and then I went to bhangra clubs; sometimes Michael or Rory came with me. It was fascinating to watch modern youth seek the peasant ecstasies of their forefathers: young Sikhs drinking themselves mad, dancing in a fury to the visceral rhythms of the Punjab. A lot of the songs were about what a great place Punjab was, and what a lucky son of a bitch you were to be a Punjabi. The chauvinist atmosphere induced male stand-offs; they'd circle each other in packs, pushing out chests and making threats. It rarely got violent; dentistry courses had to be studied, and businesses managed, come Monday morning. The girls were always hot; wearing dazzling variations on traditional dress and long, henna-tinted feather cuts, they did seductive dances taken from R&B videos.

At Ethnic News Ltd, the discourse of race was constant to working life. Being repressed and deeply patriarchal, Asian men often find the casual flirtatiousness of the black male problematic – especially when directed at 'their' women. The ones in the office got jittery whenever a sweet-looking princess started talking to some guy from the *Monitor*. Often I got Michael to flirt with a girl one of the Asian guys had a crush on; I'd sit back and enjoy his squirms as she tossed her hair and giggled at Michael's jokes. Those girls loved the attention, and led everyone a merry dance: Asian chicks tease cock better than anybody. I didn't hit on them myself; I saw the headache they held in store. A man could slaver over one for months, without a sniff of pussy; then, out of the blue, she'd be engaged to some dickless geek her parents had fixed her up with. Beautiful as they are (in my eyes, more beautiful than anyone), Asian women will forgo the fripperies of life – laughter, orgasms and excitement – for dreary, concrete certainty, just as their mothers have for centuries.

At the time, I was seeing a black girl, Marcia. I've always loved black women; they're more open than Asian girls, less whorish than white ones. She was a website designer; she was a few years older than me, and lived in Stockwell. We'd met one Saturday night at the Electricity Showroom in Shoreditch; Michael had tried his luck first, and got nowhere. She liked my quietness and girly-boy features; her five-year lesbian relationship had just ended, and she was looking for something casual. She had glossy skin, a juicy fat bubble-butt, and she always smelt of coconut. We had a good thing: she'd call me up whenever she was at a loose end; if I was free, I'd head to her flat and spend the day fooling around. She was a great girl; she taught me how to eat pussy, and what to look for when having sex, spotting the signals and making the right move. Dykes don't fuck around; if they're hooking up with a man, he has to know what he's doing. We never had the threesome I'd been hoping for, but it was fun while it lasted.

Rory was working stuff out, too; he was sneakily getting himself laid, and figuring out the scene. He started to dress a lot cooler; he discarded his nerdy pinstripes in favour of suits by Richard James, sometimes Roberto Cavalli. Something was definitely going on; he seemed more relaxed and happier by the day.

One evening Rory and I were working late, the only people left in the office. As we often did on such occasions, we took a break to have a beer and smoke some dope in the car park. We were in the shadows at the back of the building, out of sight of the security cameras. I rolled the joint, while Rory went to the off-licence. He returned with a couple of cans, and we stood together in the darkness, gently getting high and gossiping about co-workers. I'd scored some good weed; there hadn't been much of it around for a while, and this was a real treat. From the corner of my eye, I could see Rory watching me. I noticed some sort of quick, blurry movement, and turned to look at him. Staring into my eyes, he was pumping his erect penis with his right hand.

'*Feel how hard it is*,' he gasped.

'Don't be fucking stupid.' I looked at his stiff white prick, its head red and bulging; it was the most revolting thing I'd ever seen. 'Put that away.'

Rory stopped instantly, tucked his cock inside his pants and zipped himself up. He looked devastated, lost for words, and gazed plaintively at my face. 'You . . . won't tell anyone . . . will you?'

I took a long drag, watching his terror and weighing my options. 'Don't worry.' I handed him the joint, and patted his elbow. 'It's no big deal.'

From then on, our relationship really took off; Rory thought of me as a true confidant and ally. It took guts to do what he did; he'd fancied me for ages. I'd helped him cross a Rubicon in his sexuality, and this bonded us. I was happy to help him out. He was an okay kind of guy, and held regular parties at his fabulous apartment in the Riverside One building, overlooking the Thames by Battersea Bridge. He was the kind of guy I like to keep around. His father was a powerful man; one day, Rory might become one too. I was looking forward to having some strings pulled.

I sat back in my seat, smoking a cigarette and looking at my friends: Rory slow-danced with Shamir, their hands on one another's hips; Michael pressed Carla against the wall of the club, kissing her; Luca was now in the DJ's booth, playing records from his debut album, *Share My Joy*. Life had certainly moved on in the years I'd known them. To where, I had no idea.

Michael, Shamir and I were among the few darkies there that night; other than sexual difference, it wasn't a very mixed crowd. I watched the white girls on the dance floor, swirling their hair, waving their arms and strutting back and forth; they were having a whale of a time. I like the way white chicks dance: black and Asian women, coming from cultures of the drum, can be too concerned with their performance and somewhat restrained. White girls let themselves go; they pop a few pills, and the music takes them where it will. Ecstasy brings out the best in them; they surrender, childlike, to the experience, limbs loose and free, faces glowing with joy. It's the same when you fuck them. I searched my pockets for the tablets Rory had given me earlier. I washed them down with my beer and settled back, waiting for the effect. I was out to get myself laid, to help me cope: Sophie was now home, and boring me already. In a little while the pills would do their trick, and I'd move around the dance floor, looking for that big smile that says, 'You're cute!'

I'd had a bad few weeks and had been feeling like shit. I hadn't seen Sarupa since we were together in the

Cotswolds. She'd gone stone cold on me. Having promised to call me, I heard nothing from her the following week. I emailed her, and got no reply. The same happened when I stole her number from Sophie's phone and sent her a text. Whenever I tried to call her at work the receptionist tried the line, and then told me she was unavailable – instructed by Sarupa, of course. I seriously thought of waiting for her outside her office, confronting her and asking why she was being like this – but I'm not the stalking kind. I was at a complete loss. I was gutted, and left dangling.

She was, I realised, just another uptight Asian diva. She hadn't the courage to follow what her cunt was telling her, and would stick with her dopey white boy instead. It made sense: she had a lot of money, and so did he; the rich like to keep it to themselves. I'd spent the last few weeks drinking too much and thinking of what a chump I was. But tonight I stopped feeling sorry for myself: I was on the make again.

Michael came over to my table; he'd left Carla talking to an acquaintance of hers. Carla was mutton expensively dressed as lamb: she wore narrow, cropped tweed trousers and silver Prada sneakers; her short off-the-shoulder top exposed her gym-hardened torso. She was fortysomething and wrinkled around the mouth; her hair was dyed black and she kept adjusting the thick rims of her sunglasses, presumably to hide the lines around her eyes. Well connected in the art world, she was tuned into the zeitgeist and had already furthered Michael's career. She had secured him a commission for a sculpture: *Wage Slave* consisted of a clear Perspex box, in which someone sat for eight hours a day, pushing a pen from one side of a desk to the other and shuffling piles of blank paper. Michael would hire the individual through a high street employment agency, paying the appropriate fee; he or she would have exactly those rights pertaining to matters such as health and safety, lunch and toilet breaks, as prescribed by UK employment law. Michael was a new and dynamic force in British art.

He took a swig of my beer and sat down next to me.

'How's it going?' I said.

'Okay.'

'Is she having a good time?' I nodded at Carla.

He glanced at her and frowned. 'Who cares?'

'What's she like?'

Michael sighed ruefully. 'She's a maniac.' He looked at her and shook his head. 'Wants it in the arse the whole time.'

'Yeah?'

'It's freaking me out.'

I nodded.

'You ever got into that?'

'Not really.' I shook my head. 'Getting shit all over your cock . . . not a good look.'

'Ah . . .' Michael narrowed his eyes and leant closer to me. 'The chicks you've been dealing with are just rookies. You see this cunt . . .' He looked up at Carla once more. 'She's been around the fucking block. She gives herself an enema before she goes out. Her pipe's as clean as a whistle.'

I looked at him with raised eyebrows.

'Faggots do it all the time,' he said, gesturing to the homosexuals around us. 'It's a tip she picked up from them.'

'What's your problem then?'

'It's fucked up, that's what.' He took another gulp of my beer, and sat back shaking his head. 'It can't be good for you, getting ploughed out like that. Fucking idiot's going to do herself a mischief.'

'Listen,' I said. 'The anus is the locus of the Western experience. That's where stuff happens for white people. De Sade, Freud, Foucault, they knew what the deal is with the anus.' I looked at Carla: tall and thin, her movements were reserved and elegant. 'She looks like a clever woman.'

'She is,' said Michael. 'She's made some smart moves for me. She's got great ideas.'

'There you go. She's a bourgeois intellectual, they need that crap more than most.' I took my beer from his hand and took a sip myself. 'Crackers aren't like us. Their culture is all about abstraction and rational inquiry. They get so lost in their heads, they only come into themselves when something's being stuck in their behind. Stimulating that base chakra pulls them back into reality.' I picked up my Marlboros from the table and gave one to Michael. 'Our people are innately simple,' I said, lighting our cigarettes. 'We're creatures of the sun. We like to take things easy and not make a fuss. They're the ones who built boats and went exploring the world, discovering stuff. We didn't give a shit about what was out there. We were happy moseying along, beating our women and eating each other.' I exhaled smoke and reclined in my chair, watching Carla chat to her friend. 'Negotiating our differences with these people is a trip. It always will be. But it's funny. It gives us something to talk and laugh about.'

Michael swallowed the last of my beer, and nodded solemnly: 'You've got these creeps worked out.'

Shamir and Rory walked over to our table, holding hands.

'Hello, ladies.' I smiled and moved my chair to create some extra space for them at the table. I could feel a tingling in my guts; I wasn't sure if it was the drugs already working, or just a placebo effect. I felt light-headed and carefree; I was glad I'd come out tonight. I watched the girls on the dance floor moving with abandon; they were seriously loaded. I spotted a dark blonde with J-Lo highlights and a deep tan; she looked liked she'd been on holiday – probably to Faliraki or Ayia Napa. She had that easy, good-time look about her; arms aloft, she snaked her body beautifully to the music, looking me squarely in the eyes. I gave her a smile, which she returned. I nodded, and she turned away into the crowd of dancers. She'd set her stall out; I'd catch up with her later.

Shamir leant towards me: 'Have you heard from your friend Sarupa lately?' he said.

'No.' I shook my head. The mention of her name stirred no pain; in fact, I felt mildly elated – the pills had definitely kicked in. 'Why do you ask?'

'She's been chewing my ear off all week.'

'How come?' I swayed to the record Luca played, the MDMA in my blood synchronising with its beat.

'I'm helping her put on a fund-raising breakfast this week, at one of my restaurants. She's been such a fucking pain about it.'

'Why is she raising funds?'

'It's this Indravest thing she runs,' he said. 'They want to raise their profile and get more backing. There'll be lots of interesting people there, so it'll be great for the restaurant. We'll get a lot of exposure with the right sort of people. But Sarupa . . . God, what a ball-breaker! I've never worked with anyone so precious. She's been hassling me on the phone every fucking day.' He looked at me, brow furrowed and indignant. 'I'm not working with her again. What a bitch!'

'Fuck her,' I said. 'She's full of shit.'

Shamir put his arm around my shoulder; spaced out on drugs, he was being very tactile. Rory's pills were great, so I was open to his presence. 'Say,' he said, 'why don't you come along? It's on Thursday morning. The food, I assure you, will be amazing.' He put his hand on my forearm. I turned to look at him; his sneaky, narrow eyes were flitting over my face. The silly poof was going to hit on me. I glanced past his head at Rory, who stared into the dance floor, trying to ignore us. They doubtless fucked around on each other all the time, even hunted as a pair. Rory didn't seem bothered; he knew Shamir didn't stand a chance.

'Yeah,' I said. 'I might head down there. Which restaurant is it at?'

'Cuisine Kashmir.' He continued ogling me. 'Do come. It's a fantastic place, and it's going to be huge. I'll make sure you're taken care of.' He slipped his hand inside my sleeve and stroked my wrist; his touch was coarse and cold. 'There's going to be a lot of media people there. Editors and people from TV. You'll make good contacts.'

I looked at him and wanted to laugh; my restrained smirk nonetheless became a smile, which only encouraged him.

'You've got such lovely skin.' He touched my cheek. 'What do you use on it?'

'Whatever Sophie has in the bathroom.' I leant forward for my cigarettes without disturbing Shamir's attempted seduction. His technique intrigued me – it was so banal and unexciting – as did his hubris. Fairies epitomise the inanity of the male condition; through them, I've realised why chicks think so little of us. It's only a Darwinian imperative that makes women fuck us; why men would do the same, I've never really understood.

'Thursday morning?' I said, putting a cigarette in my mouth. 'I can do that.'

'Please do.' He kissed the side of my face; his lips were wet. 'It'll be lovely to see you there.'

I had to get away from him. The ecstasy had detonated, and I now wanted to dance. I scanned the floor for the girl with the J-Lo highlights. She stood watching us and smiling – she knew what was going on. I raised my brows at her, rolling my eyes, and she laughed. I stood up, patting Shamir on the shoulder and giving him a wink: 'I'll chat to you later,' I said, and headed to the dance floor. The blonde watched me walk towards her; dressed in a cream camisole and denim hot pants, she had open-toed sandals and a silver toe-ring. Her thighs were chunky and her hips broad, but she wore that outfit with a lot of confidence. I stood before her and we started dancing, facing each other. She was sexy, but wasn't the prettiest girl around; her face was wide, her teeth a little crooked. I didn't mind; I wouldn't have to put in too much work.

The weather was great, and I was feeling good. It was around eight in the morning, but the sky was clear and the sun was bright. I hadn't been out and about in town this early for a while. London is beautiful at this time of day, before it clogs with petrol fumes and the angst of ten million people. Driving to Clerkenwell, I enjoyed the magnificent view from London Bridge, the water rippling in the distance beneath me. To my right was Tower Bridge and HMS *Belfast*; peeking from behind the buildings in the distance were St Paul's and the Tower of London. Despite the rush-hour crawl, there was no stress in the air; everyone was hushed by the scale and splendour of this city, on a cool and radiant morning.

Reaching Shamir's restaurant, I drove around the block a few times to check out the cars the other guests arrived in. Indians love high-end Mercedes; I saw several parked on one street. Porsche, Lexus, Bentley and Rolls-Royce were among the other brands on show; some had chauffeurs sitting inside. I found somewhere to park and walked towards Cuisine Kashmir. I didn't feel intimidated – a good dose of fresh pussy can truly lift a man's spirits. The girl with the J-Lo highlights was called Lisa; we'd fucked each other silly in her bedsit, out of our heads on ecstasy and vodka coolers. In the morning, I asked her what my name was. She didn't know; she hadn't asked. What a girl. I was seeing her again that night.

I looked forward to meeting Sarupa. My relaxed, sated manner would show how little our encounter in the Cotswolds had actually meant. Having opened their legs, women then can't bear an offhand manner; she'd probably want me to lay her all over again. Thinking this, I smiled and had a spring in my step. I stopped and looked at myself reflected in a shop window. I was well groomed, wearing a pair of French Connection jeans and a clean, white Gap T-shirt; my sneakers were new, brown suede Adidas Campus. I didn't look the typical business type, but with my Tag Heuer watch and Burberry shades, I could be taken for a young dot-com wizard, or an ad-agency creative. If I kept my mouth shut, I'd have no trouble fitting in.

A brown, tuxedoed young man met me on the front

steps; I showed him my official invitation, and he ushered me inside. It was a beautiful restaurant. Banquettes, upholstered in gleaming black leather, stretched along walls covered in rich, green wallpaper bearing silver Urdu script. The room was huge, its centre cleared of tables, allowing people to mill casually amongst one another. Waiters bearing trays of drinks and breakfast canapés stepped delicately between them. Heels clicked against the cold slate floor; sitar music floated gently over us, playing from speakers hidden from sight. Two waiters walked by and I helped myself to some *masala chai* and a *ladoo*. Shamir's people knew how to cook; I could taste the sweet, brittle dough melt in the spicy tea and slide over my tongue. I stood in the corner, my back against the wall, and watched the hotshots in attendance: Sarupa had thoroughly plundered her father's contact book. I recognised Greg Dyke, Director General of the BBC, standing in a group gathered to one side. Virile and stocky, with a glossy bald head, he was incredibly self-assured, making animated conversation with several attentive Asian men. Greg had called the BBC 'hideously white'; he'd thrown his lot in with the coons and the coolies, and was here to be counted. Two beautiful Indian girls stood adoring Nasser Hussein, the England cricket captain; they couldn't take their eyes off his handsome face and laughed at everything he said. Nearby, Sir Max Hastings, former editor of the *Standard* chatted amiably to Lord Dholakia and Baroness Uddin. I could taste the joy seeping from everyone's pores as they basked in one another's recognition and reflected glory. A slim, sexy, older Indian woman walk past me, tossing her lustrous black hair: it was Ruby Hammer, the cosmetics entrepreneur. I was about to walk alongside her and start a conversation, when I heard a call for quiet.

Sodhilal Shah stood in the middle of the room, tapping his teacup with a spoon, wanting attention. 'Please . . . Everybody . . .' he said slowly. 'Can I please say a few short words?' He continued tapping his cup until there was complete silence. He wore grey, immaculately cut, double-vented pinstripes, a white shirt and a salmon-pink tie; a thick, clunky gold watch shone on his wrist, a gemstone ring sparkled on his forefinger. He had a veneer of refinement, undone by a residual, unshakeable crassness. 'I would like to thank everybody concerned with the organisation of today's breakfast,' he drawled in a heavy Indian accent. 'Thank you very much to Shamir Khan, who provided this wonderful restaurant as the venue.' He gestured to Shamir, who stood in the thick of the crowd, out of view; light applause rippled through the audience. Sodhilal then began a monologue extolling the virtues of the Indravest project; he was keen, he said, to nurture the 'innate genius' of young Asians in Britain, help them ram through glass ceilings and 'make the maximum possible contribution to British life'. I'd heard crap like this before, and searched my pockets for my cigarettes. Everyone else paid full attention; Greg Dyke nodded gravely, eyes focused in earnest consideration.

Looking around, I spotted Sarupa making her way through the crowd towards her father. Dressed in a lawyerly, charcoal suit with a knee-length skirt, she wore prim, flat-soled shoes; her thick, shapely calves were wrapped in sheer black nylon. She looked ashen and tired, her mouth was pursed and her eyes narrow; she seemed a little puffy, like she'd put on a few pounds. She didn't exude the happiness that radiated from everyone else, and stared vacantly ahead, almost oblivious to the proceedings. Her father turned to her, praising her organisation of the event and hard work. She smiled half-heartedly and gazed at the floor. Something was obviously wrong. I lost the desire to be aloof. I wanted to hold her, and ask her what the matter was.

The speech continued for a few minutes more; I didn't really listen to it. Sarupa held my attention; my genuine concern surprised me. Sodhilal's ramblings finally came to an end, and Shamir raised his hand and called for people to take their seats at the breakfast tables. I looked at my invitation to see which table I'd been allocated; I wasn't surprised to find myself seated beside Shamir.

'Hi,' he beamed, holding my shoulder. 'Where on earth have you been? I've been keeping an eye out for you.' He pulled my chair away from the table, and gestured for me to sit down. He was being very suave; he was in effect the maître d' of the event.

'I was hiding away in the background,' I said.

'You shouldn't be doing that.' His smile lingered, as did his hand on my shoulder. 'It's lovely to see you here.' Clean-shaven, wearing blue, Edwardian-style Alexander McQueen pinstripes, and a wide-collared, lilac embroidered shirt, he wanted to promote an avant-garde air – the dapper young Pakistani restaurateur, on the cutting edge of his community. To me, he looked conspicuously homosexual. He was taking a risk, dressed like that; none of his family and associates knew he was gay – I was probably the only one here who did. Subcontinentals can be naive in such matters; the unwitting hints he let slip no doubt passed them by.

He introduced me to his father and younger brother. The old man was quiet, almost indifferent to the prestige of the morning's occasion; a typical North Indian patriarch, he wouldn't allow himself to be moved by his son's success. His brother, Tariq, was a skinny and bespectacled medical student. He was in awe of the coup Shamir had pulled off; celebrities and power brokers were all around, he could barely finish a sentence without glancing up at someone impressive. Figures of all sorts of authority were here: politicians, media players, celebrities and chief executives of corporations, councils and government agencies. Two tables away from us sat Sarupa and her father; to Sodhilal's left sat Patricia Hewitt, the Trade and Industry Secretary. Sarupa seemed removed from the general conversation; my sense that something was amiss grew each time I looked at her.

The breakfast became difficult; the food was good, but I had no appetite. I did my best to be affable with Shamir and the others around me, but had no interest in them. My thoughts kept turning to Sarupa; I found myself stealing occasional glances at her. Somehow, looking vulnerable and unwell, she was more beautiful than ever. I nibbled at a *pakora*, trying to forget her; it was no use, and I didn't try eating anything else.

'Don't tell me you're off your food too,' said Shamir, noticing how little I'd eaten.

'What do you mean?'

'Your friend's not feeling up to much either.' He nodded contemptuously at Sarupa, almost sneering. I felt a pang of hatred for him as he did so. 'She's really acting out of sorts today,' he said. 'She's being very strange.'

'What's wrong with her?'

'God knows. She's been so bloody awful to work with. She's taken issue with everything . . . the decor, the cutlery, the table planning, the food . . . She's been impossible.' He leant closer and lowered his voice. 'Fuck knows why I'm helping her out on this thing. Between you and me, I think she's a fucking junkie.'

I looked at him in dismay.

'I'm not kidding,' he sighed. 'The way she's been behaving. So fucking erratic and pissy about the arrangements. Look at her . . .' He glanced sideways at her. 'She looks like shit. Her face is so *pasty*.' He frowned. 'And she keeps disappearing into the toilets. I've been watching her all morning. She can't sit still for ten minutes. I bet she's done a good few grams today already. Look, there she goes again.'

I glanced up to see her walking towards the bar, to the staircase leading down to the toilets. She held the handrail tight, unsteady on her feet, and gingerly made her way downstairs. I sat fidgeting in my seat: 'I need to use the bathroom too,' I said, and hurried after her.

The toilets were on either side of a small lounge; a deep leather couch was against the wall. I sat on it, taking out my cigarettes. I had a smoke, waiting for her to appear, hoping no one would turn up and interrupt us. My nerves were on edge. I smoked my cigarette apprehensively. The door to the ladies' opened; she emerged ruffling her hair and looking at the floor. I stood up, not knowing what to say; I dropped my unfinished cigarette into the ashtray beside me. She stopped in her tracks on seeing me: until now, she'd not noticed me all morning.

'Hi,' I said.

'Hello.'

We stared at one another; a few seconds passed without a word, and she began walking towards the stairs.

I touched her arm. 'How have you been?'

She stopped and looked at me: 'Okay . . . You?'

'Okay.' I looked into her face. 'You alright? You seem a little off-colour.'

'I'm fine. Just a bit worn out from arranging all this. I've been too busy for my own good.' She looked at the floor. 'I'm surprised to see you. Why are you here?'

'Shamir's a friend of mine.'

'Oh . . .' She raised her eyebrows, mildly interested. 'I hope you enjoy yourself. I'm sure we'll chat again.' She began walking away; I held onto her arm, stopping her.

'Why didn't you call me?'

Her face turned towards the staircase, she sighed, as if too bored or tired to reply. I held her arm a little tighter.

'You completely ignored me . . . Like it was nothing . . . Why did you do that?' I slid my palm down her forearm and held her hand; it was limp and unresponsive. 'Why did you cut me off? What the fuck did I do to deserve that?'

She pulled her hand away from mine and looked me in the eyes. 'What do you think would've happened if I'd called you? That we'd run away together?' Her stare was hard and uncompromising. 'I have a fiancé. I'm getting married. We have plans . . . We have a life.' She sighed again and shook her head. 'Nothing's going to happen between us, Puppy. I didn't want to lead you on.' Her forehead tensed and she closed her eyes, tightening her lips; she seemed nauseous. 'Excuse me,' she said, stepping backwards. 'I have to use the bathroom again.'

227

'Are you sure you're okay?' I wasn't angry, only sad and concerned for her; she'd said nothing I hadn't guessed already. She wobbled a little; I held her elbow and began walking her to the ladies' room. 'What's the matter?' I asked. 'Are you sick?'

'I'm pregnant.'

I stopped and gawped at her.

'Don't worry,' she said, reading the look on my face. 'It's not yours.'

I was about to ask how she knew, but realised what a stupid question that was. I bowed my head and quietly said, 'Congratulations.'

'Thank you.' She stopped at the door. 'We're thinking about bringing the wedding forward,' she said, pushing it open. 'Maybe do it next month. We're going to Mauritius, we might do it there and tell everyone we couldn't wait.' She turned and looked at me. 'I don't know why I've told you all this, it's not really any of your business. We haven't told anyone yet.' Her stare hardened again. 'I'd appreciate it if you kept it to yourself.'

I nodded in compliance, watching her gaze.

Her face softened; she smiled and squeezed my arm. 'Thanks,' she said, and walked into the bathroom.

I stood there for a few seconds, desolated. I stumbled into the men's room and into a cubicle, slumped onto the toilet and sat gazing into space, blank and unthinking. I felt exhausted; my guts were heavy, weighing me into my seat. Eventually I heard myself breathing and came to my senses. I went to the sink and washed my face with cold water. Drying myself with a hand towel, I stared into the mirror, making sure I looked okay, and then went back upstairs.

At the top of the staircase, I saw Sarupa and Shamir standing at the bar; they were bickering, trying to keep their voices low and not draw attention to themselves. They patently despised each other; arranging this event had set them at one another's throats. Sodhilal Shah stood beside his daughter, giving Shamir a hawkish look as she

228

berated and jabbed her finger at him. She said something Shamir found intolerable, and his restraint broke: '*Fuck off!*' he hissed, loud enough for me to hear. '*If you're feeling like shit, you should be at home, not here, giving me a fucking headache!*'

The gloves were off. '*If I'm sick,*' she hissed back, '*It's because of your food . . . You filthy queen!*'

Shamir gasped; the insult was astonishing. 'How dare you!' he squealed, and flounced away in disgust.

'The food made you sick?' asked Sodhilal, putting his arm around Sarupa's shoulder. She didn't reply, and he held her close. They had a short conversation in Gujarati; her voice sounded so different, speaking her parents' tongue – fast, animated and less assured. 'I will get somebody to look at this place,' said Sodhilal, hugging her once more. 'Bastard. Who does he think he is, talking to you like that?' He whispered something calming in her ear, and went back to his table.

I watched her propped against the bar, staring pensively into a cup of coffee, not taking a sip. She caught sight of me, and we looked at each other for a moment; her face expressed nothing, and she turned and walked away. That was the last I saw of her. I left the restaurant, and made my way back to West London.

I'd smoked half a bag of weed, flicking through the music channels on TV. Now that I didn't pay rent, the compulsion to find work or take an interest in things had gone. I had no aim in life. Other than my bitty music reviews, I hadn't written an article for nearly a month; I hadn't pitched any ideas for over a fortnight. Sophie, however, had found purpose: she'd enrolled on a four-month aromatherapy and shiatsu course at a college in Westbourne Park. I'd pretend to be asleep as she got ready in the mornings; when she'd gone, I'd get up and enjoy the empty flat. I'd spend the day getting high and watching junk on television. Sophie didn't mind; she was happy to indulge me. She didn't mind anything I did, as long as I was still around.

She kept the fridge stocked with expensive food – a lot of it from Fresh & Wild and Harvey Nichols – and she left cash on the mantelpiece, in case I wanted to buy or do stuff during the day. She was a nutcase and it frightened me. I'd developed a mild anxiety; I was sure I was getting into a rut I wouldn't escape from. I smoked a lot more weed to calm myself down.

Women cultivate imbecility in men; infantilised by overindulgence, men become dependent on them. This meets two pathological female needs: martyrdom and security. A woman will tolerate a useless slob, if he's predictable and unlikely to leave; that same slob provides copious reasons to complain of the sacrifices she's made, proving her stoicism and moral perfection. This phenomenon is played out every day on daytime TV, on shows like *Trisha*, in which women drag their men on stage ostensibly to remedy their laziness and selfishness. It's bullshit. Those women only seek the misty-eyed empathy and applause of the bovine, self-righteous audience – itself overwhelmingly female. I pondered this as I staggered about the kitchen, heavily stoned, scratching my beard and thinking of what to have as a snack. I'd worn the same jogging pants for a few days now; they'd acquired a range of stains and a strange smell, but they fit so nicely I didn't want to take them off. There had been a notable increase in my waistline in recent weeks, as I nibbled on Gruyère, truffles and Green & Black's butterscotch chocolate; none of my jeans were comfortable anymore. Sophie, of course, remained as thin as a rake. She'd made a gilded cage for me; life here was so easy, I was slipping into lassitude, becoming a sort of pet. She wasn't the brightest girl, but even dumb chicks can outsmart most men.

I spread a big piece of focaccia with a thick layer of tapenade, and took it back to the lounge, along with a bottle of beer and a tub of ice cream. I fell onto the couch, began eating and turned on MTV; I switched back and forth through the channels until I found a song I liked. I was about to try masturbating to a Destiny's Child video when my phone rang. It was Michael.

'What's the deal with your friend?' he asked.

'Who?'

'The Asian gay boy. Rory's boyfriend.'

'What about him?'

'He's a fucking gangster. You never told me.'

'I don't know what you're talking about.'

'He's on TV. On BBC1. The cops are looking for him.'

I put my dick away and changed channels; the lunchtime BBC London news bulletin was on, screening a photograph of Shamir. '*What the fuck* . . .' I gasped. 'Let me call you back,' I said to Michael. 'I have to see this.'

The bulletin changed scene, to a smart, earnest-looking young reporter standing outside Cuisine Kashmir; a police cordon sealed off the pavement around the restaurant. My head was muggy from smoking dope all morning. I had a lot of trouble concentrating on what was being said; for a moment I thought I was hallucinating. The gist of the guy's report was that Shamir was wanted for people-trafficking and heroin-smuggling, running the operation out of one of his smaller restaurants in Shepherd's Bush. Drugs and illegal labour were smuggled from Pakistan, then stored and distributed from a property he owned above the restaurant; some of the people brought in went to work in his kitchens. I was impressed; I didn't think the faggot had it in him. He was a real Al Capone.

The story was kicking up a stink. A lot of bigwigs had been to the Indravest function he'd hosted last month, and were now busy explaining away their association with him. After the Hinduja and Mittal scandals, New Labour had got themselves mixed up with yet another shady Asian business figure; a lackey from Patricia Hewitt's office was in the studio, giving the presenter some spiel dismissing any connection with him. This was big news, made bigger by the fact that Shamir had vanished. He'd eluded the police sting, and was now nowhere to be seen. None of his family were among those arrested; there was no evidence implicating them. No one knew where Shamir was.

I picked up my mobile and phoned Rory. The call went immediately to voicemail; I left a message, saying I hoped he was okay and to call me if he needed any help. I sank into the couch, open-mouthed and dismayed. I changed channels to News 24, keeping it on for the rest of the day in case anything more emerged.

Shamir was on the front page of each edition of that day's *Standard*. The press was loving this; it was a heady brew of its favourite preoccupations: political sleaze, drugs, race and immigration. Once they'd figured out the gay angle, this story would rocket to the moon.

It was almost five in the evening when Rory got back to me; he was calling from a payphone.

'Puppy . . . come over . . .' he panted. 'I have to see you . . . I need your help.'

'Sure,' I said, 'I'll be right there.'

'Straightaway . . . please.' He sounded like he was about to hyperventilate.

I took a cold shower and drank a large cafetière of coffee – I still hadn't woken from my marijuana binge – and left to meet him. The Riverside One building by Battersea Bridge wasn't far away, and I had the Mini Cooper at my disposal; I was there in fifteen minutes. On the way, I got a text from Sophie; it was Friday, and she wanted to know what we were doing that night. I had a thing about North African food, so told her to book a table at Momo and I'd see her there for dinner.

I parked behind the building and walked into the immaculate white foyer. As usual, the guard behind the desk made me tell him which apartment I was visiting, though I'd been there a hundred times before. I got out of the elevator on the sixth floor and walked to Rory's door.

He stank of liquor and didn't look at me when he let me in. Rubbing his temple, he walked back into the lounge, staring down at the yellow, polished wooden floor. I followed him and made myself at home on his sofa – a thin black number from B&B Italia – facing the floor-to-ceiling windows that overlooked the Thames. The windows were open, offering a beautiful view of Chelsea Embankment, Albert Bridge and West London as far as Trellick Tower. It was the second week of September; the summer light had dimmed, the view was balmy and serene.

Rory's father bought the flat as his London residence; it cost over £400,000 – the building was designed by Norman Foster – and now, ten years on, was worth double that. A million doesn't get you much these days; the apartment was small, with only one bedroom and a small, stylish kitchen. But it was somewhere to bring a high-class call girl or a mistress; it didn't need a lot of looking after and was in a great location, with a smart, spacious lounge and a view that held your gaze all evening. I'd seen a lot of sunsets and a few sunrises from here, drinking good red wine and light-hearted on ecstasy.

Rory walked to his drinks trolley and fixed himself a large whisky and soda. His jeans were fashionably faded, and he wore a Dries Van Noten crochet sweater over his paunch; the heels of his black loafers clacked against the hard floor. On the wall behind him was an original Gary Hume; it was a human profile, painted in bold shining colours. It was an exquisite and restrained work of art that somehow stopped short of gaudiness and kitsch. Rory loved modern art and design and had superb taste in these things. He walked back into the centre of the room, staring into his tumbler. He hadn't made me a drink or even offered me one. He stopped and looked at me; narrowing his eyes, he asked, 'What's with the beard?'

I rubbed my bristles; I hadn't shaved for maybe two weeks. 'I'm thinking of taking my Sikhism seriously,' I said, not knowing what to say. 'I need to get back to my roots.'

He stared at me quizzically. 'You're looking quite beefy. Have you been working out?'

'Yes,' I lied, sucking in my gut and adjusting the waist of my jeans. I'd left the top button undone so they'd fit, holding them up with a belt; the buckle was scraping my skin.

'You look good,' he said absent-mindedly. He continued pacing back and forth in front of the open windows; the evening air breezed through them, cooling the room.

I could hear traffic in the distance. I looked past Rory, and stared at the river, its water moving slowly eastwards. Across the Thames was Cheney Walk; I remembered that Duncan had a property there. My thoughts turned to Sarupa. I wondered if she was there now, looking in my direction from an apartment no doubt as lovely as this. 'How are you?' I asked, trying to forget her. 'I saw Shamir on the news. Things look pretty messy.'

'Really fucking messy!' He threw down his tumbler; it exploded, scattering glass and splashing the floor with whisky. He made me jump; I'd seen his hissy fits in the office, but not this sort of anger. 'Why does everything always fuck up for me!' He glared at me in a fury. 'Why, Puppy?!'

'I don't know.' I squirmed in my seat; he was unnerving me.

'Everything was going so well,' he sighed, lowering his head. 'We were in love. We were fucking happy . . . And now it's fucking finished.' He began crying; the sobs came from deep within, he gasped between tears. He stood there crying for a while, his arms hanging uselessly at his sides. He was in bad shape.

I didn't know what to do. I thought of putting my arms around him, but decided not to. I sat awkwardly on the couch instead. 'Have you heard from him?' I asked.

Rory nodded slowly and looked up. 'Yeah. But it's all been very furtive. He's terrified the police are listening in. He's got me scared, too, that's why I called you from a payphone.'

'Do they know about you two?'

'I don't think so.' He shook his head. 'None of the

people involved with this knew about us. He kept every-thing hidden from them.'

'So you weren't in on this thing? The drugs and stuff.'

'God, no!' He looked at me with a sincere face and wide eyes; he was telling the truth. 'I knew fuck all about it. I didn't know a thing until this morning. I found an email he'd sent me last night. Then I switched on the TV and saw him on the news.'

'What did he have to say?'

'In the email? Not a lot. I phoned a call-box number at lunchtime. We had a chat then.' He walked back to the drinks trolley, kicking pieces of glass out of his way, and poured himself another whisky. 'You want anything?' he said, gesturing to the bottles.

'I'll have a vodka and tonic.'

He fixed me a drink and brought it over, then went back to pacing back and forth. 'He'd only been doing it for a couple of years,' he said wearily. 'He was winding things up, he wanted to go completely straight. He only did it to raise capital. He needed start-up money for the new restaurant. He wanted to do something sexy and upmarket.'

'He told you this?'

'Yeah . . . He only ever wanted to make enough money to get the restaurant up and running. He's not a criminal, just an opportunist. Stupid bastard.'

'Drugs and smuggling people. That's heavy shit.'

He nodded, looking at his drink. 'It is. But it's not how it seems. It wasn't dozens of people packed into crates and hidden in lorries. They did it in small groups, every-one was looked after. They drove them in people carriers and put them up in nice places, and they got them here safely. They were educated people with money to spend, not village folk. He wouldn't exploit anyone that way.'

'What about the drugs? How did he get into that?'

'Everyone came from Pakistan. Once in a while he got them to bring some heroin with them.'

Outside it had darkened. The lights on Battersea Bridge

were switched on; the dim headlamps of cars drifted in the distance. I shook my head, amazed by the whole situation. I wondered why I was surprised: people love money, and will do a lot worse to get it. Shamir was reckless, but no less moral than most. I had no ethical problem with his scam: people can shoot all the junk they want, and niggers need a way to sneak in, now the door's been shut to them. What's wrong with getting high? What's wrong with wanting to get into the West and having a slice of Whitey's pie? He stole it all from us anyway.

Rory sloshed petulantly about in the puddle he'd created, splashing his ankles with whisky and dispersing bits of glass further around the room. Someone else would have to clear that mess up, probably some African contract cleaner, earning the minimum wage. Watching Rory, I felt the shiver of disgust I sometimes feel when I look at white people. I knocked back my vodka; I was getting into a bad mood, and didn't want to. 'How did it all start?' I asked, wanting to occupy my mind.

'It's a long story . . .' he sighed. 'A friend of his had a couple of cousins who needed to get into the country. So they got together and worked something out. That was about three years ago.' He furrowed his brow and began massaging his temple. 'He was going to stop it all over the next month or so. He was already slowing things down. He can't believe that it's all fucked up now, when there's so little going on.'

'What happened? Did someone rat him out?'

'God knows. He hasn't got a clue.' Rory started violently rubbing his face. 'He thinks it might have something to do with a health inspection that happened at Kashmir. He'd moved some people over there for a couple of days, to keep them out of the way, when the inspectors came around to do a spot check. He didn't think anything was too obvious at the time, but maybe something was. Maybe they got wind of things.'

'When was this inspection.'

'Last month, a few days after that function he had. The one you went to.'

'Oh fuck . . .' I'd grasped what had happened.

'What is it?' said Rory, looking at me with interest.

'Nothing,' I said, shaking my head. 'I was just thinking how crazy this all is.' I didn't tell him I'd realised Sarupa was behind it. She told Sodhilal the food had made her sick; that's what caught Shamir out. I saw how it happened: Sodhilal called a high-ranking friend – maybe the head of a local authority – and put someone on the case. Maybe my imagination was running wild, but the scenario was too plausible, the facts too congruent for me to think otherwise. My gut reaction was too instant and compelling to discount. One throwaway lie had caused all this. I sank back into the sofa, dizzied by my sudden comprehension. 'What's going to happen now?' I murmured. 'What's Shamir going to do?'

'He's trying to get away. There's some people he knows, they can get him out of the country. But they want paying.' He walked over to me, crouched down and fumbled under the couch. He stood, up holding a large envelope. 'Puppy, I really need your help . . . You don't have to do this, but it would mean everything to me if you did.'

'Did what?'

'Take this money to him.' He held the envelope out to me.

'Where is he?'

'He's in some awful, squalid dump in Haringey. It's a place the really poor bastards stay when they get here from wherever. The police know nothing about it. It's driving him mad. He's got to get out of there.' Rory looked at me, his eyes tearful and pleading. 'Help him, please. These people, the ones who can get him away, they've got him over a barrel. They want the money upfront.'

'How much is it?'

'£20,000. I've put more in there, in case he needs it . . . It's the most I could raise without having to ask around or do anything suspicious. I wish I could get more.'

I looked at the envelope and wanted to laugh; right now, I couldn't raise a hundred without asking around or doing something suspicious. The difference between us was staggering. 'That's a lot of money.'

'Yes . . . When he gets to Pakistan, he says he'll arrange for his family to pay me back. But I don't care. I just need him to be safe.' Rory knelt on the floor before me; he put his hand on my knee, lowering his head. 'Please . . . please do this for me, Puppy.'

I reached out and took the envelope from him. It was fat and heavy with promise; I held it with both hands. 'Why don't you do this yourself?' I asked. 'Why are you roping me into this? It's a big risk you're asking me to take. You want me to throw myself into something that's none of my business.'

Staring at the floor, Rory took his hand from my knee and tugged at his short hair. 'I know . . . It's nothing to do with you, I know that. But I can't do it, Puppy. I'm a fucking coward.' He looked up at me in despair, his eyes red from crying. 'This whole thing scares the shit out of me. I can't handle it. Please do it for me, Puppy. You're much braver than I am.'

I could hear my heart beating; I was scared too. I stared at the envelope: a little brown parcel packed with freedom. 'Okay,' I sighed, trying not think about it. 'I'll do it. Tell me where to take it.'

'Thank you! Oh God, thank you!' Rory lurched forwards and hugged me. 'The address is in the envelope.' He held me tightly; I could feel his body heave with each sob. His face pressed against mine, his tears slid down my cheek and along my neck. His legs buckled under him and he slumped to the floor, pulling me with him. I gently lowered him down and sat beside him; curling into a ball, he pushed his face into my torso and held my waist. I folded my arms around him; he was shaking with pain, exhaustion and relief. His crying was too agonised to bear. I held him close, resting my chin on his head; I rocked from side to side, wanting to soothe him. Through the open windows ahead

238

of me, I watched London descending into darkness. A cold breeze blew inside, and I shuddered. Summer was pretty much finished.

I watched the city glide past from the window of the taxi. I couldn't remember when I'd last been in a black cab; they're so expensive. We drove along Bayswater Road, then down Park Lane. I turned to look into Hyde Park: Horse Guards in uniform sat on beautiful dapple-grey horses, taking them for an evening stroll. We took a left onto Piccadilly, moving towards the centre of town. It was the start of the weekend; London was filled with people drinking outside pubs or walking hurriedly to a social rendezvous. Heading through Haymarket, I looked at my watch. It was twenty past seven, and I was worried I wouldn't make it in time. Sophie was sat at a table in Momo, waiting for me; I'd sent her a text saying I'd be late. I thought of Shamir chewing his fingernails in anticipation, desperate for me to arrive.

I was relieved when the traffic thinned on the Strand. I stared out the window at the theatres and hotels, at the people thronging the street. I felt sick, but determined. I rubbed my clean-shaven face, and tried not to dwell on what I was doing. Before getting the cab, I'd taken a while at Sophie's flat to shower and clean myself up; now I looked like the photo in my passport. I clutched the holdall resting in my lap, bulging with a quick, poorly made selection of clothes; I'd buy whatever else I needed later on. Rory's money was stuffed into the pockets of a couple of pairs of jeans and the denim jacket I'd packed; everything else was in there just to fill the bag out. Life can turn on a split-second decision. A few lives would turn on this one.

As the cab turned onto Waterloo Bridge, I almost gasped; I was nearly there. I checked my watch. I had fifteen minutes to get to the station, buy my ticket and board the train. I'd phoned ahead to make sure seats were available on the last Eurostar of the day. I'd stay in Paris a few days, relax and see the sights, maybe hit on some French girls. But I was planning to get to Amsterdam; I had to be somewhere people spoke English. I took out my wallet, getting ready to hand the driver some of Rory's cash.

I kept my eyes wide open as we crossed the Thames: that was the last I saw of the city. Ahead of me, lit up, were the Royal Festival Hall, the London Eye and the National Theatre; soon I'd be at Waterloo and on my way out of here. I thought of those I was leaving. A lot would happen to them in the following weeks: my brother would have his wedding, Sarupa would marry, too; Luca's mother would die, and Michael become a father for the second time. Rory and Sophie would be devastated, and Shamir hung out to dry. Thinking of all this, I felt like a cunt – but that was nothing new. I wasn't afraid, and that was more important. I was in the clear. What would Rory do? Report me to the police for stealing the money he'd raised to help Shamir abscond?

I turned to look through the rear window; I got a view of the Embankment and Cleopatra's Needle, and was emptied by it. London had been my home for almost thirty years; I'd known nowhere else. She was the gorgeous, faithless old whore that bore me; she'd never shown me any love, but had shown me the world and its workings. For that much, I was grateful.

October 2004

HOT WIND, BLOWING from the desert behind me, takes the scent of my body with it out to sea. Sweat pours from my forehead; droplets linger on my eyelashes, then splash against my cheeks. Eyes shut, I focus on my breathing; my abdomen held in, the air fills my chest, opening my ribcage and pushing against my spine. Inhale matches exhale; the flow is firm, steady and continuous. I listen to its rhythm, and gaze into the blackness inside.

It's a difficult posture, Janu Sirsasana B. Sitting on my buttocks, left leg outstretched before me, right heel tucked under my crotch, my thighs almost make a right angle; leaning over the straight leg, I grasp the sole of my foot in both hands and listen to my breath. Not long ago, this was impossible; my hips were too stiff. But the Egyptian heat warms deep into my limbs, releasing them. I feel the discomfort and surrender to it, sinking into the darkness behind my eyelids. I count my breaths, controlling their pace; each one pulls me further into the posture.

I sit up, clumsily push myself into a press-up, and perform a Vinyasa; I sit back down to perform the same posture, now on the opposite side. Inhaling, straightening my spine before reaching forwards, I look up and glimpse the shimmering water ahead of me, and the hazy outline of Saudi Arabia in the distance. Closing my eyes, I submit again to the limits of my flesh and the abysm of my mind.

A shanty Sinai beach resort, Dahab lies eighty miles north of Sharm el-Sheikh, on the Gulf of Aqaba. Right now, it's a ghost town. Last month, a suicide bomber killed more than thirty people at a nightclub in Taba, a hundred miles up the

241

coast. The place was full of Israeli kids; they were sitting ducks. Dahab was quiet when we got here; the war in Iraq was already keeping tourists away. Now it's empty. I don't know how much longer I'll have a job; there's nothing to do. I spend my time doing yoga, and looking at the sea.

I came here with hope. I'd spent the last year penniless, drifting around Europe, cadging whatever work or favours I could get. For a while, I shacked up with that old fruit, Marcello; once I'd got some dough out of him, I hightailed it. The dirty wop kept trying to suck me off; when he figured I wasn't interested, he wanted me to fuck his niece while he peeped through a hole in the wall. I spent the next six months flitting around Italy and then Spain, waiting tables, serving drinks, labouring in fields and building sites; a couple of times I found a woman with money to spend. Last April, I went to Ibiza; I wanted to be there early, bed myself down before the holiday season began. There I met Donald and Jane. They ran a yoga centre near Puerto San Miguel, and offered me a job. A pair of ageing hippies, they said they liked my 'energy' and put me up in their villa; eventually they asked me to help out at the centre.

Donald is a sinewy long-haired Californian, his wife a skinny, English middle-class bohemian. They wear kaftans and ethnic jewellery, read books by Ram Das, recite Sanskrit prayers and eat a meagre, strictly vegan diet. Their skins are dark orange, and have that scaly texture that comes with too much sun; their frames are lithe and bony. They're in their fifties and think they've defied age and transcended the material world. In truth, they're just loopy white people, growing old, underfed and in denial. The West repeats itself in India as farce; India repeats itself in Westerners as tragedy.

I flunked around for them – cooking, cleaning, gardening and greeting guests – in exchange for a room, three square meals and a hundred euros a week. It was peanuts, but I didn't mind; the weather was great, and it was the most stable thing I'd had in a long time. For a fortnight I watched the morning yoga class from my bedroom window; it was held in the open air, on the front lawn. At least

242

twenty people would be there – the centre was always busy – making a phalanx of elegant shapes for three hours at a time. I was intrigued, but reluctant to join in. Being Indian, I'd never done any yoga; I've known almost none that have. Baffled but impressed, I'd watch the crackers line up each morning to say their collective *Om* and perform their salutations. White people love doing yoga; with so much bad karma to shake off, that's no surprise. Finally I decided to join in. Don kept pestering me with bullshit about developing 'super-consciousness', and I wanted him to shut up.

It was in the last session of my first week that I felt something. Lying in Savasana – 'corpse pose' – at the end of class, exhausted after practice, eyes closed and breathing deeply, I had a vision of my mother. It was nothing spiritual, just an honest realisation of how much she loved me. I felt her love in its purity, freed from her fear and confusion. I felt her pain at never having given me this, and at not knowing where I was. I've done yoga every day since. I often think of her during practice; sometimes I hear her voice, speaking to me when I was a child, or quietly reciting *kirtan*. I feel I know her a little more each time, and the urge to see her grows.

In August Jane and Donald fell out with the owners of the centre; the relationship had been difficult for months. They'd planned to set up on their own for years, and now they took the plunge. Dahab seemed like a good place to start. The rent was cheap, and it was an increasingly popular spot on the hippy trail. Donald wanted a hand and offered to pay for my travel; he'd been good to me and I fancied a change, so I accepted. The bomb went off just days after we got here; the tourists cleared out straightaway, and the yoga instructor Don hired decided not to show up. The place is now deserted, apart from a few New Age fruit-cakes and Bedouins carrying bundles of unsold hash. The hoteliers and barmen don't come outside anymore; they know there's no one around to hustle. Jane and Donald burn incense and offer prayers to Patanjali; they wear un-convincing smiles and hold one another's hands in long stretches of silence. Their savings went into renting a complex here – with twelve rooms and a courtyard – and taking out ads in alternative lifestyle magazines. The dream was still-born, and they're heartbroken. I don't know what to say to them, and only think of when I might leave and where I can go.

I finish my morning practice and sit cross-legged, staring at the sea. I practise on the roof, a private space from where I can see for miles. I achieve perspective here. Behind me is the Sinai and nothing but sand and rock; ahead is the sea, beyond that the Saudi desert. The view is austere and beautiful.

I begin my yoga at nine in the morning, four hours after Don and Jane; I like to start when the day has warmed. It's now almost eleven. Soon the heat will be unbearable. I take a moment to watch the sunlight explode and sparkle on the surface of the water, which is deep blue; beneath it are vast chasms and fantastic coral. Dahab is a great place to go diving.

I pick up my towel and wipe the sweat from my naked body. My skin is rich and dark, like raw cane sugar, and has an almost golden hue. It's the darkest I've ever been; it looks amazing. This is how nature meant for me to look, browned under an Indian sky. I stand up and wipe the moisture from my buttocks and genitals, then wrap the towel around my waist. I can feel the sun pressing on my head, and make my way downstairs.

I go into Don's office, sit at his desk and switch on his computer. I look at the website of an airline and check the times and prices of flights to London. I have to go back some time; I need money, and have nowhere else to earn it. Michael's promised me his couch for a while, and is trying to find me work. He's the only one from my past I communicate with. He emails me quite often; he thinks I'm bumming around for the sake of it. He doesn't know why I left. His career in art is going well, and he sends shots of his new son, Joel. The boy has an open, happy face, and I long to meet him. Luca is no longer in touch; after Kate died, his emails grew more incoherent and infrequent, and finally ceased. I have no idea where or how he is; nor does Michael.

I never contacted my family. Thinking of my kid brother, my heart is heavy. Maybe it's the yoga, probably it's just age, but I know the value in them now. I can feel the courage to meet them rising. It won't be long, I'm sure.

I go to a travel website and look at destinations in India. There's a yoga school in the south that interests me, in Mysore; I plan to check it out. But I want to see so much more. I want to visit Benares and the village where the Buddha was born; more than that, I want to see Punjab and the village that my mother left. I've been there once, when I was a child. For a long time after I remembered only the scorching sun, the poverty, and the pain in my body, wracked by diarrhoea. Older now, I remember a great deal else: the enormous sense of space, the depth and complexity of the people, the unaffected love of relatives I had only just met. I want to arrive in Delhi, knowing this time I will kiss the tarmac, like my mother did, with tears falling from my eyes. But first I have to get away from here.

Don says he'll pay for my ticket home; he brought me to Dahab, and feels obliged to help me leave. But he's ruined. I can't wait for him to raise funds and have written him off. I'm asking Michael to lend me the money. I sign into my Yahoo account to send him an email. My inbox has two unread messages. One is junk mail, offering me erection-enhancing pills at a knockdown price; the other is from sarupa.shah@haw.com. I catch my breath and hear my heart pound. It has no subject heading, but there's a document attached: Rekha.zip. My breathing is slow and deep; my stomach, though empty, wants to heave. I open the email:

Bhupinder,
I think you ought to know that we have a
beautiful daughter.
Sarupa.

I hold the desk with both hands to stop me falling; my legs are trembling, my head spins. The sensation is intense, almost overwhelming: shock, nausea and mounting exhilaration. Blood throbs through my temples; my eyes bulge from their sockets. I look at the attached file: Rekha, is that my baby's name? I click on it and it begins to download. It's a big file, and the process is slow; I know it contains film and pictures. I almost scream to make it hurry, but want no one to come to the room. My palms are cold and wet, my face hot and my heart thumping. I stare at the screen and wait.

Acknowledgements

I'd like to thank:

Liz, for helping me to write this book and change my life; Julie, for throwing her clout behind me when it mattered; Robert, for knowing a good thing when he saw one; likewise Dan and Rachel for giving me a break; Jason, for sensitive and intelligent editing; Suzanne, for putting together such a great cover; May, for being so upfront; Sue, for fervently getting the word out; everyone else at Vintage – you've been fantastic about the whole thing.

God Bless. Lots of love,

Nx

www.randomhouse.co.uk/vintage